I0748404

THE NEXT GREAT DEITY

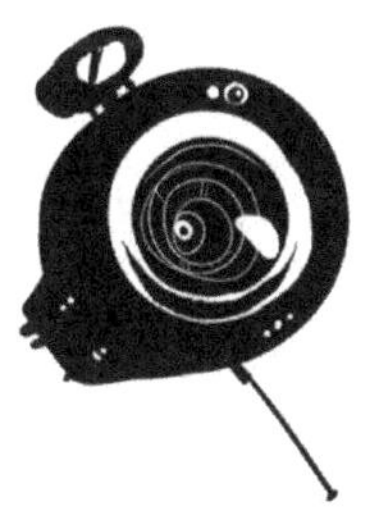

Written by Millard Crow

Cover Artwork by Vincent Rogers

Cover Design and Interior Artwork by Vincent Rogers, Millard Crow

ISBN 978-1-7335578-0-1

Chance favors the prepared mind.

— Louis Pasteur

The New Heart

A single pendant bulb funneled its weak light from the rafters. It had the simplest job in Heaven, and it performed it well.

Its cone of light illuminated a six-foot-tall wall of circuit boards, each uniform in their small size and fitted together like overlapping scales. The tracks and pads on each printed board were identical, with the lone exception of a blue board in the center of the electronic display. Its only component was a plug for a patch cable, which poured to the floor and snaked far into the darkness of this dry, cold, tomb of a room. It was a monument of meaningless technology framed by soot and shadows.

A door opened and gave a brief flash of full light onto the scraped up concrete floor. Two sets of feet brought their expensive sound into the dim storage area, and their high heels and dress shoes echoed between the walls. Behind them, a heavy vessel dragged.

"So this is it, huh?" a low, baritone voice asked. The ocean was in his mouth—it spat and sloshed with every sound he made.

High-Heels gave a sharp "*Mmm-hmm,*" in reply, and stepped into the light. She approached the wall of electronic boards and laid a red painted nail on the center. Her dust colored eyes burrowed into the circuitry, and her walk crisscrossed with the curvature of the cable. She heard the slight hum of new life rattle the boards, smiled, stroked through her chin, then sashayed back into shadows.

"So, I think it's time to open 'em up."

"I don't drink," Ocean-Mouth lied. Latches swung open on the vessel. Ice shifted. Bottles popped. Two glasses clinked together. "Not at all, not one drop," his mouth grew wetter as it slithered around its club whiskey. “But tonight’s good. I’ll make an exception.”

High-Heels agreed, “It’s all great.”

The boards started to move on their own, as if they were sucked towards the patch cable. They had a slow and instinctual movement programmed into them by an imperceptible force far beyond the capabilities of their individual circuitry.

“It’s all good.”

As the boards gathered towards the cable, their trajectory went upwards and outwards like waves against a rock.

“I control the likelihood,”

But waves would remain water. *These* currents were something different—as the boards rose and broke away, they turned to bone and began to reform.

“Of thread of fate being shred,”

The distinct shape of a square pelvis slowly emerged, lifted from the waters of wires. Soon, a spine. Ribs. More boards started to cover the bone, then melted into stringy layers of blood and muscles.

“Those in my way *can drop dead.*”

Shoulders emerged, then arms. The centerpiece patch cable was an umbilical cord in the navel of the flesh-less, dripping *thing*.

“I have never heard you say that before,” Ocean-Mouth tilted his bulbous head.

Staccato clacks echoed as High-Heels turned. Though shrouded in near-darkness, her eyes burned enough to be seen for a mile.

“I’m just saying,” he attempted a clumsy clarification, “I didn’t know you needed to do that. The whole... rhyming thing.”

"Shut up. I don't. This is just..."

"I'm sorry. I was just wondering," he muted himself with more whiskey.

"This is an important moment for me. I want this to be fun. Can't you have fun? Have you ever, like, tried having *fun* before?"

"It's... it's fine—"

"If I want to make a dumb-ass nursery rhyme to make this pivotal moment *for me* a little more *symbolic* and *mystical*, let me."

"Jesus, I'm sorry."

"You're damn right you are." Click-clack. She turned away from him.

"Jesus. Look."

"Hmm?"

A skull began to form; it was canine in shape, but had more of a forehead than a human would normally be comfortable seeing on a dog. One could interpret the in-progress creature as a werewolf, but its shorter stature and thin muscles wouldn't inspire much fear in any prey.

"Why does it have a dog's head?" Ocean-Mouth asked.

"It's what it chose."

"Chose? Wait. Y-you mean..."

As soon as the creature's throat gained a functioning set of muscles, it released a horrible shriek burdened with the pain of creation.

"I gave it the catalyst, but it's building itself in the image it thinks will work," High-Heels rubbed her hands together. "This... is *beautiful*."

The shrieking skull disagreed as muscle formed over its cheek bones.

"It's birthing itself."

Fur and flesh began to sprout outward from the patch cable in its navel. Since enough muscle had covered its neck and maw, it blurted its first words:

"DEWEY... DEFEATS... TRUMAN!"

The canine's eyes were lidless and yellow behind layers of meat. Were it capable of an expression, its grunts and cries indicated it wouldn't have looked much different than the horror its sounds expressed.

"...WAS... INCORRECT!"

It ripped its head forward and stray circuit boards flew off the rack. They landed and skidded across the floor, past the high heels of High-Heels. "The... Chicago Tribune..." the flesh had covered most of his body and started to creep along the face of the creature. All of his words shivered, "...printed the headline... preemptively... but they were unable to recall copies... before... " the monster hemorrhaged as lids formed over his eyes in time to paint the arch of agony on his bestial face, "...before... before... before the REAL RESULTS CAME IN!" He ripped an arm forward and another set of blood splattered circuitry flew from the rack.

Ocean-Mouth sidestepped some of the airborne boards, his slimy hands clutched to his chest. "What the hell is he doing?"

"Rationalizing!" she clapped.

"You can cook... hamburger meat... in an oven at 350 degrees for 20 minutes," the canine-man grunted, and ripped his other arm from the rack. "Or... or... or at 450 degrees," he popped his back free and tumbled forward. The momentum ripped his legs from the rack. He landed in a pool of his own blood, his freshly grown gray fur already stained deep, dark red.

"O-o-o-or... or on a grill... over charcoal... or on a s-s-stove... top. W-why... Why... Why are there... so many ways to cook hamburger?" He lifted himself up to his elbows. His wide, busy eyes stared at himself in the bloody reflection. "A-and... what's hamburger?"

A long silence passed between the three, with Ocean-Mouth and High-Heels transfixed by the manic ramblings of their invention, their creature, their child.

"WHAT AM I?!" the bloody dog-man screamed.

A small squish could be heard as the umbilical patch cable was tugged from his navel. It pulled away and he followed it with his eyes to red high heels owned by long and sculpted legs glued into a tight white mini-dress. Her hip was cinched with a red velvet band the exact same hue as his blood. A gold cross glinted in the dim light between breasts that could have started the Renaissance. At the moment the creature's eyes reached her face, the pendent light shone above her; into her moons for eyes, into the electrically charged waves of hair, into her expertly trimmed beard that folded into itself with an impossible maze-like volume.

"A contestant," she twined the patch cable between her fingers. Some blood flicked off of the end and stained her dress. She didn't mind. "I'll have someone come clean you up, sweetie."

Air pushed out from the spaces between the vent and dispersed, and its slight, subtle hiss harmonized with the overworked air conditioner.

In the hottest part of summer, the AC's condensation leaked into the drainage pan. To help with its aural union, the bathroom door underneath the vent was kept wide open. These combinations of industrial sighs were annual, and in the cool complexes of Queens, fleeting. Typically, they only lasted from June to September. (Unless the end of May showed up early to party.)

Tonight, he thought as he pointed multiple microphones around the vent, *I'm gonna get it.*

When he turned the gain up all the way on his condenser microphones, the concept of privacy escaped. Gain, in recording terms, specifically refers to the power of the microphone signal. The smoke-scented man always turned the amplifier's gain dial with a slow restraint while he held one ear close to the headphones. He listened for the details of the most overlooked moments of life in an attempt to capture them with an artistic system as specific as the audience willing to listen to it.

With this methodology and equipment, he could record the taps of his roommate's fingers on a desk, or the clinks of Bach's collar. (Bach being his pet German Spitz—the microphone was good at picking up his many barks and scratches, too. Given how loud Bach could be, that's not quite a selling point, though.) The soft buzz of a guitar amp was too much noise to escape, even when in a different room. At its highest setting it can capture silence, turning it into a tangible sizzle when recorded. He didn't just want capture sound, though—his intention was to mold it.

With a flick of a keyboard key, the smoke-scented man hit record. Thirty seconds passed. A minute. Five minutes. He barely moved during this time, and if he did, he did it with an underlined purpose.

During this session, he:

Brushed his fingers across the desk.

Preformed loud, open mouth breathing.

Rubbed his hands through his brittle stubble.

Took a sip of coffee.

A few sips.

A giant, impatient, nerve calming gulp.

Theodore Flores's phone vibrated suddenly on his desk. The recording-ruining buzzer scored enough of a jump to splash coffee onto his war-torn tank-top.

"Fucking...! *No*!" he held his arms wide in frustration as he stared into the ribbed, stained cloth. Ripped back into reality, Theodore clicked the keyboard to stop the recording, then pulled his phone screen to his face with angry scrutiny. When he saw the name "Matt Meelkop" across the ID, his expression unraveled from furrowed grimace to a perplexed, lip-pursed surprise.

"Hey, What's up, Matt?" he stared at the blown out square of sound on the waveform.

"Not much, man," a fried voice croaked on the speaker. "Just confirming our appointment for later."

"Oh, yeah man, yeah. We're still on. I didn't forget."

He forgot. Sort of.

His world of sound had consumed hours he didn't expect to lose. Theodore worked when he needed to. He preferred a nomad's life where days were mushy hazes of creation and sleeping, maybe eating food if he was feeling adventurous. Now that he was at a place of semi-professionalism in his art, this lifestyle put him in some small danger when it came to the business side of making music. That's where Matt, theoretically, would come in.

Mr. Meelkop was a producer associated with the record label "SmallSound". Appropriately named, SmallSound's artists tend to play with quiet, layered samples and textures more than volume and bombast. Theodore ran into Matt at a concert years back and the two thinkers, full of opinions and alcohol, sparred with smiles over the ups and downs of this odd genre—something Theodore might not have done at all had he known he was talking at, not to, someone affiliated with the style's label of origin.

Theodore's flailing hands and obsessive knowledge of the sampling process didn't irritate Matt as he thought it might have. He used this, and their subsequent pleasantries, as motivation to push himself to make his own album. After an irresponsible amount of time and money spent, he was on the precipice of signing with the company he wrote reader-less essays about years prior.

Matt wanted to hear the demo before he committed to a contract. As he had mentored Theodore during the creation process, the aspiring sound artist didn't fear rejection—barring any Chernobyl-level disaster, like, say, forgetting what day it is.

Theodore clawed through his bedroom and tossed discarded clothes and forgotten bills that had settled into the crust of the floor. "Yeah, no, I have a demo. I've got three tracks done, minus some percussion on track two. Yeah, that's the one I wanted to come in to work on."

In a particular pile of apartment debris, he excavated a USB flash drive. He set it aside and juggled his phone between his hands, neck and the table. With impressive cell phone gymnastics, he exchanged one set of tattered clothes for another, and stuffed the drive into his book-bag. A laptop, a set of portable speakers, and a pair of headphones were rammed in with modest regard for their safety.

"I'll be there. Bus ride isn't too long and we still have plenty of time. I'm excited too, it's my wildest stuff I've ever done. Yeah. I'll see you soon—"

Theodore would later remember this promise as he ran up to the bus stop. He was just a minute too late to get on, but just in time to watch the city bus turn off the main road and disappear from view.

"Sssssssshit!" his mustached top lip inflated as he opened up his phone. He tried to figure out how he could still make this meeting—hope was not lost, but he'd have to get creative. He didn't want to spend money for a ride-share or taxi when he already had a bus ticket. It wasn't that he didn't have the money for those alternatives, but he had lived the life of someone who *didn't* have the money for so long that it was just second nature for him to be as thrifty as possible.

There's another bus stop a few blocks over that goes to Jackson. If I hurry I could probably make it in time, he thought, and pieced out a plan with the routes left around him.

His jog began. His dexterous weaving around fellow pedestrians was impressive considering his steady diet of caffeine and cigarettes. The black, bulky backpack around his shoulders didn't slow down his broad frame, though it did contribute to the sweat that slid down his back.

He cleared a city block with a pavement-slapping dash. The next block had less people and obstacles—he was surrounded by the broad, blank sides of tenant-less buildings, parking garages, car rentals, and consultants. Places you wouldn't be at unless you had to be there. At this time, few people were.

He passed by an alleyway. In the corner of his eye he caught a flash of odd colors, a dance of peach skin and denim.

Theodore skid to a halt, his lips glued to keep the sound of his runner's breath through his nose. The vague shape from his peripheral vision stuck to his mind. To his back was the narrow alleyway he just ran past. He could hear the frantic scuff of shoes. A deep, muffled impact halted the scattered dance, before something made a sharp, metallic click.

Theodore took off his backpack.

A voice hissed. Another one whimpered. Theodore turned back towards the alleyway and brought one sweaty leg over another. His hand, dotted with black hair to the knuckles, trembled on the brick wall. Theodore was close enough to hear:

"Get your fucking wallet out, faggot."

Jeremy's Playground

A knight lumbered deep into a nearby clay cave. The only light was from his torch, which was lit with a flame that couldn't die on its own. The flame's magic waned and flickered with the breath of its source—a wounded mage at the cave's entrance. These two friends, knight and mage, were battered after a battle with a fearsome monster that had terrorized a local village for months on end.

In the dead of night, the beast would screech and bellow and chase anyone and anything in the streets. Every single night this happened. His roar would boom down every corridor in town, and rattle within the earth and hillside. The diurnal was forced to become nocturnal, oppressed by his wicked, snarling song. Livestock disappeared. Crops were scorched. The people could not live this unnatural terror any longer.

Upon arriving, the two heroes heeded the townsfolk's pleas to vanquish the monster. They were certain it would be no trouble for such decorated veterans of battle. Monster slaying was one of the simpler services they offered, and with a reasonable fee.

After their encounter, though, the pair realized they had underestimated the brawn and wits of the beast. The knight, whose armor kept him in much better condition than his ally, had instructed his friend this: "If I do not return by sundown, release your concentration on this flame. Warn the town to leave these lands. If we cannot stop this thing, no one can."

He thought such brave words were noble and necessary, but he didn't believe them. Instead, he believed there was no need for this light to go out, no need for these good people to worry about their sleep or way of life. Not tonight. Not ever again. The warrior now knew the beast's weapons and ways, and was prepared.

The knight approached with his sword drawn. The cave's dusty maroon walls flickered in the torch light. As he went deeper, the pungent mineral fetor clogged his nostrils and lungs. Despite his wet eyes, he noticed another source of light up ahead, greater than the flame he held.

"Alright," he rolled his sword-holding wrist.

The faint glow came from a pool of lava just further ahead. He found claw marks along the jagged floor, and a trail of blue blood contrasted with the red clay. In their last encounter, the knight struck a blow into the hide of the beast's shoulder—this trail, the reward.

The beast was indeed magical in nature, this much he knew from the spells it cast from its enchanted axe. But how did it *dive* into the lava? Could it survive its melting temperatures? And if so, how was the knight able to pierce it at all?

In response to his internal dialogue, a large bubble began to form in the middle of the pool. It didn't pop: as it rose, it's circular form clumped and became defined. Its outline morphed to a hunched back, slabs of muscle covered in heat resistant scales. The wound that it had just suffered was gone, healed without a scar.

What sort of sorcery is this?, the knight thought.

As orange magma dripped and slid off the beast, he raised his horn-crowned head and stared with pinpoint eyes.

"Hello!"

No, that's all wrong, the knight thought. *That's not the voice of the dragon-man. These two just battled each other. He'd say something menacing and dramatic, like—*

"Hell-o-*ooo*?"

The child shook his head in surprise and glanced up.

He may have towered over him, but this average height, suited man only appeared massive from a 9-year old's perspective. He was a younger man with a deliberately bald head that caught the midday sun on its polished surface. His eyes hid behind large dark sunglasses of an unusual, shifting color. While his eyes were not visible, the rest of his smarmy face, unfortunately, was.

"Hey kid," the man's smile pulled at his cheeks with a snapping elasticity. "Mind if I talk to your friend?"

"My friend?" the child was seated on the wooden boundary of the playground, the divide between plain grass and jungle gyms. He turned to where, he thought, the rest of the children would be. They were not. The child rubbed the back of his head in confusion—he did have a tendency to space out, but even if he was playing in his head, he should have noticed if anyone left.

"They're gone?"

"No, he isn't. You were just talking to him, silly!" the suited man placed his hands on his upper thighs and bent down. The child, baffled, leaned and looked past the adult.

There were no people. No birds. No dogs. No moving cars. No wind. No noise at all, just the crinkle of the man's cheap suit.

"What's your name, kid?"

"Jeremy. W-where are my parents?"

"They're right there, Jer!" the man turned and pointed towards a nearby empty bench. That *is* where the child remembered them being—he and a group of five other children were on a day-trip, as they often were since their parents were all friends. Now, there was only absence.

Jeremy blinked. "No they—"

"Oh, *yeah*! You can't see them. Well. You see," in a fluid spin of inhuman grace and dexterity, the man squat next to the child, one arm wrapped around his shoulders, while the other jabbed a finger into his chest, "and that's not a pun, kid."

"Uh," the child was confused.

"That's because I've cast a 'spell' on you. You get spells, yeah? I mean, you're sitting here thinking about 'wizards', and 'knights,'" the man let go of his shoulder so that he could air quote and grin and condescend.

"Um," the child's eyes darted around, looking for help.

"I'm assuming because the ol' parental units over there let you play D&D with them, yeah? Your newly forming, easily distracted, tomato sized brain is laser focused on this *cool* little adventure you've cooked up! All on your little own! Well, okay, it wasn't on your own, you're basically making fan fiction of the, what, *five* stories you've experienced in your life? But still. IMAGINATION!"

"I don't understand," Jeremy whined with increased unease.

"How do I say this?" he turned his sight towards the bench as he adjusted his suit jacket. His hands moved wildly in front of him, as if he was trying to unlock the words he wanted to say from an invisible box. "We're kinda... sorta... in your mind right now. You're still at the playground, for sure." He stomped a foot on the ground, as if the thump of soil against sole proved his point.

"...What?"

"This is really where your body is, I promise," his tone darkened, and his patron-smile disappeared. "You see, I could *forcefully* talk to your friend, but that gets *really* messy and cruel and I'm... just... not that sort of guy. I'd rather ask for permission from you because I would prefer to be nice."

Jeremy grabbed the hem of his shorts with his fists.

"So, *come on*, Kiddo! Lemme talk to your big, red brain-friend for a minute or so, and you can go back to playing in your head and eating ice cream with your weirdly progressive parents or running around in traffic or... something. I'll be on my way and no one will know this happened."

A tear began to go down the child's cheek. Though it seemed certain he would burst into a loud, messy cry, a different energy erupted from his sockets.

An explosion of darkness spiraled outwards from his face and consumed the entire landscape. In a near instant moment, the world became the red clay cave Jeremy's knight was previously in. The knight was nowhere to be found, though: alone stood the suited man as he held his lapel in front of the lava pool.

"Who dares..." a voice burbled from its depths.

"No, it's 'Who dares?'" she smiled, then clarified further in Spanish. "<It's a question. A really angry one!>"

The student nodded and resumed reading aloud in English.

More than once, when she explained what she did in Honduras, a friend or family member would call the student's accents 'broken'. Each time, Mrs. Alleyne would correct them: "Their accent is not *broken*, it's *in progress*," she'd say while twirling the cross necklace near her throat. "These children are learning, after all. What they're doing, at the speed they're doing it, is incredible."

Robin Alleyne was not native, but the 43-year-old's Spanish was decent enough to get her by for the first few months of her stay in Honduras. It was remarkable she was able to navigate Copán Ruinas as well as she did with only her college education to support her. It's one thing to learn a second language for a written test; it's a different task altogether to semi-competently speak it with locals over an espresso.

Sometimes 'semi-competently' was all she could manage. Any grammatical error or word misuse would get scrawled down into a small notebook she kept with her for the sake of reinforcement, no matter where she was. Robin knew that experience was the strongest teacher—and any problems she ran into with Spanish, surely her students would encounter with English.

Julio, one of her younger students, glazed his eyes a little bit as a jumble of unfamiliar prepositions assaulted him from the page. Julio liked to learn and he liked Mrs. Alleyne, but the day was nearly through, and so was he. He was tired and could not shove any more English into his brain, particularly prepositions. Nothing new was going into the cup of his mind without spilling.

The overflow was enough to draw his wandering eyes to floor where he saw a pair of dark, discarded sunglasses. The scraggly haired lad leaned down and hooked the edge of his finger under an arm, then pulled the glasses up. After a brief examination, he whispered to the girl seated next to him.

"<Are these yours?>"

"<No,>" she shook her head.

He held the glasses by one of its chunky arms and scrunched his face. He noticed, depending upon the angle that light would hit the lens, it would change color subtly—like a moving oil spill. *Maybe they were Mrs. Alleyne's?*, he thought.

After a glance at the clock, Julio opened the arms and brought them to his face.

I'll put these on and see if she notices. These things are huge. I bet she'll laugh, he grinned outwardly at his inner plans.

"<Okay, so, the bell is about to ring,>" Robin clapped her brown and calloused hands together and smiled. "<Everyone did really good today! We made great progress, so I'd like it if you just finished the chapter over the weekend, okay?>"

As predicted, the bell cawed and trilled to end another school day. Robin high-fived and head patted various children as they left, but one remained seated. As the crowd thinned, Robin looked and saw the bespectacled Julio, hands clasped on the table expectantly. The adult sized sunglasses took up an unintentionally large portion of his face.

"<Julio, it's time to go,>" the teacher stifled a laugh at the face-to-glasses ratio.

Julio rolled his head and popped his neck, not a hint of humor anywhere on his face. "Robin," he executed the perfect cadence of a bored corporate suit, “If you were god, what would you change about the world?”

Her smile shrank. “That was... <that was a very good English sentence, Julio.>”

Alley Chance

"You understand *English*, you mop-headed fag?"

Though the smell of three day old body odor and booze was enough to pin the hapless old man against the wall, the gun jabbed into his ribcage helped keep him in place. His eyes watered, partially in fear, partially in submission as each of his senses were mercilessly attacked. He slid up to the tips of his toes as the barrel of the gun pressed hard into him through his sweater.

The robber's long, stringy hair clung around his face underneath his drawn hoodie and framed his crazed eyes. He was considerably shorter than his victim, but that mattered little now. "You wanna die?" he spat.

"I-I-I..." tears streaked down the older gentleman's face from behind his sunglasses. He didn't have a wallet, and was too buried by adrenaline and fright to say so.

Suddenly, the blare of police sirens pierced the air and echoed through the alleyway. Both the robber and the robbee looked up in surprise—they were in one of the more secluded parts of Queens, and this crime-in-progress had only just started. The police were never in this area, and not this close, this fast, if they were.

"S-shit," the terrified robber slid back from his mark. He just wanted some cash. In his mind, the risk became too great. He bolted away from his would-be donor towards the opposite end of the alleyway.

The victim's jaw hung wide as he wiped away the tears from underneath his sunglasses. The sirens continued to shriek, but as he looked towards the street, he noticed the blank walls remained dusk-lit. No police lights flashed on them, or in the windows of buildings across the street, or in the reflective paint of nearby parked cars. The sound of the siren never got louder as they would from an approaching vehicle, and it never stopped as if the police had arrived on the scene.

He lumbered forward towards the alleyway exit. As thankful as he may have been, there was something *off* about the sirens. When he reached the mouth of the alley, he found the true source of the sound.

A Hispanic man sat cross-legged just outside the alleyway, his back against the wall. A black book-bag was crumpled to his side, with a lit up cell phone perched on top of it. In front of him sat an expensive set of portable speakers of sleek and modern design, plugged into a laptop of equal excellence. In sharp contrast, the plain-clothes man was unremarkable—broad and fit, perhaps, but disheveled. There was an attempt to style his pencil mustache, but the effort was undermined wholly by the rest of his unshaven stubble.

The laptop played a video of a police siren, ten hours in length.

The mustached millennial looked up, brow furrowed into a mess of wrinkles born too soon. The shrill sound cut abruptly as he paused the video.

"You alright?" Theodore asked.

The older man wheezed, hunched with mental exhaustion. "How on *Earth* did you know that would work?"

"Are you kidding?" he laughed. He picked up his cell phone and thumbed idly. "Listen, the police station is nowhere near here and you would have given up your wallet a lot quicker if you had one."

The older man clutched the chest of his sweater. "Y-you gambled my life that he wouldn't shoot me when he heard the police...?"

Theodore frowned and closed the laptop. He unplugged wires with sharp tugs. "*Huh*. I thought I was saving it."

An awkward silence buried the two, only occasionally interrupted by Theodore's clicks and shuffles as he packed up his belongings. He slung his full backpack over his shoulder and pointed down the street. "Sorry to scare you, man. This isn't the best area to walk through. Go take a right over there and you're back to the shops. I'll go with you if you want."

"Y-you're.." the old man spluttered. "You're Theodore Flores, aren't you?"

Theodore's posture straightened. "Do I know you?"

The old man's skin stretched with his smile, and his brows raised high. The oil-colored sunglasses he wore seemed to shift with the afternoon light as his head rocked backwards. He laughed like a revving motor, gradually louder and longer, as uncomfortable as his stare and twice as obvious.

"This wasn't how it was supposed to be..." the old man laughed and rasped. "This wasn't how we were supposed to meet."

"It's good to meet you," the bald-headed man tugged his lapel and anchored his hands underneath the fabric. "Taninim."

A hulking beast erupted from the lava and landed with a cave-shaking thud. Molten gunk splattered across the floor and on the man's jacket and hand. He flicked it off his suit, which had started to catch aflame. With a few swats, the flame not only went out, but his clothes were completely repaired.

"I guess it's for the best that this kid has no idea how lava works."

The dragon-man stood nearly two feet taller than his suited intruder. His nostrils flared. His pinpoint eyes shook with rage. His war-sculpted, scaled upper body was bare of cloth save a neon strap around his shoulder. The strap, impossible it may seem, survived the heat of the lava—as did the gold guitar it was buckled to.

"But I'm able to survive because I know the lava isn't real. I'm in control of my form in this illusion. This body you're in still has to play by *his* rules," the suited man rubbed his jaw. "Why are *you* heat resistant?"

Taninim had all the historically inaccurate appearance of a rock star—clingy leather pants, a gaudy skull belt, and various trinkets on his wrists and fingers. He even sported a nose ring in his snout, with a long chain hooked up to one of his many horns.

"Literally every single thing on you would melt in the lava, even if we pretend for a second that you're fireproof. Unless you also fire proofed your..." the suited man looked Taninim up and down, "*...electric guitar*?"

"Who DARES enter my most AWESOME LAIR?!" Taninim bellowed as he cracked a sick lick from his musical axe. It's unclear where the sound came from, as the guitar wasn't connected to anything. Even if it were hooked to an amp, he'd be hard pressed to find a plug for it in a cave. The sound seemed to merely exist because Taninim made it so.

The bald-headed man laughed and held a hand up incredulously. "Wait, wait, wait. What?"

Taninim pointed the head of the guitar towards the suited-man. "State thy name! State thy purpose of intruding upon these hallowed grounds, or face my wrath!"

"Okay, look. So I probably shouldn't admit to spying but... like, weren't you just fighting a knight? With a sword?" the bald-headed man gestured towards one of the cave's many tunnels. "Am... am I the only one that sees the inconsistent theming here?"

The dragon-man took a powerful step forward. His nostrils billowed smoke. For the first time, the suited-man reacted with hesitance, and took the slightest step backwards.

"Look, look, look, I'm a talent agent. I came to make you an offer."

"What does a TINY HUMAN like you-"

"Stop."

Taninim blinked.

"Not human. Also, just... stop. I know this isn't you," the suited-man drew a line with his finger between the guitar and the dragon-man. "You're just an imaginary friend. This whole place is you. I don't know why you've centered yourself in this form, annnd I don't care. I'm talking to *you*." He sucked in a breath with slow, saliva-coated disdain, and let it coat his annoyed sibilance. "Not whatever this stupid thing you're role-playing as."

Taninim's eyes fluttered. He staggered backwards and held his head. He asked again, more meekly now, but still with the undercut of rage, "Who dares...?"

The suited-man's smile melted away. He took off his sunglasses and revealed pupil-less green eyes. "I told you. I'm a talent agent. I've come to make you an offer that I think you'll like."

"Robin. Let me word this another way," Julio said as he opened his hands. "You're someone who uses their position as a teacher to try and shape the world. But your *position* on this planet is just... so... *small.*"

"<This is a prank, isn't it?>" Robin backed away until she felt the edge of her desk bump into her rear. Her eyes searched the pastel painted classroom for cameras, evidence of a film crew, anything to explain Julio's new voice.

He stood up out of his seat. His clear and stern tone commanded respect his small stature had yet to earn. "Does this sound like *a joke* to you?"

Robin circled the desk slowly as she locked eyes with what she once believed was her student. The stone cold confidence he possessed smothered the air of the classroom. Julio didn't learn to speak perfect English like this in an instant, she knew that couldn't be. This thought was not a slight to Julio—the human mind cannot command a new language without training and usage.

But what's the explanation? she thought. She wondered if he always knew English, or if he was reciting lines from memory—the latter of which she ruled out because, if this were the product of a script, he couldn't have responded to her. She clutched the cross around her neck and opened a drawer, her touch light and her movement slow. She prayed.

"Personally, I don't see it," Julio muttered. "But I want to give you a chance. So tell me. If you were god—" he stopped when Robin leaned a bit too far, too quickly, into the drawer. The desk creaked. Julio noticed. She gulped. They both stared with probing intensity. "What are you doing?"

Theodore shuffled his weight between his feet. "Um... what?"

"Sorry. How rude of me," the old man patted his jean pockets down.

"How do you know my name?"

Theodore, who moments prior looked for a sociable way to leave, was bolted down by the gravity of this stranger's knowledge. He studied the wizened lines on the old man's face. The frailty of his limbs and the unkempt garden of curly hair didn't match the darkness in his tone.

"I'm a talent agent," he smirked, the evidence of his terror-induced sweat had evaporated in the evening heat. "I was on my way to meet you, anyways. How lucky we both are."

Theodore's gut turned. "A... talent agent? Wait, are you with SmallSound? Do you know Matt? He just told me we were going to..."

The old man pulled out a small, cheap business card from his back pocket.

"...talk about my demo. Um," Theodore pointed at the card. The sharp, confident movements of the old man uneased him, "I thought you didn't have a wallet."

"Oh, I don't."

The old man flicked his wrist. In a brilliant streak, the card left his hand, zipped through the air and plunged deep into Theodore's chest. It slapped into his center like a knife into beef and forced a gurgle from his throat.

"And I don't know who Matt is, sorry."

Theodore's laptop-protecting backpack cracked expensively into the sidewalk as he stumbled backwards. Though the card was buried into his chest, no blood poured from the wound, or split the fabric of his shirt. It simply sat in his front, as if the flimsy square were part of his body.

"I know that you're a musician, though," the talent agent walked forward, hands in his pockets. "And you just mentioned a demo, so I'm *guessing* you were going to meet someone from your record label. Are you already on their label? Or were they interviewing you, or...?"

Theodore's chest erupted from around the card. The pieces of his upper body separated into perfect squares, which floated like soft, delicate bubbles into the air before they faded away.

In a normal explosion (if you were an unfortunate viewing party) you'd expect to see the blood and guts of the deceased. But Theodore was quite alive, and though his eyes rolled back into his head from intense pain, there was no typical evidence of bodily harm. The place where his chest once existed was gone, and what remained was a glossy, plastic cavity in the shape of the squares floating from his person. Each cube that flicked off his form burbled away like the drizzle of blonde coffee from an espresso machine.

"Well, I guess that doesn't matter, now," the talent agent shrugged. "I didn't read your bio that closely. Wasn't a lot there that mattered to me."

"What... the fuck..." Theodore managed to gasp as he writhed. He grabbed the pant leg of the talent agent, "...are you doing to me...?"

The old man squatted down, tsk-ing his pale, pained victim. "Listen. There's no sense in being mad at *me*. If you didn't want to change the world so badly, the card wouldn't affect you at all."

By this point, the shoulders up of Theodore's body remained. As the lines of separation drew over his mouth and ripped apart his jaw, the talent agent casually arched back up, stretched, and walked away. Before the strange spell could take Theodore's hearing, the old man stopped and said one more thing:

"You can't hide your intentions where you're going, Theodore. So you might as well be honest with people. It's the only way you'll win," the old man turned back and smiled.

"Thanks for saving me, though. That was real nice of you."

"You only get to be an imaginary friend for a short time, Taninim. He'll grow up. This form will be useless to him, a distant memory. He'll be embarrassed by you, and simultaneously enraged that he can't earnestly see you. You will no longer be a toy, nor a tool, but an admittance of the weakness of his mind in an increasingly real and grey world. And that's if you're *lucky*. At worst? You will be forgotten. You will be *forgotten*, Taninim, and he will not use you because he will not *need* you. You will atrophy, and you will *die*, and your essence will float in a void of regret for *just long enough* to be mistakenly hopeful that the next human mind won't be so shitty to you. This is the *truth* of the temporary world you live in—and it's an optimistic summary at best, since those leukemia tests haven't come back yet, have they? Still have another week to find out whether Jer's about to go battle a new dragon, right?"

The dragon-man's fist curled and his arm flexed with a hot hatred that made the lava he emerged from seem inviting by comparison. The talent agent noticed.

"Or, you can potentially be given the power to make any of his dreams come true. He'll lose you in the brief time you're gone, sure, but that's not any different from any rainy day blues, now is it?"

Taninim exhaled smoke, "What are you trying to say?"

"Those that earn the right to play god can make any world real... even this one," the talent agent stamped his foot down onto the cave's floor. "All you have to do is win a small contest. And if you do, you can do a lot more good for Jeremy than you ever, ever could otherwise. And he *needs* good, doesn't he, Taninim?"

Robin's Risk

A blur of white leather rocketed towards Julio's head. Robin Alleyne, it turned out, had an excellent pitching arm.

Perhaps, as an English teacher, she didn't have much use for it in her life anymore. Practically speaking, Robin hadn't needed her pitching arm for a long time: You don't *need* to be able to trace the red stitched outline of a baseball on touch alone to learn Spanish, or complete your 4-year bachelor's degree. You don't *need* to know the difference between a four seam and two seam fastball to get married, or to get divorced. You also don't *need* to practice opening your hips so your cutter explodes with more speed. You don't *need* anything about baseball in your life to do most things.

Robin's love of baseball had nothing to do with *need.*

Julio didn't know any of these little details about Robin's life, and even if he did, he probably had no idea a typical pitch reaches between 80-90 miles per hour. He also missed his brief opportunity to appreciate Robin's subtle adjustment to the power in which she threw—a conscious decision made to accommodate for the much closer distance between Robin's arm and Julio's skull than a standard regulation ball field.

As the sphere of sport cut the air towards him, his nerves lit up. In a twitch, he flicked his wrist. A white blur of his own flew from his hand—a cheap business card with unlikely speed and weight.

To his eyes, there was no clearer destination for the baseball than his face—and perhaps a less skilled pitcher would have cracked open his brainpan. The cutter pitch gets its name for its ability to break slightly as it reaches its target. Robin's cutter curved round the child's cheek and skimmed past the skin. It was just enough for Julio to feel the heat.

Robin wanted to cut *a little* sooner, but nobody's perfect.

Julio's magical pitch with his card, though, hit square in middle of Robin's forehead. Wordlessly, she toppled behind the desk. Julio also fell backwards, though it was just from his late reaction in trying to avoid the projectile. He stared at the speckled ceiling from behind his sunglasses, and panted as the previously pitched baseball rolled back to rest beside him.

"You... you..." he stammered. "You CRAZY BITCH! Isn't this one of your *students*?!"

He rose to hands and knees and fumbled his way towards Robin's desk, his limbs in tangled argument with themselves. His intention was to retrieve the card from what *should* have been the evaporating body of his teacher, but as he turned the corner, the adult-sized chair Mrs. Alleyne would sit in slammed into him and knocked his small frame down.

Flat on his back and dizzy from the blow, Robin was able to leap up and pin Julio by his wrists. As his vision clarified, Julio stared into the wild, furious eyes of his teacher—or rather, the furious *eye*.

Half of Robin's head was completely gone, separated into light squares of flesh that floated away before they disappeared into nothingness. The energy that cut away at her body came from the humming, drilling business card—but as it tried to further serrate her existence, it ran into the roadblock of her will.

"You. Are not. Julio," her cross dangled from her neck and clanked against the frame of Julio's sunglasses. "Who are you?"

"I'm a talent agent," Julio spat as he struggled. "You know what? No, fuck you. How are you able to move?"

"He was just here, where did you take him?"

"Listen! This is his body, okay?! I'm just here to-"

"Are you a demon?"

"I'm a talent agent-"

"You're possessing him!"

"Calm down, you bitch! Stop! Look, this dumbass kid is fine. I'm not from this world, lady, this is my only way to talk to you-"

"Then go back to where you belong!"

Robin grabbed Julio by the shoulders and shook him. She had no clear understanding of the situation—all she could do was just try and shake the devil out of him.

"We wanted to make you an offer-" Julio's voice vibrated as he struggled to push Robin's wrists off of him.

"Let him go!" she screamed. She slapped Julio across the face and knocked the glasses off. She then recoiled, shocked by his unnatural, pupiless green eyes.

The glasses skid across the floor.

"N-no!" Julio cried out. His hands free from Robin's momentary shock, he clawed towards the frames. Just before he could reach them, they vanished, and his palm smacked into the hard titled floor where his glasses once were.

Both teacher and student remained frozen: Robin's swiss-cheese body leaned against a wall and Julio's weary form splayed face first on the ground.

"W-what are you?" Robin finally asked.

"<Mrs. Alleyne...>"

Robin straightened up in surprise.

Julio climbed back to his hands and knees. His eyes, though drowned in tears, were clearly brown. "<Mrs. Alleyne, I'm so sorry.>"

Robin sucked in a lung full of conflicting emotions and pulled him in for a hug. "Shh, shh," she combed her fingers through his hair. "<It's okay, it's okay, it's okay. It's over now. Come on, don't cry.>"

"<It's not over Mrs. Alleyne,>" he sobbed. "<I could hear his thoughts...>"

Robin's hands froze in place.

"<He's going to take you away. It's my fault. I... I put on the->"

Robin pulled Julio away from her and looked him in his eyes. He couldn't believe she was smiling.

"<Do you hear him right now?>"

He sniffled. <"N-no...">

"<Then I'm glad,>" she pulled him back in. "<Tell me about what you remember... when you're ready.>"

Julio was sure he could remember and explain plenty once the tears stopped. Unfortunately, he would never know: As his body was brought forward to her chest, Robin's form crumbled like a house of cards. Whatever will she summoned to stave off the business card's ability was no longer good enough, and Julio crashed through her remains.

He caught himself with his palms, and the squares of Robin's body floated past his face. The business card that wiped her from existence landed in front of him. There was an emblem of an octopus, and the text "Cthulhu Allman Waters—Solutions and Design" was emblazoned across the card's face.

The Path

Squares of matter twisted and wobbled with the slick, oily film of time. They plopped together like cosmic gelatin, and their substance hardened as they condensed. The cubes lathered and settled into the form of Theodore Flores, who opened his mouth with a jolted inhale. He looked around.

There was nothing ahead, behind, or above him. He floated in a void that stretched forever, like the universe itself was made of bleached paper. He tried to shake his balloon-mind free from dizziness—and as he did, he saw that below, too, was a vast sea of nothingness.

As his legs dangled in negative space, he realized his dress was wrong. "Wrong" in the sense that those clothes were not what he put on that morning, or recently, or for several years.

"Uh..." Theodore tugged at the lapel of a suit he no longer owned. "Wh... what the fuck is this?"

But *he knew* what the fuck this outfit was. He was wearing an iridescent lavender suit of exquisite cut and proportion. His darker silk tie lassoed around a matching shirt's collar, relics of a decade Theodore actively chose to forget.

At the time of the talent agent's assault, he lived the type of life where he'd schedule what days he would eat packaged ramen. When he was younger and roamed the casinos of New York, though, it was a lot more time-efficient to eat whatever was inside or around the gambling den. For those days, and since it never hurt to make connections, Theodore chose to splurge on a nice suit. *First impressions... you know how it is,* he may have said then. (Poker—technically illegal in the state only if you payed a fee to play—was nonetheless possible to profit off of if you knew where the players went to play cash games. Theodore, a child of the generation first gifted the internet, learned of these shifting locations quickly.)

It was a suit nice enough to trick his way into games with people that had a lot more money to spare than he did. Here, in the void, he could hear the poker chips of the past chatter in the crinkle of the suit he presently wore. Fake names and fantasies to mask his college-debt reality whispered to him from the collar.

"I... I sold this..." Theodore spun around and upside down as he lost his grip on direction and sanity. "I wasn't wearing this..."

Before he could regress too deep into his overloaded memory, a slight whistle broke his concentration. He looked forward and saw an indistinguishable dot; a speck of matter far in the distance.

It grew. No—it got closer. The whistle sharpened.

"What-"

At a breakneck speed, Robin flew perpendicularly towards Theodore. Their heads crashed into each other and exploded like red fireworks, and their corpses ricocheted off into the void. They tore through the fabric of nothingness. Their speed reduced them to streaks of light. There was no way, by their understanding of the universe, that they could have survived such a collision.

Cthulhu's Balcony

"Fucking *finally*," Ocean-Mouth poked at the little umbrella in his martini with one of his green face tentacles. He watched the ultra-bright collision of stars from his balcony.

Two streaks of light broke through the foaming sky, then split away from each other like repelled magnets. One flew towards a hundred-story, color-shifting building. The other angled down towards the (accurately named) Forest of Golden Trees. From his vantage point, Ocean-Mouth could see the destination of these falling stars were roughly a few miles apart.

He laid in an reclining beach chair of expensive taste and let the lime sun soak into his thin, mucus-producing skin. On the other side of the balcony laid a large obelisk, who rested in its own beach chair with a foil reflector tilted to redirect light onto its smooth, obsidian surface.

"Oh man, that's like..." the obelisk paused. "...*really* far away. At least five minutes of flying."

Ocean-Mouth sighed and sat his drink down.

"Which one was it?" the obelisk asked.

"Guy went to the hotel. The girl was the one that landed in the forest," Ocean-Mouth twirled his legs to the side of his chair, and began to push himself up.

"Girl went to the forest, huh? That's not the contestant you're supposed to watch over. Sit down and relax."

"You know if Jesus finds out we didn't tell her the humans arrived, she's going to lose her mind, right?"

The obelisk titled as if to talk directly at Ocean-Mouth, despite the fact it had no appendages or discernible face. "You're not staff. She has people for this sort of thing. Enjoy your down time for a few more minutes, because you know you won't have *any* once this shitshow begins."

Ocean-Mouth rubbed the wet surface of his head as he tried to figure out which he was more uncertain of: Jesus's anger over their schedule or his own anxiety over the show. He adjusted the oil-like sunglasses on his face. "I guess I must've missed them coming in. I must've napped or something."

"There you go," the obelisk rotated back to the green sun. "We're judges. Let the peons do the work. Besides, I think there's a few contestants trekking through the forest right now. They can show the girl the way to the hotel."

"You think?" Ocean-Mouth raised a brow.

"Pretty sure. They both came from Hell. It's either contestants there or Luci. Either way, that human woman will get to where she needs to be before the show starts."

Ocean-Mouth sneaked an olive into his mouth, smearing it with the natural slime of his face tentacles. "Ah. Great, I guess.."

They laid still for a while, motionless and lazy. Then, Ocean-Mouth sat up, lifted his sunglasses, and scanned the landscape with his his pupil-less green eyes.

"What's wrong?"

"I swear, the one going towards the hotel..." he worried, an audible lump choked out of his throat as he observed one of the comets. "It was going to land in front of the building, then changed mid-air. It'll hit the side of the building now..."

"It's still going to the hotel though, right? It's fine."

"I mean, I guess, but... how did that happen?" the octopus-man turned his hips and rested on an elbow. "I didn't do that, and that's never happened before."

“Who cares? Maybe it’s just windy over there. Relax, Cthulhu.”

Cthulhu cared, and he knew the wind had nothing to do with the course correction. But when the obelisk floated another apple martini over to him, the weight of his anxiety crumpled under its fruity allure.

Taninim's Song

The dragon-man leaned against the color-shifting window. He had been left alone in the waiting room with nothing to entertain him except some plastic plants and uncomfortable, bizarrely polygonal couches. A soft angelic choir hummed from speakers in the corner of the ceiling, accompanied by the backbeat of brush drums and Hammond organs.

The only real entertainment there came from what he brought with him: his guitar.

Taninim's golden guitar was not just the main source of his power—it was a symbol. Jeremy, the human child who gave him life, was the son of a heavy metal musician and her #1 fan, whose livelihoods were an obvious inspiration for the world of swords and scales he kept himself in. Taninim, a creature born from the subconscious mind, cherished this symbol above all else.

He had been brought to the hotel by a creature that called itself a "talent agent," who had assured him that staff would arrive soon with further instructions. By now, Taninim had deeply regretted not specifying what "soon" meant. He spent his time laying on, or against, everything in the waiting room. He'd idly noodle up and down the neck of his guitar in some desperate attempt to make the music over the speakers more interesting. A new song faded in—though considering it was just another muted, jazzy Hammond organ, a less accustomed listener would be forgiven for not noticing the difference between these elevator-appropriate jams.

Taninim blew smoke from his pierced snout and grimaced. He had had enough.

He shoved one of the couches over to each corner of the room and systematically unplugged the speakers on the ceiling. When his claw tips brushed against each audio jack, a golden energy sparked briefly from his hand and the plugs that he grazed. The dead silence of the unplugged speakers was eradicated by a loud, idle buzz. Once he was finished, he returned to the center of the room and took a wide stance. He let the guitar drop low to his waist by its strap.

"Let's rock," Taninim shook his hand. It sparked golden.

Using his claw tips, he strummed a mighty, window-rattling power cord. Each of the speakers blared his notes in unison with the volume of his noisy stab. He nodded eagerly and bounced back and forth between his feet while he wailed away at a fast, chugging progression. He lost himself to the music and bounced around the room, jumped off furniture and punted plants. Had the riff not been so tasty that he shut his eyes with delight, he might have saw the spiraling comet hurtle towards the window of the room.

He slid on his knees across the floor at the end of a held high note. As the volume dropped from his passionate playing, he realized the windows were still vibrating independently of his solo. He opened his eyes.

The room was aglow with a neon green light. He turned his head to look out the wall of windows, and at that moment, they shattered. Taninim's body was swallowed by light as the energy comet smashed into, and through, the room.

Ishta-Devata's Vision

Two women sat together in the Forest of Golden Trees. It was not the bark that the forest got its name from, but the metallic leaves that these trees would shed year-round. If viewed from far away, these shiny leaves would catch the green sun, sparkling like a massive sea of hoarded coins.

A single leaf fell and drifted to the leg of one of the women. She almost brushed it away absentmindedly, but then noticed that the leaf was the exact same tone as the metallic skirt and chest plate she wore. She picked it up by the stem and twirled it and compared its hue to that of her armor's.

"Get enough of these and I could make a pretty cool crown," she mused. "I could wear it under my helmet. Hell, *on my helmet*. Shame they're so fragile, though. I wonder how many layers I'd have to stitch together to keep em' sturdy."

This was Athena. She was the daughter of Zeus, a god so (formerly) popular that their family, at one point in time, owned real estate in Heaven. Earth didn't believe in the Greek gods anymore, but still studied them, revered them. Theirs was a legacy she could squander on lazy luxury if she so desired—but she didn't. For her, living meant leaving the comfort of familiarity. She wished, however, that she had any reason other than *this one* to leave the House of Olympia.

"You're getting impatient," the other woman said with a sing-song giggle as she placed her teacup down to plate. She traced the outer rim with one of her blue fingers, "I promise she'll be here soon."

This was Ishta-Devata. She lived a similarly privileged life of the daughter of a family whose clout exclusively came from the years of praise they received from humanity. She was a gentle soul who could taste the difference of air between cities and describe it to you in fluid poetry. Her presence could cool anything when heated—a quality she needed to balance the fiery disposition of her companion.

"I'm just saying, had I started gathering these earlier I could've made crowns for both of us," Athena sighed, letting the leaf get carried away by the breeze. "We'd be queens of this forest. Probably would have had enough time to fight a bear and form a government of birds before your 'prediction' came true."

They both dreamed of moving to Heaven together, but not under these circumstances.

"This isn't a prediction, my dear. A prediction implies observation, or making a conclusion based off evidence," the other woman brushed a long lock of curly black hair from her cerulean face. "A prediction is more impressive than what I do, because a *prediction* implies I've put effort into its discovery."

Suddenly, an explosion rocked the forest. The crash of timber and screaming animals reached a momentary crescendo before it died back down to a heavy silence. Neither woman seemed phased by this development, but Athena did rub her face in annoyance.

"Alright, Ishta," Athena said. "What should I call it?"

"Well, since I saw it with my eyes, I guess it'd be a vision, wouldn't it?" Ishta smiled. Athena stood up, then offered her hands. Ishta pulled herself up in her grip, "Thank you."

"Well, I hope your future visions are more specific. Let's go find her."

They headed, hand-in-hand, in the direction of the explosion. A sulphur smoke choked the air as they got closer, as did the haze of disturbed pollen and soil. Ishta covered her mouth with the silk, heavy sleeve of her free arm. Athena soldiered ahead and pulled the blue maiden behind her, scanned the area like a hawk, noted every tree top and bush, and sought any twig snap not from her own feet.

They reached a massive crater, some 20 feet in diameter and depth. The earth in, and around, the crater was a charred, smoking black. Ashes of bark and leaves sprinkled down, birds and squirrels laid with their bodies burnt and broken on the forest floor.

Oddly, as the pair observed the devastated land, the crater shrunk in diameter and lifted in depth. In the center of the cavity was a human skeleton, red and black from its fiery travels.

"No way," Athena said. "That's a human. That's really a human! Look at it, why, there's no magic in that thing at all! And... oh my word, look! Heaven can heal here, this far away from the hotel?"

"The hotel isn't the source of the healing, after all. The whole planet's surface might have this property."

As the soil in the crater lifted and filled, stringy layers of muscle and tendon grew from the bones. Athena looked around and saw that the same magic occurred to the creatures and trees destroyed by the blast—bark slowly built back up and regained its unsullied tone. Dead birds were reattached to their wings before they took flight.

Ishta rubbed Athena's shoulder. "If your sister really came to this place, then she's still alive. We'll find her. I promise."

Athena sucked her lips in briefly at the mention of her sister, but kept focus on the regenerating skeleton. The crater had filled now, and this skeleton had reverted back its original form: a middle aged umber skinned woman. Even the clothes she wore—a sharp geometric top and dyed jeans—returned from incineration.

The woman, Robin Alleyne, shook her head from side to side. Dirt from the ground fell from her face. She opened her eyes and saw two women standing above her, staring—the Greek warrior and the bejeweled, blue skinned princess. One's face was tight and intense, the other soft and curious.

Reflexively, she crawled backwards. "Where am I? Who are you? Where's Julio? Uh... h-how long have you just been staring at me?"

"Are you okay?" Ishta clapped her hands together. "Tell me how you feel."

"Can..." Robin squinted in confusion. "...Can you answer... *any* of the questions I just asked?"

"Oh, who are you kidding, Ishta?" Athena soured. "Of course she's fine. Look at her."

"Are you two... dressed up for a play or something?" Robin raised herself to her feet, but then tumbled back when she took in her surroundings. "Oh, whoa, whoa. What the hell are these trees? Is this a movie set? How long did it take to make all this? Is that green spotlight supposed to be the sun?"

Athena sneered. "Do I look like an actress to you? A charlatan?"

Robin slapped away dirt from her clothes. She scrutinized the tall, blonde, sharp-faced warrior up and down. Her braids were packed tight around her head, likely to fit in the Corinthian helmet tucked under her arm. Fussy, sheer fabrics made up her skirt and clothes under her golden armor, needlessly and intricately pleated and detailed with the smallest floral applique.

Her bronze, round eyes waited for Robin's answer with an unnecessary intensity.

"Yes," Robin said.

Ishta covered her face to mute her giggle. The warrior's eyes widened. "You dare mock the great Athena?!"

Robin raised an eyebrow. Ishta stepped forward and lightly pushed Athena back, taking a tone that cooed and commanded. "Oh, stop trying to scare her. She just got here."

"Hey, you two aren't..." Robin lowered her head and took another step back, "...you aren't talent agents, are you?"

"Oh, no, no, no," Ishta peacefully glided towards Robin and extended her hand. "We're contestants, like you. My name is Ishta-Devata."

Athena pursed her lips.

"I'm Robin," the teacher hesitantly took the soft blue hand in a shake. "Listen, I'm not competing for anything."

Athena lowered her brow.

"If you're looking for a talent agent, it'll be a while. All of staff is notoriously hard to get in contact with... outside of, perhaps, the camera crew and hotel staff," Ishta turned and pointed through the dense forest. "If we go this way, we'll make it to the hotel in 20 minutes or so. I'll show you our quarters, and we'll see about contacting staff."

"Our *quarters*? You don't understand. I'm not staying."

Athena closed her fist.

"Robin, I'm only saying this because it's an important lesson for you to understand," for the first time, the soft, pastry-like smile was gone from Ishta's face. "You do not get to choose when you leave here."

"Like hell I don't. These guys attacked one of my students," the lines of annoyance drew over Robin's face.

If there was more to that thought, neither Athena or Ishta found out. The punctuation to her complaint was a bladed spear tossed into her chest. The pole arm knocked her back into the bark of a tree and pinned her there.

Robin gurgled and her eyes rolled back into her head. She hated that her last thought was how this had happened twice to her in the same day. Unlike the last time Robin was blindsided by a projectile, though, her blood covered the ground underneath her five foot flight. Her vision faded and the chill of death seeped through the veins of her arms, legs, and chest.

Then she came back to life. Her lungs filling with a loud gasp. There was no blood, no spear. She laid with her back against the tree—light-headed and bewildered, but otherwise as healthy as a person that hadn't been stabbed.

Athena stood over her, and shadows fell over her face as she glared down. She let the spear rest against her shoulder.

"Welcome to Heaven," she said. "You weren't listening, so I figured I'd chime in."

Robin clenched a pile of leaves into her fist. "W-what...? Heaven?"

"No one can die in Heaven. But don't think for a second that means you get to do whatever you want."

"Athena, that was completely unnecessary," Ishta grabbed and lifted the front of her layered red skirt, ran over, and pushed herself between the two. Athena's muscular, wall-like build only relented because it was Ishta.

"Clearly it was, if she thinks she has any power over talent agents."

"You... you stabbed me," Robin stood back up to her feet, and stumbled around and away from the duo. She kept her eyes locked on Athena as she warbled around. "You're insane."

"Robin, I apologize for Athena's rudeness. She's trying to understand you, and you should try to understand her, too."

"She *stabbed* me," Robin's backwards gallop contained enough fear and anger that she stumbled gracelessly. "Nope, I'm outta here. Peace."

"Actually," Athena ran a finger across the edge of her spear's blade. With a tap, the blade vibrated, hummed, then disappeared in a flash of light. "If you want to go home, that's the last thing you want to do. You can either run around lost in this forest for the rest of your life, or you can follow the only two people you've met that understand how this world works. You're from Earth, right?"

Robin stopped. Even if Athena's no-nonsense suggestion contained a drop of logic, Robin swore she could still feel a phantom pain where the spear entered her scar-less chest. "Earth...? You think just because you put some blue paint on and spent some money on a set that I'm gonna believe I'm not on Earth anymore?"

A flaming skeleton cooled its ashen bones with magnetized meat and fiber. The corpse cobbled itself together into a fine suit, and once fully healed, Theodore opened his eyes.

While there was more scenery than his last displacement, there was no time to appreciate the fact that he was, well, *somewhere.* Unfortunately, he had no more information than this because *somewhere* was currently on fire.

His lungs sucked for clean air, but all that they received was a wall of sulphur smoke. The battering his coordination took from the heat caused him to tumble around like a knocked over barrel. His teary eyes blurred his vision. He reached a hand out to find something to pull himself up on, and found a bumpy leather surface—thin and cheap on its own, but the white fabric protected a pocket of fluffy stuffing. This was, as far as he could make out, the arm of a couch. When he pulled himself up, though, he stumbled back to his knees as the remains of the furniture flipped onto him. The couch arm, which was woefully unequipped to handle Theodore's large frame, was all that remained of the still smoldering sofa.

Theodore coughed and kicked the former-couch off of his body. As he tried to climb back up to his feet, the same furniture arm flew back into him and knocked him flat.

"What the hell..." Theodore groaned.

He sat back up and shrugged off the pain in his spine. He noticed the smoke, which a moment ago was almost completely disabling, had cleared to thin wisps. The smell of sulphur was faint. To his surprise, a perfectly maintained white leather couch sat in front of him. Its back was a bizarre asymmetrical polygon—clearly an attempt at something modern and whimsical. Theodore winced, personally feeling it looked better when it was obscured by smoke. And destroyed.

Breaking the silence was a soft, inoffensive Hammond organ that waltzed from a small speaker in the corner of the ceiling. Theodore stared into the grill of the speaker both in disgust at its tinny, cheap sound, and in confusion. Its feel-good groove gave him mood whiplash from the burning building he could have sworn he was in the moment before.

"Hold on. This is..." he wagged a finger in the air, "...a cover. This is 'Haunted' by Poe. And it *sucks*. Why would you water down such a great song like this?"

He brought himself to his feet and raked his thick, curly hair backwards. He went to brush the soot off his suit, but it was no longer there—instead, the lavender fabric was as perfectly pressed as the day he had it tailored.

"Uh... Uh..." a voice choked out.

Theodore froze. He wasn't alone.

"UWAAAH!" a sandpaper cry howled from behind Theodore. It rattled his ribcage and soul.

He spun around to see the source of the roar; a hulking beast, humanoid in shape but monstrous in frame. Theodore, not at all a small man, would likely need his highest jump to reach any of the several horns the dragon-man was crowned with. He'd need to clone himself to out-muscle the serpent's obviously well cultivated physique. He'd need a more wild lifestyle to wear its rebellious leather studded pants and wrist cuffs, or its intimidating nose ring and chain. He'd also need a well paid tailor to customize these to his size—and he'd still look more out of place in them than the dragon did.

Perhaps most importantly, before he could say anything, he'd need context as to why this impossibly-toothed man was sobbing a waterfall of tears over the remains of a guitar. To be fair to Theodore, he would also need the understanding that the wild thing in front of him was real, and not the product of any of his most recent head trauma. As Theodore could neither jump that high, bulk up that quickly, or have that knowledge, he lacked all the required prerequisites to comprehend this spectacle—so instead, he just stared and mouthed half-formed expletives to himself.

The dragon-man sat on his knees, hands held at the small flames that consumed the wood and strings of his golden instrument.

"MY GUITAR!" the dragon screamed. "NO! NO! NO! That's my most valuable possession!"

The dragon-man brought a leather-cuffed wrist to his drenched eyes, choked back a messy sob, and then froze in stiff silence. He rose like embers and opened his pinned, enraged eyes.

"You."

Theodore clenched.

"*You* did this."

The dragon-man plodded forward. His shoulders swung with each furious step. The swell of his anger dragged his body. The scales of his chest began to glow as a deep orange light source formed within, and his eyes rolled back into his head.

Theodore panicked and looked for an exit. The pink-and-gold waiting room was mostly empty, aside from its ugly furniture, plastic plants and terrible music. Despite its busy-on-the-eyes wallpaper and gold adornments, there was little there to hide behind or use as a weapon.

"Wait," Theodore blurted.

Smoke billowed from the dragon-man's nostrils, and his chest expanded three times its normal size. The smooth scales of his front slid to their maximum stretch during the expansion, and revealed a thin, heat resistant membrane between them. His eyes glowed with the flames of vengeance—only slightly dimmer than the actual flames building within his chest.

"Waitwaitwait! Your guitar is fine!"

The dragon-man stopped, turned his head, and unleashed a massive fireball onto a nearby plastic plant. The powerful blast incinerated the cheap pot it sat in, and blew out the wall behind it. The eruption and subsequent explosion toppled a terrified Theodore over.

"What did you say, you *runt*?" the dragon-man snarled.

Theodore adjusted his collar. "Y-your guitar. Look at it again."

With a whip-like head turn that jangled his piercings, the impossibly-toothed man let out a shriek of delight when he saw that Theodore was telling the truth. Where there was previously a pile of ashes now sat his golden guitar, glittering in the neon sun that streamed through the room's singular windowed wall.

"YES!" The dragon-man leaped and scooped up the instrument. He cradled it like a large, awkward child. "Yes! Yes!"

Theodore held his hands on either side of his head. He turned to where a plant had just met its untimely end—except there it sat, its plastic leaves defiantly artificial and undamaged. He looked at it, then at the dragon, then at the walls, then at his suit, then back at the potted, unharmed plastic.

"So, I saw *Jacob's Ladder*," Theodore stammered. "Am I dying? If you're supposed to be my Danny Aiello, I don't mind just skipping to the end."

The dragon-man curled his scaled brow in confusion. "Danny... Aloe vera?"

"What," he pointed at the plant, "the FUCK is happening here? What are you, where am I, What is..." he spun with his arms out, throwing his question to the world around him, "what is ANY of this bullshit?"

His plea echoed. Only the soft jazz from the speakers answered. Theodore turned back to the dragon-man, whom was still on his knees, clutching his guitar. He had curled away from Theodore a bit, as if this monster had just been spooked by something.

"Those are bad words."

"What?"

"Those are bad words. You shouldn't say them."

"*What*? You nearly cooked me and you're trying to tell me about what's *bad*?"

"I'm sorry," the dragon-man teared up. "I just don't know what I'd do without my guitar. I should have known better. I just... I just didn't think the other talent agent would be right about this place."

The blubbering lizard, despite his intimidating presence, was not the same enraged beast he was a moment ago. *He's like a child,* Theodore thought.

"Talent agent? Were you kidnapped too? What did he say to you?"

"K-Kidnapped?" the dragon-man wiped a tear away. "What do you mean?"

Theodore curled his lip. "Exactly what I asked."

"I... I agreed to come here. Why wouldn't I want a chance like this?"

He squinted. "A chance like what?"

"To become god."

Theodore tilted his head. The dragon-man's frank answer hung in the air while the bland jazz simmered.

"Okay, before I venture too far into this conversation I just want to go ahead and note, out-loud, that I'm talking to the subject of a *Judas Priest* album cover about becoming god," Theodore started to pace, yelling aloud at the walls of the room. "If any hidden cameras would like to come out and tell me what show all of these incredibly illegal pranks are for, that'd be great, because I'm fucking *done* with jokes today. Who wants to be the person to give me a rational explanation? Who wants to get their *asses* beaten and/or sued out of existence? Anyone?"

"He told me that this place would heal anything," the dragon-man whimpered.

Theodore stopped pacing. "I'm sorry?"

Taninim strummed the guitar to check its tuning, then started to twiddle with its machine heads.

"He said, 'Everything can be healed in Heaven.' The talent agent, I mean. I thought you were one when I saw your suit," he noodled up and down the neck of the guitar, doing anything to avoid eye contact. "I'm sorry. I shouldn't assume things. My name is Taninim. It's nice to meet you, and please... please understand that I'm really, really sorry about getting mad at you. I just get worked up sometimes. Would you like to hear a song? I could play a song to make up-"

"I'm going to stop you right there," Theodore quickly held up his palm. "'Heaven?' Not that I even believe in that, but people need to be abducted into *Heaven*?"

"I-I told you I wasn't abducted. And the shark should have explained all the rules about this place to you," the dragon's scaled lip-line frowned.

"The shark?," Theodore rubbed the nose of his bridge.

"He's the only person from staff I've met since I came here. They told me they'd be sending someone here soon but you're the only person that's shown up."

"Cool, okay, whatever. If he can tell me where the legal department is, then point me to him. Any more animals I need to know about?"

"You have to find a camera. The shark lives in the cameras."

Theodore walked over and grabbed the neck of Taninim's guitar, muting its strings with his palm. Taninim stiffened his back and lowered his voice.

"Please don't touch my guitar."

Theodore, unblinking, put his face next to the rows of teeth. "Then *start making sense*."

The two sets of eyes locked in a clash of uncomfortable testosterone. The elevator jazz on the speaker paused all its instruments in coincidental suspense, except for the clueless prerecorded bassist unaware of the mounting tensions.

"Go ahead. Keep your hand there. See what happens," Taninim said.

"You're not the only god damned musician in this room. I was one meeting away from having my work published with a company I loved on my own terms, and one of those jackass 'talent agents' fucked that up for me. He literally *drugged* and *abducted* me."

Taninim pulled the guitar out of Theodore's hand with a snarl, but his scaled expression softened with sympathy. "W-why would they do that? It's just a reality show. I had to agree to be here."

Theodore's head shook in a boggling tug of war between disbelief and hysteria. "*What*? A *reality* show?"

A polite knock interjected from the other side of the room's only door. Both the guitarist and the sound engineer looked up towards the jewel encrusted handle as it wiggled with gentle concern.

"Y-you should really talk to the shark. If that's a cameraman, he'll be there."

The door opened. On the other side was a misshapen mound of human flesh, asymmetrical in proportion and structure. A semblance of clothes was tacked onto what could most charitably be described as a chest. There was only one limb there that was relatively human looking—an evenly toned arm, bent to hold up a tiny, blinking camera. It was a stretch to call this drooling mass a cameraman, but in the brief moment Theodore got to observe the creature, he knew this was what Taninim was talking about.

Nowhere, however, did he see a shark.

"How dare you talk to her like that," Athena said. She snapped her hand to the side, and another spear sparked into her grip. "Ishta's patience with your blubbering has been infinite, which is still not enough to get through to you."

"Athena, wait," Ishta said, her huge smile commanding the attention of both. "Think about what she just said."

Athena stared into the soil. "You... can see her?"

The absurdity of Athena's question spun Robin in place. "Can I... are you... are you serious? Can I see the lady in the technicolor makeup we've both been talking to?"

Athena's face twisted with such instant agony that it immediately brought her to one knee. "Forgive me, Robin. I could not see Ishta's blue skinned form for a very long time. That you can see her—as she really is—shows your depth of character. And you did it with no magic at all... incredible."

Robin's brow had furrowed to the extent that she could have caught another chucked spear from Athena between the crevice of her forehead's confusion. "What? No. My character isn't determined by my being able to see skin color," after saying that out loud, she wretched. "Oh god. No. I've actively been trying to fight against that idea my whole life, in fact."

Ishta held a sleeve to her mouth to cover her giggle, but the crescent of her eyes betrayed her amusement. "Athena, why don't you tell her what you saw when you first met me."

Athena breathed embarrassment through her nose, and kept her gaze down.

"I saw myself," Athena muttered.

Ishta took soft steps over to Robin, and the leaves that she walked on crunched thankfully underneath her. "Robin, you are now in a realm of magic. You have seen the healing that hangs in the air. You've been pierced by the ever-present War Chest of Greece, and suffered no damage in the process. You've seen the strange beauty of our Golden Trees, and you haven't run screaming and crying at the rationalization that you are very, very far away from your concept of reality. You have instead challenged me, and remained clear of thought in your goals. It is the clarity in your determination that has broken the fog of my ability. "

"Your... ability?"

"When people see me, they see what they desire. Sometimes it's material. Sometimes they see their perception of god. Sometimes it's sexual. It depends upon the person, the mood, the moment. For those of... particularly thin thought, my disguise may never be broken."

Robin listened, a finger to her chin. After a moment, her eyes widened and she directed a machine-gun wheeze at Athena. "So which one was it for you?"

"You will not *mock* me," Athena rose.

"Athena," Ishta raised a hand, and the blonde warrior exhaled obediently.

"So you know," Robin fished her cross necklace out from under the ribbed collar of her top. "This is all very difficult for me to believe, even after experiencing it. I have my own idea of heaven. This isn't it. And if you are supposed to reflect some desire I have, well. This *still* isn't it."

"I think you're doing a fine job," Ishta countered with a smile, a suggestion which initially confused Robin. "We would probably struggle on Earth, too. Listen, I have a compromise I'd like to make. Maybe even a bet, if you're interested. Let us go to the hotel together. That is where the talent agents that brought you here are. Let's watch, together, the way other contestants perceive me. When you see that they have wildly different ideas of what I look like, you will know that you have seen through me in a way that almost no one else can."

"I don't... understand why I should care about that."

Ishta clasped her hands over Robin's and drew her near. Robin wanted to pull away from the saffron-scented woman, but when their eyes locked, she found herself captivated by the silk of Ishta's voice and skin. The song of each syllable spiraled into her mind and soul, the softness in her every subtle movement submerged Robin in a sea of droning echoes.

"I also want to know what the talent agents are doing. And it's precisely the fact that I know that something is wrong in Heaven that makes me your ally, not your enemy. Helping you helps me. *Please* let me help you."

After an uncomfortable pause, Robin was able to shake her head and pull away. She looked between the warrior and the maiden, then huffed.

"I'll go to the hotel, but let's make something clear: you will need to earn my trust. I normally assume the best out of people but you pretty much ruined that by stabbing me, even if... even if I'm fine for some reason," Robin took a heavy gulp of forest air. "You can tell me along the way what I'm walking into."

"Gladly," Ishta smiled. "Anything you need to know, ask."

Robin sucked her lips in, squatted, and took a golden leaf from the ground. It shimmered like metal, and crumbled like paper with the slightest squeeze between her thumb and index finger. "Start... with what brought you two here."

Athena led with a map and strange compass she summoned from thin air. It was Ishta that explained Athena's story, as if the strong-willed warrior didn't want to tell it herself: Her sister, Eris, was a fan of the television show these three had all tried out for at an audition. Eris had, at the time, been selected as a contestant and after she left, Athena had received her own invitation. She was excited to be on the same show as her sister, until she tried to call Eris and tell her of her acceptance.

"It was only an hour since she left to go to the show," Athena crinkled the map when she interjected. "I don't remember her saying goodbye, but she's gone. Her belongings are gone. Her number doesn't go to her voicemail anymore. I might sound crazy, but I can feel it. If she's not there... if she's not at this show..."

Robin's mind was hung up on an important juxtaposition: "Wait, this is... a TV show? What the hell sort of show is this?"

The Camera Shark

Theodore opened his eyes. "No... not again."

He had been transported into an aquamarine tinged room of economical size. What it lacked in space, it made up for in the buzz of electronics—everywhere he turned, there was a flashing display, or black-and-white CRT TV spying on a hallway. Drone-like cameras whirled around him and blinked their red-recording eyes with curiosity. Their metal supports stretched into portals of disconnected darkness. On a monitor, he spotted Taninim: the scaled guitarist had brought his face near the camera, and his forest of teeth took up a large part of the frame.

Behind Theodore, a whirling hydraulic pump creaked on. Pressure chambers hissed with release, and a doorway appeared where one did not seem to exist before.

"Oh! Hello, hello!"

The shark waltzed in with a corked bottle of wine in one sandpaper gray hand, and two clinking flute glasses in the other. The bottom of the glasses rested in his counter-shaded palm, which he lifted up in a mixture of wave and invitation. Theodore briefly thought the smile of this creature was warm, but realized it was a trick of the light—there was little movement capable in his shark mouth, and little emotive power in his black vacuums of eyes. The head of this killing machine was stuffed into an ensemble of bubbly personality. A champagne trench coat billowed over pleated trousers. Ornate turquoise dotted his cuffs and collared shirt. Any animal instinct left in the bipedal fish-man's blood had been drowned in fine fashion and alcohol.

"You must be..." the shark walked over to a clipboard on a cluttered desk. "...Theodore! Theodore Flores, right? Am I right?"

"This might be a wild assumption, but I guess you're the shark."

"Mark! Mark Sharkman. Friends call me Markie."

"Mark it is, then."

"Would you like some wine, Theodore? I got this Port wine here. I also have some kava, if you're feeling wild. I think I like kava more, but that's more of an acquired taste. It's not pretty to look at, kind of looks like garbanzo beans run through a blender. And its taste... well, it's pretty disgusting, if I'm being honest. But my word, does it calm you down-"

"No."

"Not a drinker, eh? That's alright!" Mark tossed the wine flutes over his shoulder, popped the cork, and started guzzling. The wine splashed down his mouth and neck. This shark's feeding frenzy was atypical for its species, but resulted in roughly the same amount of red stains along his face. "Everyone has their own way of partying. I don't judge."

After downing an entire bottle of wine on his own, Mark hiccuped and pirouetted over towards a stool, clipboard in hand. "Alright! So I suppose we should get down to the boring part. I know the talent agent gave you the elevator pitch on the show, so let's jump into-"

"No."

Mark looked up from the clipboard. Possibly in confusion, but with his coal eyes and stiff smile, it was difficult to tell. "I'm sorry?"

"They didn't tell me anything."

He tapped his clipboard anxiously. "Should've made kava. Okay, well. I'm sure they at least told you-"

"Nothing. Your talent agent kidnapped me, and now I'm your problem. I don't know what's happening, and I want to go home."

Mark craned his head around and hoped if he viewed Theodore's stone face from different angles that he'd gain more insight into his meaning. "I don't... understand."

"I want the number to your legal department, and I want a ride home. I didn't agree to any of this, and I don't care what I have to do to get out of here. For the record, I *am* aware I'm talking to a man in an animatronic Shark-Mask. I am also aware of the fact that this is, apparently, a reality show that I didn't consent on being a part of. Either that, or this is all a dream, one of which I don't like, and one of which I will continue to bitch about until I wake up."

"Theodore... first off, not a mask," he circled a finger around his finned head. "Second off, I've been working here for longer than your family tree has been growing. The talent agent's business cards *do not work* without consent from the soul of the transported. Are you sure you're not just getting cold feet?"

Theodore's crossed arms tightened around his chest.

"Where in my body, exactly, is the soul located? The heart? I know my blood's there. My head? My brain does a lot of work, but seriously, I've never seen a soul on a CT Scan before. What does a soul look like? Is a soul admissible in a court-of-law?"

"Hey, I'm sensing some negative energy right now. I'm telling you, man, that kava will help us calm down—"

Theodore's eye twitched. "I will *ne—ver* calm down just because someone told me to."

Theodore saw that shards of the flute glasses Mark had tossed earlier had not reformed. He grabbed the empty wine bottle from the desk, smashed it against the corner, and brought the jagged top to Mark's neck.

"So, uh, I can see that you're very upset," Mark said.

"Whatever that 'healing' thing was over where I met Taninim, apparently takes a longer amount of time to kick in here, if it does at all. So, question: do you think if your body dies before the 'healing' kicks in, you'll *stay* dead? All this mystical bullshit is new to me, and I gotta say, I'm feelin' *real* inquisitive right now. Of course, it would be easier just to let me go home, and probably less painful, so ... "

Theodore marched Mark backwards with the serrated wine-top against him. The two toppled onto the desk, and Theodore's larger frame pinned the shark-man down effortlessly. If Mark's toothy, unchanging expression was difficult to read, his relaxed tone wasn't.

"Huh. I've seen some unique reactions to contestants being brought on the show, but this... is... certainly a new one."

"Take. Me. Home."

"You cannot go home until the ritual is complete. And by ritual, I mean your time on this show. I'm not being difficult. I'm explaining how things work around here."

Theodore spoke through gritted teeth and pressed down harder on the shark. "I don't care about your 'show.' I'm not asking you to take me home. I'm telling you: take me home, or get filleted." He twisted Mark's arm above his head, and pushed the edges of the broken glass into the shark's chunky neck with enough pressure to punctuate his seriousness. Mark did not struggle, and his obsidian eyes did not blink.

"Theodore, I'm afraid you're going to find that Heaven is a unique place where threats of death are on the weaker side of intimidation tactics. This is also a touch out of character for you, and not a path I think you want to go down *again*."

Theodore's eyes widened at the emphasis on "again" and he immediately hopped away from Mark. The shark-man, like a zoo-keeper trying to keep conservative movements around a dangerous attraction, peeled himself off his own desk slowly, hands held out. "What the *fuck* would you know about my character?" he straightened his posture like a cobra before a bite.

"Well, a lot, silly! That's why I'm here! I am the interviewer." Mark curtsied with the long tail of his champagne coat. "My job is exclusively to get to know you and film your intimate reactions. I try to be the smiling face that introduces you to Heaven, but, well, something clearly went awry for you to have exploded into the side of this building the way you did. Also—for future reference—if you're going to stab me, I wouldn't aim for the throat. Shark skin is notoriously thick, you'd probably never make it through with that. Go for the eye, that's a lot more vulnerable."

Theodore dropped the broken bottle top and held the sides of his head. "None of this is real. I don't understand. I don't get... *this*. I don't get what's happening."

"Hey, hey, hey, let's just take this a step at a time. I'm here to talk you through this. I'm sorry that whatever idiot agent you got didn't do a very good job at explaining things, so let's just go right to the beginning," Mark shifted through some of the cluttered papers on his desk. He ripped a sheet from a pile and held it up, and a whirling camera behind him nodded in approval. "Here we go. So when you were talking about your 'dreams', I'm guessing you were talking about the record label you were in contact with, SmallSound. They wanted to hear the demo for the album you wanted to release with them, right?"

"I was literally on my way there, when-"

"Yes, the timing was awful, but I think you'll be a lot happier when you turn around and look at Taninim."

Theodore turned back to the monitor he saw earlier. Taninim's maze of fangs still took up most of the frame.

"Wait, has he been looking into the camera this whole time? It looks like he hasn't moved at all. Is the screen broken?"

"Time moves differently here in my Camera World—a Heaven second probably hasn't passed yet. It's a much slower pace within the camera than it is outside. And I suspect the same is true for the path between Heaven and your planet—"

"You 'suspect?'" said Theodore. "So you don't know. In addition to it being scientifically unsound, you can't even *bullshit* me properly."

"I have two points, Theodore. That was number one."

"Get to the convincing one."

"You won't need a label if you win."

"What?"

"The show. If you win, you won't need anyone's help ever again in anything that you do. The prize of this show is beyond anything else anyone can ever offer you. All this anger at your situation clouded you from asking the simplest and most important question: What is the name, and premise, of the show you were chosen for?"

Mark fished around in the large pocket of his coat, and produced a cheap plastic card. Theodore bristled predictably at the sight of a stranger producing a card in front of him, but Mark assured him that this was not an attack, but a gift.

"Theodore, it's not just a coincidence you're in Heaven. Whether you choose to believe it or not, you're not drugged, nor are you dreaming. You're actually talking to a sharp-dressed shark (and I should know, since I dressed this handsome man myself.) And yes, you were just having a spat earlier with a death-metal loving dragon. You are at the surface level of the magic that gets drawn to Heaven, and I promise you the show will just get crazier from here on out. All these spirits and creatures—you included—are here for the same thing: they all want to be the winner of the most popular reality show in existence, *The Next Great Deity*. You should be *thrilled* to be among them."

He walked up to Theodore and placed the card into his palm.

"Contestants are chosen by a committee that monitors the potential and power of a living thing's soul. The odds against any single entity being chosen for this show are infinitely small. You, my friend, were chosen to compete because something in you was loud and bright enough to get noticed. And if you really don't want to be here, if the power that comes from being a god is really so unappealing to you that you would willingly tangle with someone that has as many teeth as I do, then I have simple advice."

Theodore scanned the text of the card. It came in a small paper half-envelope with a room number on it—35-D. On its back was a thin black magnetic strip, with childishly illustrated instructions on how to use an electronic card reader. Theodore drew the card out of its envelope and looked at the front—a bubbly, winged logo emblazoned the name 'Heaven's Heart Hotel.'

"All you have to do to go home, is lose."

Theodore flinched.

"If I lose, I get to go home? That's it? Is this the... like, eating bugs type of reality show, or make-a-dress type of reality show?"

"I'm not allowed to spoil anything, obviously. But if you were picked specifically to be here, I imagine there's something in your skill-set the hostess was impressed by," Mark did his best to smirk. "I suppose you don't eat bugs, typically."

"Not yet," he sighed through his nose. "So, when am I going to sign a waiver? For my protection, of course. I'm assuming a show as important as you claim this bullshit is will also have a 'Contract of the Gods.'" He mocked and finger quoted his hypothetical legal document.

"Theodore, you were just hurled across time and space and your body is fine."

He pointed the hotel card at the shark. "Yet you can't send me back as easily."

"Nope. The transport spell binds you here in Heaven until you are officially removed from the show... or declared winner, I guess, but judging by your reluctance and attitude, I doubt you'll be here long."

"Fair enough..." Theodore poked at a blinking drone that got too close to him, and it recoiled away into the darkness. Mark attempted a frown, disappointed his jab didn't land—was Theodore not competitive? Or did he just not care? "If I lose any time on Earth, though... if this costs me anything in my career, I'll find a way back here, and I'll be coming for you."

"Me, specifically?" Mark laughed. "And after I offered you something to drink. How rude."

"Or the next most important person that pisses me off. I was hoping that'd be your moment to tell me who I should talk to next. Or should I just come out and say it plainly? 'I want to talk to your manager.'" Theodore paused. "It feels gross to be on this side of that sentence."

"It's as difficult to spot as a hummingbird's wing in flight, but I think I'm finally starting to see your sense of humor. My 'manager'... you'll meet her soon enough. In the meantime, though, maybe I have one more thing to show you to convince you there's no ill will here."

Mark hooked arms with Theodore and walked towards the wall. He clicked his sharp teeth together: the same hissing door from before opened up, and a gust of air pushed into the tails of his coat. It led to a well lit tunnel that endlessly stretched. Lemon yellow paint, fluorescent lights, and an infinite supply of alcohol lined the walls forever into the distance.

"Reality shows have to construct a story from both the footage, and the interviews with the contestants. I can live in these cameras, but I can't make the camera move on my own, so the shiqq—that's the lumpy guy you saw earlier—helps me get around. Isn't that interesting?"

"No."

"With the way this Camera World works," Mark continued on, unfazed, "I can film in here, then send the footage to the editors. Do you see what I'm getting at? I'm a valuable asset to the show. In front of you is how they pay me: with a world of liquid delight. Now, sadly, because of Heaven's healing abilities, I can never drink myself stupid, but the fact it takes longer to heal in here means I can at least keep a happy warmth in my cheeks. I also get food, but, the wine's better."

"Why are you showing me this?"

Mark wrapped an arm around Theodore's shoulder. Despite his rigid facial structure, his toothy smile seemed authentic, if but for a brief moment. "If there is any way at all of breaking the spell, I promise you they will accommodate you. I'm being paid to drink and play armchair psychologist. Trust me. Or, at least relax and just enjoy this one chance you're getting. You might accidentally have fun if you let yourself go." He then clicked his teeth.

Theodore opened his eyes, his reflection in the lens of the shiqq's camera.

"Ah, you're back!" Taninim said. "What's that in your hand?" Before Theodore could shake the fog from his head, Taninim suddenly had a hotel key of his own between his fingers. "Ah, I'm back! He forgot to give me mine. Turns out we're roommates."

Theodore rubbed the bridge of his nose. As his jet-lagged brain eased into reality, he understood that Mark gave no inclination that he was going to send Theodore back to the hotel—it just happened. It stands to reason, then, that he could have kicked Theodore out of the camera at any point if he wanted to. He allowed Theodore to grab the bottle, to threaten him, to argue with him. The implication forced the sound-sculptor silent—he could be caught there at any time, instantly, for any reason.

The shiqq oozed out of the doorway, grunted incoherently, and tilted its head towards an ornate golden elevator. Cards in hand, the musicians left behind the dull jazz of the waiting area and went on to their destination, room 35-D: Third Floor, 4th hallway, 5th room.

“Yeah, I get it,” Robin said.

Mark navigated the planes of her face, in desperate search of sarcasm or dishonesty. “You do?”

"You do interviews, and this place is like a pause button. Is there, uh, something I’m missing?"

"No, you’re fine. This is just...” Mark was staggered by the difference between the two humans he just met in succession. “It’s just a nice change of pace for me. Most people have more questions.”

“You said I’ll be meeting the person in charge of the talent agents soon... that’s all I wanted to hear.”

“Right. Yes. Well, good luck, Robin!" Mark clicked a triangular tooth and Robin instantly vanished from the room. He brought a flute glass of earthy-colored liquid up to his mouth. "Laser focused, that one. Kind of surprised a school teacher is here, though. Both of those humans are... odd choices for our show. In fact, I don’t think I can remember a time where we brought ordinary humans on."

Mark’s hand froze in place as he raced through his sludge memory. All the years blurred together in the oceans of his mind and became a smear of faces, stories, and ambitions. Eventually, it took too much effort to navigate, so he slurped some of his Kava. He nearly retched, but then sighed blissfully.

Robin opened her eyes.

In her hand, and in the hands of Athena and Ishta, was a hotel key-card with a corresponding room number: 24-C. The three looked up at the hotel’s shifting pastel colors with trepidation. A shiqq adorned with a bell-hop’s hat wriggled a misshapen hand around the door knob to welcome them in. The mutant-guided tour led them through cathedrals of rooms and hallways, then to a pearl encrusted elevator. The red-and-gold extravagance of every centimeter of space was a touch nauseating to Robin, but this perhaps isn't a huge surprise: her mind was in another time and place. She worried for Julio, and for the drama she must have caused by disappearing. Would he get in trouble? Would the school? What would life be like once she got back?

She, unlike Theodore, believed in the magic of this place without worrying about "how" it existed. She couldn't deny what happened to herself up until this point. Where she took issue was the idea that anything here in this commercialized, self-indulgent machine of a building could be called "Heaven." This wasn't the Heaven of her parents, or of her church, or of anyone she ever knew. It was just a building. A beautiful one, perhaps, but still just a building far below the standards of eternal salvation.

Athena, leading as she always did, swiped her keycard into 24-C and pushed in. A coat of blue paint immediately slashed across her face.

"Oh my god! Oh my god! I'm so sorry!"

The source of the offending splatter was a blue-green serpent-woman, and the evidence dripped from the flat brush in her hand. Glittered fins sprouted from the sides of her head, which fanned out in embarrassed surprise. White, almost translucent hair popped out of the top of her reptilian head, teased and molded with the height and weight worn by a televangelist's wife. The sway in her scaly hips and her midriff exposing tank top would have never been allowed onto the TV network her massive hair was so clearly borrowed from.

She dropped the brush onto the lined plastic below her feet, her velociraptor like legs thumping into its crinkly surface as she left. "Oh god, I'm sorry, let me get a towel for you."

"There's sharks *and* lizards? How many humanoid species are there here?" Robin whispered to Ishta.

"Lots of people believe in heaven, my dear," she said. Robin inhaled slowly as she unpacked that sentence.

Oshunmare scooted back, towels and apologies in tow.

"Why... on Earth... are you throwing paint at the door?" Athena growled as she buried her face into the ragged cloth. Robin and Ishta stepped over buckets of unsubtle red, restaurant green, and reduced-price yellow.

"When the talent agents told me it'd be a while before the show began, I thought I'd have some fun," the lizard-lady wiped her hands clean, the paint easily coming off her smooth, slender scales. "I mean, look around here. Everything's white. The rooms are huge and bland. I can't believe this is the same building that has *gold nuggets* on top of *gold door handle*s in rooms with *painted murals* buried on *gold walls*. They gave me permission, I promise. I didn't do this to anything other than the door, and look! Look how much cooler it looks. Right here."

The lizard scampered to the far end of the living room, past strange shaped furniture, and motioned for the three to come over. In the sterile white room, the door was coated in a rainbow array of paint, with splattered streaks that radiated outwards. This supernova of primary colors enchanted Ishta and Robin. To Athena's eyes, it was kitschy and annoying. She continued to rub blue off her face.

"I'm Oshunmare, by the way," the lizard-lady said. She shook their hands by clasping both her claws over them. She held Ishta's hand a bit longer, and her scaled lip-line curved in reverence. "I... I didn't think you'd be here, Aida-Wedo. I'm so honored. I hope we both do well."

Ishta looked to Robin with a sly grin. The earthling grimaced, knowing she could not see what Oshunmare saw: where the human saw Ishta's blue skinned form, Oshunmare saw Aida-Wedo, the majestic sky serpent of the Fon people of Benin. To her, she clasped the coiled end of the snake's tail, and peered happily into the rainbow colored eyes of her personal hero.

"I'm afraid I'm not who you think I am," she smiled. Oshunmare tilted her head, blinked, rubbed her eyes, then tumbled backwards as she finally was able to look past Ishta's illusion. The snake dissolved into a human. "Wh-whoa! Did I... Did I just have a stroke? Is this what a stroke is like?"

"No, that's just what disappointment feels like," Athena sighed as she helped the scaled painter back up to her terrifying, weaponized dinosaur feet.

"Does anyone else hear that?" Robin lifted a finger in the direction of a far off room. Muffled rumblings could be heard from behind a door.

"That's our other roommate! There's five rooms here outside of the living room, so I guess everyone's made it," Oshunmare said. "In there is Santa. Aren't we lucky? Well, that's what I thought when I found out who she was, but she's been yelling at her phone pretty much since she got here. I've probably said five words to her. Santa's not nice, y'all."

"...Santa?" Robin tilted her head. She knew what she heard, but she needed confirmation.

"Yeah!" Oshunmare nodded.

From behind the door, a loud crashing sound jolted the group's senses. Some furniture in that bedroom had met a temporary end.

"THERE'S NO FUCKING RECEPTION HERE," a loud, husky woman's voice screamed. Silence passed for a moment. "Oh, good, GOOD. The fucking TABLE fixed itself but their fucking CELL SERVICE WON'T."

"Good ol' jolly Saint Nick," Oshunmare's fin-ears flattened.

The Boys Of 35-D

The furry creature bashed into the door of 35-D with an aggravated fury much larger than his frame. He was raised shoulders and snarls as he stomped into the barely buckling entrance, and he cursed loudly to rile himself—and anyone else within earshot—up.

Behind the dog-punk attempting property-damage stood a tall, slender bug-man, who rested against the wall with one of his sets of arms folded across his front. His golden, bored eyes were exhausted, and they flinched with every kick the heavy door took. Lapels and tassels decorated his asymmetrically-cut blue suit with the honors of war, but there was no sign that this soldier was going to help, or stop, the assault against the apartment entrance.

"Why?" Bam. "Won't?" Bam. "You?" Bam. "Open?!" the dog-punk yelled.

"The door does not equal the problem," the purple-grey bug-man muttered through an electronic collar around his neck. The device translated the clicks and scrapes of his mandibles into a sing-songy, digitized voice.

The dog-man's shoulders fell in a sharp jerk. He twisted his head to look up to the tall bug-like bystander. His snout turned into a snarl.

"Shut the fuck up," the dog-man said. In comparison to the decorated veteran, this punk was clearly a civilian of a different culture—he wore bleached jeans and a poorly frakenstine'd Death Grips/Britney Spears t-shirt that, due to its stitching, read "Britney Grips." A pair of sky blue sneakers aided in his volley against the door. Custom fitted for his canine head was a flat-brimmed baseball cap that sat high enough to intentionally show off the underside of its visor. A brazen fashion choice, indeed, since the underside of the brim was obnoxiously bright pink, adorned with a houndstooth pattern of thousands of tiny cartoon middle-fingers.

"What is 'fuck?'" the bug-man asked earnestly. "Translation failure, I suspect. Please define. I lack belief you asked me to lock sex up."

"How long till your collar starts working properly?" the dog-punk asked.

"Estimation of full calibration: 48 hours."

"Right. Don't talk till then, Stephen Hawking."

"Please explain. Talking required for calibration. 'Stephen Hawking' did not translate."

"Christ."

The dog-punk tightened his hat further down onto his head and walked to the opposite hallway wall.

"What is 'Christ?' Did not translate. Is this 'name?'"

"Shut up," the dog-man hunkered down. "All I have to do..."

All the power in his compact body surged through his legs and pushed him into a hop. He brought his leg close to his chest in mid-air, and like a pumped shotgun, unleashed an explosive kick into the door, next to its handle. His other foot ground into the floor and gave him stability. The lock broke, metal bits and screws flew, and the door swung wide open.

"...is get through!"

Standing triumphantly with one leg in the hallway and the other in the apartment, the split-second the dog-man spent in victorious glee was enough of a distraction to negate his accomplishments. Powered by Heaven's air, the screws flew back into place, and the door slammed shut. The sudden slam knocked the dog-punk over and sent him rolling back into the opposite wall.

"Fuck, that was fast..." the crumpled dog-punk groaned as he fixed his askew baseball cap.

"I mentioned at the last time, the door are not the problem," the strange soldier said.

"Your translation was better that time, but you should still shut up. *God,* it's like listening to a phone's predicted text being read aloud."

"If everything heals here..."

"I KNOW everything heals here!" dog-punk punched the wall and kipped-up to his feet. "Listen, if I can break the door down and get in, I can just unlock it from the other side after the door heals itself. I just wasn't ready for it to heal that fast... I'll get in this time."

"Would it not be more of a logic to correct the problem of our unlocking cards?" the soldier held up a hotel key-card between long, slender fingers. "Subject Shark issued, Subject Shark possibly replace?"

"Do you want to be the one to tell someone working for *gods* that their shit doesn't work? Especially when you're about to be tested by the same deities? No, this is a challenge. This is intentional."

The dog-punk walked back to the wall again and lined up.

"Everything here is a challenge. I just *know* it."

His next attempt was the first thing witnessed by Taninim and Theodore as the gold elevator doors slid open. Kick, run, open, close, tumble, scream. Taninim cringed as the dog-punk took a particularly nasty bump into the opposite wall, while Theodore just stared, his hands jammed into his pockets.

"Do you think they're contestants too?" Taninim asked.

"*Furry-182* and *District 9* over there? Sure, why the hell not?" Theodore stepped off the elevator. With a glance at the sign on the hallway wall, the pair saw that they were spectating two creatures trying to break into their room—either as roommates or intruders. Theodore lifted his hand in a weak wave. "Hey."

The dog-punk rolled to his feet and glared at the two musicians. The soldier, who would have fallen asleep against the wall had it not been for the canine cacophony, opened one eye to observe. He couldn't be bothered to do anything more.

"Who are these jackasses?" the dog-man said as intentionally loud as possible. The bug soldier didn't respond. Taninim was taken aback by the sudden rudeness—his meeting with Theodore may have been tense, sure, but it arose from a misunderstanding. This creature, shoulders arched and head hung, seemed eager to swing a fist right out of the gate.

"Excuse me!—" Taninim wanted to complain. Theodore placed a hand on Taninim's shoulder calmly, which took the guitarist by surprise.

"It's alright, man. No need to get worked up."

Though Theodore started that statement with a relaxed tone, he didn't give the reassuring look the dragon-man expected to see. Instead, the human and the dog just glared at each other. An uneasy silence fell between the two groups, and when Theodore started talking again, Taninim gulped down a terrible realization.

"He's just barking. It doesn't mean anything."

This was going to escalate.

Santa emerged from her locked bedroom with a chunky mobile phone in her hand. When she entered the living room, Robin was initially pleased to see another human. (This rationalization forgets Athena because Robin had, perhaps unsurprisingly, lost empathy for the woman that stabbed her.)

Santa was a tall, heavy-set woman with fire-hydrant red hair that spilled off one side of her head. It was wild and rebellious and in stark contrast to the sharp-shouldered power suit she wore. If her hair didn't perfectly match her high-heels, Robin would have never believed that the owner of that color would wear that navy-blue suit. The more Robin observed, the more she doubted she was in the company of another human; Santa's hooded eyes were Saturday-night-bar-sign blue, and what she thought was an odd bald spot on the side of the business woman's head turned out to be a glowing star within the strands of hair. The star always remained in the same place at every angle, its shape and light created by the hair itself.

"Carol! Oh, thank Heaven you're here," the woman wiped her forehead with a red, white, and blue handkerchief she produced from her suit pocket. "Why weren't you answering your phone? How did you get here?"

Robin looked around to see who Carol was, then realized she was looking at Ishta. After a few moments of confusion, Santa recoiled as Ishta's disguise melted, and the group of women explained Ishta's ability to her. Introductions commenced. Robin's handshake with Santa was limp and hesitant.

"That's rude, why would you do that to people?" Santa asked Ishta.

"I can't help it, my dear. As in, it just happens, and I've learned to live with it," Ishta said. She added with a smile, "But I admit some small amount of amusement always comes about thanks to this... 'ability', I guess you could call it."

Santa shrugged off the absurdity of Ishta's claim and accepted it just as Oshunmare did. The willing acceptance of reality-bending magic surprised Robin here just as much as the first time. Perhaps more so, since Santa's face was perceptibly human, star-hair notwithstanding.

"Well, this is just great," Santa walked to the balcony window of the living room. She looked to the setting neon-green sun, and hoped for a glimpse beyond it. "It's end of day by now, I have no idea what's happening in the office, I only really came here to increase my company's visibility and..."

"Company?" Robin asked. She was genuinely perplexed, and not just because the name 'Santa' pulls up some *particular* imagery that didn't quite fit the power-suited woman. Everyone that Robin had met thus far talked of gods and magic and spirits—hell, she was standing in Heaven, if these eccentrics were to be believed. But Santa talked of her office, her company—things typically not thought of as necessary in the afterlife. What need is money to a god? What could a spirit possibly gain from an economy?

"Don't you know me? I'm Santa Inari! I am the spirit of industry! CEO of Capitalism! Why do you think Christmas even exists? It didn't just invent itself, you know. It was one of my best ideas," Santa beat the side of her chest with pride, but then her smile melted into apparent frustration. "I haven't taken a day off work in a very long time. Carol's my secretary. I just wanted to...

keep tabs. Winter's not far off, gotta make sure we're ready for the season, you know? We get most of our testaments then."

"Testaments?" Robin almost exclusively associated that word with the Bible.

"Testaments," Santa repeated herself, only louder. When she realized that wouldn't suffice as an explanation, she clapped her hands and tried to catch the words she needed. "Um, it's our currency here. Humanity's love of gods manifests itself as coins. In return, we work to influence Earth. Remember when Captain LaRue saved all those Koreans? I don't want to brag, but I made a *huge* acquisition of Imoogi Inc. just a month before."

Robin shook her head.

"Well, uh," Santa Inari frowned. "It was great. Believe me."

Robin looked around the room, trying to rationalize the juxtaposition of magic and microwaves, of CEOs and Greek goddesses, of blue women of flesh and scales. The four girls she was with, despite their supernatural appearances and abilities, chatted among themselves in an ordinary manner, about ordinary things—their excitement, their interests, their tastes. They sat on couches and drank water out of glasses (or vodka, in Santa's case). Oshunmare rapidly shot a long rainbow tongue in and out of her glass like a snake. Athena played foosball and accidentally shoved a rod too hard and broke the table. No worries, of course—the table healed itself thanks to Heaven's air, and Athena continued on without interruption.

A god wouldn't need a place like this, would they? Robin thought. *Gods wouldn't need a reality show... or water, or alcohol, right?*

"But why do you have a company?"

The women all looked up. Robin had no idea that she had retreated into her own mind, and blurted out a question to a conversation the rest of the room had moved on from.

Santa Inari laughed. "You think this suit paid for itself?"

No, of course it didn't, Robin thought. *But that means there's an economy. There's people like these guys in here... out there.* She looked towards the window. *I'm in one very, very small part of a much larger world. This can't be Earth, but they're speaking English and everything around me looks like... a really nice, normal hotel room.*

"Robin, are you okay?" Ishta placed a hand on top of Robin's thigh.

Even though Robin already "knew" the wild information pounding the front of her thoughts, she didn't believe it until Santa casually talked of her company—her job. Her livelihood. *Her life.*

"I'm fine. Sorry, I'm just a little overwhelmed," she leaned back into the chair and forced a small chuckle, though the puff of air that came out of her mouth sounded more like exasperation than a laugh. She knew in that moment that whether or not they were gods didn't matter. She was alone in every way she could think of. "So, uh. Why does everyone want to be here, anyways?"

Theodore popped back into the Camera World. He shook in surprise as his cells settled into their new position. Once he knew where he was, he scrunched his face and turned:

"Fucking hell, Mark. It's been five minutes."

"Oh, man, has it?" the shark spun around in his swivel chair and frantically slapped keyboards. He was in a completely different suit, though one of equally meticulous pleating and complexity. This one was deep red, like his wines, like the blood of the prey of his Earthen counterparts. "Sorry. I've been working, or drunk. It's easy for me to lose track of stuff like that," he paused his typing, his hands hung in the air before he spun to face Theodore. "That... that sounded a lot more sad out loud than I meant it to be."

Theodore had noticed the change in wardrobe and mentality. "So wait, if time moves differently in here... how long has it been since you last saw me?"

Mark shrugged and went back to typing. Theodore concluded that the passage of time didn't matter to the shark—and if it did, Theodore would never be able to read the concern on his toothy, goofy face to figure it out. In a sea of magic monitors and tentacle-like cameras, the shark was honed in on the minutiae of his work. He spun dials to rewind through footage, he flicked levers to switch camera perspectives, and smacked the sides of monitors that began to dim.

"Why did you bring me back in here?"

"Well, normally, I interview people for the show. We talked about that, yeah? I'm absolutely going to ask you about this little altercation after it happens, but..."

The shark flipped a switch on one of his monitors, and a red-blinking light went off. With another snap, the whirling cameras in the room powered down. They drooped as the electricity cut from their conducting veins.

"Just be careful, okay?"

Theodore scoffed. "I'm not sure what I can really do to him, given the way this place seems to work?"

The shark's swivel in his chair was slow, rhythmic, side-to-side. He waited for the right words to surface in his mouth.

"You're being recorded now. These are your introductions to the audience. I just wanted you to..."

Silence. Mark struggled.

"To...?"

"...be who you want to be. Look, just don't hurt the puppy too badly if things gets out of hand."

Theodore smirked. *Where was this coming from?* he thought. *Is this fish toying with me again?*

"I thought we established last time that more teeth equals more fearsome? I also fundamentally disagree with the description of him as a 'puppy'. That thing out there is a werewolf, albeit a kid-sized one, and I know I shouldn't judge based on the way he's dressed, but he looks like a 90s teenager. I grew up in the 90s. Those kids were fucked up even without fangs. Why aren't you more worried about me?"

"He doesn't have a record."

Theodore's smirk soured. He looked away at a stray monitor. "I don't like you, Mark."

"That's probably understandable," Mark tapped his fingers on the desk. "Shall I send you back?"

"Yeah. Go for it."

With a click of his shark teeth, Mark made Theodore vanish from the Camera World. While Mark had told the truth, Theodore thought the shark meant *his* record. He thought the shark meant he knew about a past Theodore had attempted to keep hidden—a mistake in his youth, a moment of violent weakness, and a permanent hook in his heart. The hint of his sin was the most real thing he had encountered in Heaven, and he didn't need its reminder.

The shark meant it both ways, though. Among the clipboards and files on each of the contestants, the dog-punk's profile sheet was almost completely devoid of details of history and accomplishments. When Mark contacted production thinking it was a mistake, they informed him that, no, they *had* sent him everything and, no, there are *no mistakes* in Heaven.

It was the same dismissive stance production gave Mark when he expressed surprise at two ordinary humans being brought onto "The Favorite Reality Show of the Gods" (as it had been advertised for several years), and the odd circumstances they both claimed led them there. There was a line, Mark considered, between the two events. "Production is interested in trying something new," was the terse and official statement regarding their inclusion. It didn't sit right with the shark, even if it's a perfectly valid reason for a reality show to do anything.

There was something about the nature of Theodore that appealed to Mark. Perhaps it was the wine swirling in Mr. Sharkman's head, but he considered that if he could plant a seed in any of the contestants to keep a watchful eye on the dog-man, it would be the already frustrated and cynical human forced to be there with him. It was either him or Robin, and from Mark's brief encounters, he believed he could manipulate Theodore purely through the fact Theodore had more to hide and was more desperate to leave.

Theodore opened his eyes.

"So you think I'm just BARKING, huh?"

Theodore sighed. "Here we go."

The dog-punk swayed like a child imitating a boxer, hovering between each side of Theodore's face. He spat with machine-gun vitriol, his fangs bared as he tugged Theodore's tie out from his suit, insulted his stupid mouth-brow, and questioned his masculinity. Theodore just stared down at him and kept the shark's words in the back of his head.

"You fucking pink-ass bitch, you think you can do anything to me? You think just because a caterpillar died on your goddamn lip that you got what it takes to fight me? Wanna box in that cheap-ass suit you got from Prince's trash can? Huh? Huh?"

"Sorry, Mark."

When the dog-punk lifted his hand, it was likely just to jab a finger into Theodore's chest. But the world will never know if it was a punch or posturing, for when he lifted it up, Theodore quickly snatched the dog-punk's wrist, twisted it behind his back, and shoved him hard into the wall. The musician drove his other forearm into the dog's back and knocked the air out of him. Theodore, nearly twice the dog-punk's height, easily pinned him against the wall.

"I'll fucking kill you!" the dog-man growled. His slobber flung against the gold wall.

"Can you, though? *Really?*"

Taninim moved towards the two, hands held out in worry, but his hesitance kept him from doing anything other than blubbering "G-guys. Guys."

"So, look, I've had a bad day," Theodore said. "And it sure seems to me like you're not doing much better. It's easy to throw a fist. Trust me, I want to. Right now, right in the back of your skull, I can see exactly the place where I could drive my knuckles in to make you see colors you've never conceived of. But what does that *do* for me, exactly?"

The dog flattened his ears. Theodore pulled his face closer to them and lowered his voice to a boil.

"Maybe in a different time or place I would lay you out for coming at me like that. At some points in my life I *know* I would have. But you know why I didn't? Your friend over there. All this time you've been kicking at this door, yelling at me, yelling at the world... he hasn't moved. Not an inch. Not even now. Just content to park against that wall and let you make a fool of yourself. Now I'm going to wager that's *probably* because your endearing personality hasn't won him over."

The bug's mandibles clicked. The collar didn't translate it, but that's not a surprise since no two people scoff the same way.

Theodore cranked the dog's arm with each word—"I can't. Imagine. Why."

"F-fuck you, man," the punk whimpered.

"Whatever 'this' is, isn't going to fly here in this apartment. You are not going to start fights like this anymore, and neither am I. You got that?"

The dog-punk gave a sad, angry nod, and no longer struggled.

"Good. Let's try this again."

Theodore let go of the dog-punk's arm, spun him by the shoulders, and took his paw-hand in a firm handshake. It was a fluid enough motion that the dog, whom was still in adrenaline-pumping confusion, went along with it.

"I'm Theodore. It's nice to meet you."

The dog snarled and shoved. He didn't want to make eye contact with anyone, but with Theodore in front of him, the bug behind him, and the door he couldn't open to his right, he just stared at the wall, hands defiantly on his hips.

"Hmph. Well it doesn't matter, we can't get in anyways."

"Generally when someone introduces themselves, you introduce yourself back. It's polite."

The dog-punk took his cap up, combed back through some fur, then readjusted it back to his scalp. He said in a low tone of embarrassment, "I'm The Internet."

Theodore's head rotated around his neck as he failed to process properly what he just heard. He hung on his opening vowel as he tried to figure out how best to ask, "I'm sorry, you were named after the Internet?"

The Internet snarled and pivoted and got right back into Theodore's face. "Do you not have ears, you cigarette-scented shitbag? I AM The Internet. And I just looked up every "Theodore" on facebook and didn't see your ugly ass in any profile pictures. So tell me, are you shy, or just a liar?"

"I..." Theodore closed one eye. His brain slowly shut down under the weight of the idea he was talking to "The Internet." "I don't... I don't *have* a facebook. You're *allowed* to not have a facebook."

"Well then, I hate you *even more* than I did before. Everyone should be online."

"How are you 'The Internet'? What does that even mean?"

Click.

"Hey, guys!" Taninim said as he pulled his key-card out from the door. He motioned as he pushed his back into the opening door, playing a happy, celebratory riff. "I got in!"

"Oh, look," the bug's digitized voice sang. "Subject key-cards were the source of all problems. Subject 'The Me' was the right one."

Back in the Camera World, in a notebook meant for his eyes only, Mark Sharkman took note of The Internet's fierce independence and standoffishness. He was, after all, the one that gave him a blank key-card, and not by accident. Why the bug-soldier never used his working key-card, though, he did not understand. Given the poor quality of his translator, he just had to chalk it up to a misunderstanding.

The women of 24-C were initially tight-lipped at Robin's inquiry. It was a simple enough question—"Why do you want to be on *The Next Great Deity*?"—but the refrigerator's hum and settling ice in half-drunk glasses answered sooner than the contestants did. This was a group that was aware of the lens of the camera, and they tried to choose their words carefully.

"We all want to be goddesses, of course," Mrs. Inari finally said.

"But aren't all of you... powerful already?" Robin almost said 'gods,' but caught herself. She pointed towards each of her roommates. "Athena, you can make weapons appear out of thin air. Ishta, you can make people hallucinate. Oshunmare, I'm sure you can do something out of this world, and even if you can't, no offense, you're a lizard-person. That's extraordinary to me because I didn't think you existed."

"None taken. You're a human, we know humans bounce between beliefs better than anyone."

They shared nervous laughter.

"My point is..." Robin waved her hand as if to shield the topic from Oshunmare's barb. "You are all beyond what we can do on Earth. It still feels like a dream, here. This place is crazy and I can't shake the fact that I have seen all of you in textbooks or heard about you in myths."

"And you're worried about the fact you haven't run into any of your own myths here," Ishta added.

On one hand, it was an obvious statement about the cross necklace Robin wore. On the other, Robin had kept the particularities of her own beliefs to herself, intentionally so, because she didn't understand where she was in the universe. How do you tell someone about your faith when they demonstrate a power within themselves far beyond anything you have seen?

For her, even the most evangelical faith was about sharing experiences in a positive way. Robin was always celebratory with like-minded individuals, and used this to find common ground at parent-teacher meetings, or to get to know her community through choir, little league, mission trips to South America, drinks with the neighbors as they announce the good news of their first incoming organic gift from God. If the individual she was talking to didn't share her faith, then it became a billboard, a type of mechanism to explain the good decisions in her life and the strength that she's shown through the darkest times: her worries, her trauma, her grief. Her divorce.

"I'm not sure I appreciate my beliefs being called a myth," Robin said through a forced smile.

"Oh, well, no one else here does either," Ishta laughed.

Robin pushed her sigh through her nose when she realized that the other women were still chuckling, and it was here that it felt pointed in one direction. These were unrestrained chirps of agreement she may have shared in the past with a church member about a liberal, an atheist, or just a fellow church-wife that couldn't season a meal properly to save her life. The circling ice in her water was not enough to distract her from the realization of how in over her head she was in this strangely modern and supernatural place. Robin rarely drank, but she felt a desire brewing for the vodka in Santa's grip.

"Being strong doesn't make you a god," Athena said. She kept her hands busy at the foosball table, and her bottom lip twitched each time she reacted to the ball bouncing off a corner.

Robin shifted. "It doesn't?"

"Spirits can be strong. Demons can be strong. Bears can be strong. Anything can be strong if it works hard enough. But a god's limitless ability to 'create' is something else altogether, a separate category from all other things. Everything that you've seen thus far is a parlor trick compared to what a god can do," Athena scored a goal from across the table with a trick shot off the motionless enemy figures. "You feel overwhelmed because you are weak and small. That's how we *all* feel compared to the most powerful gods. Especially those of us that have previous experience."

"Athena, there are ways to word that more politely," Ishta said.

"And speak for yourself, I'm rich," Santa laughed.

"But you still need a secretary," Athena said. "You still depend on others. True gods don't need anything or anyone."

Robin, used to the world of the classroom, raised her hand meekly. "What about angels?"

"Tch. Just another way to earn a paycheck," Athena practiced passing between two handles. "Janitors with wings."

Santa rolled her eyes and took another shot of vodka straight from the bottle. The alcohol gave her the power to, finally, properly answer the original inquiry:

"To your question, Robin. If I win, no force in Heaven or Hell will be able to match my production capabilities," Santa said after a long, happy *"Aahhh,"* from her drink. "If I lose, I get to have my face and name out on the most popular TV show in reality. I couldn't refuse something like this, because I benefit either way. I'm gonna win though, so you bitches watch out."

Oshunmare folded her raptor like legs onto the couch. "I just want to make beautiful things. The great thing about being a god is that you have the ultimate paint brush in your possession."

"I want a harmonious world," Ishta said. "Calm and tranquil, a place anyone would want to be. This is the place you have to go to achieve that, so here I am."

"I want a world of no ambiguity," Athena, bored of foosball, walked over to the group and sat down in a chair apart from them, legs and arms crossed. "Where strength and justice are above all else."

"What about you, Robin?" Oshunmare asked.

Robin rubbed the side of her face. "I didn't want to come here."

"W-What, why?" Oshunmare gasped.

Robin watched as Ishta's face fell, and with a glance she caught Athena's glare. She remembered that they, too, were suspicious of the talent agents because of Eris's absence. Ishta's promise on how other contestants saw her "in a different way" proved to be true. All at once, it clicked that openly talking about her distrust of the show to the wrong people might not be the best idea. Even if she didn't know whether Santa and Oshunmare were "the wrong people" or not, she knew she would need some sort of guidance through this strange-yet-familiar world. It was then that she decided that, to learn why she was abducted, she needed to measure what she did, and did not, reveal.

"I wasn't sure if this was for me," Robin said. "I didn't know if I deserved it."

"Well, you are a human, after all," Santa raised her glass. "You guys can't make up your minds on anything."

They laughed. Athena leaned in, resting her elbows on her knees. "I hope you continue to think that," she smirked. "You'll be doing us a favor by laying down. Not all of us can win, after all."

It was at that exact moment that a burst of light erupted from the center of the apartment. An intense pressure disturbed the furniture like a strong, brief breeze through tree leaves. Hovering in the origin of the shockwave, directly above the glass living room table was a floating sheet of paper, which glistened with glitter and hummed with a strange, soft, angelic choir. The women were startled—Ishta the least, whom barely moved except to turn her sight towards the light, and Oshunmare the most, whom scampered in terror behind the couch.

"Uh, so," Oshunmare delicately combed her bouffant of hair back into shape, "I'm guessing that's for us."

Robin took charge and grabbed the sparkling paper out of the air, and hoped the show's nature would be revealed in its text. It was crisp stationery with flowery ink handwritten script. She had expected something that glowed to burn to the touch, or shock her, or... something. Once it was between her fingers, though, it was just textured paper with fine writing.

"Dear contestants," she read aloud.

Theodore extended his hand out to the medal-adorned insectoid.

"Guess we're gonna be roommates, too, huh?"

The bug-man observed the human hand in a studious, unblinking manner. His two antenna, which arched from the top of his head and fanned out to either side like long, thin pigtails, flexed and bounced with curiosity.

"Subject You appears to be doing the handing of something to Subject Me, but there is a lack of thing to be doing the handing of," the bug's voice-collar translated his sparse clicks.

"This is... a greeting. I'm greeting you."

"A custom of introduction I am not being of the awareness. For this, Subject My Soul apologizes. Subject I contains the name Zargah," the bug lifted a long, slimy, three fingered hand outwards, and it froze in mid-air parallel to the floor in awkward imitation. It was clear to Theodore that it was going to remain there without guidance, so he took the moist bug-hand between both of his own and gave it a gentle shake. Zargah clasped his remaining three hands on top of Theodore's, each making a wet smacking sound. He shook much harder.

"An intimate and powerful greeting. Subject Theodore's hands are warm but soft, like uncooked *Kzgkh*," Zargah said. "Subject I am of believing Subject We all will learn new things through acquaintance."

Theodore slowly withdrew and made his way into the kitchen to wash away his freshly coated hand. "...Yeah. I agree."

Almost immediately upon his entrance, The Internet paraded around the apartment. He whirled, stomped on couches, and let his roommates know what he thought about the tangy plastic smell of counter-tops, of the balcony view of the Forest of Golden Trees, and how unfortunate it was going to be in the morning when it would inevitably blind the living room with too much light.

His monologue was ended abruptly. In a blinding blast of light, a mystical stationery had appeared. It happened at the same moment Internet had decided to stand on the living room table and gloat about how they could do anything they wanted to the apartment's furniture and it wouldn't matter since Heaven's air would just clean up any messes they made. As if to condemn his flippancy, the paper appeared exactly where he was standing.

"Why?" The Internet yelled through fangs and tears. The paper had fused into the nape of his neck, askew just enough so he could see its corner in his peripheral vision. "Is that paper? What happened?"

"Did Subject Internet read it? Perhaps the answer—" Zargah began to suggest.

"NO I didn't read it you IDIOT, how can I read it?" The Internet barked back. "Oh my god it's like my entire neck is just one giant paper cut!"

Taninim put his hands under The Internet's armpits and lifted him down from the table. He folded open the paper and began to read aloud, each crinkle and flex of the page netted a yelp out of the dog-punk.

"Dear Contestants,

Congratulations! You've made it into reality's favorite competitive TV series, The Next Great Deity! *You are the best and brightest stars we could find in existence—everyone's waiting to see what you can do! Come meet me at the rooftop, and let there be fun!*

I'm so excited!!!!,

J♡ !"

"There's, like, exclamation marks after every sentence," Theodore read along over Taninim's massive shoulder. "Four after that closing at the end. Amazing."

"Just rip it out," The Internet cried. "*Please.*"

The group exited their apartment with a collective nervous energy. They were escorted by a camera-wielding shiqq to the floor's elevator, and on the way up, each were interviewed by Mark Sharkman—

"I was born ready for this," The Internet told the finned interviewer. His tightened hands refuted his confidence. "And they better be nice to me after all that bullshit in the hall. That shit hurt."

—his Camera World barely stole a second of their time—

"I don't know where all of this is leading," Theodore rubbed the side of his head. "But I'm living with a guitarist, a roach, and an angry dog. It's like I never left Queens."

—It captured them on the way to the biggest challenge of their lives—

"I'm gonna do it. I'm going to do this for you, Jeremy," Taninim said with a slight tremble in his snarling voice. "Wait for me. I won't be gone long. I'll be your knight."

—and framed them perfectly against the backdrop of their ambition.

"Define 'Heaven,' translation failure," Zargah said.

Mark Sharkman sighed, "Never mind," and sent the bug back without much argument. Interviewing him was pointless until that damn collar worked right.

Through corridors of gold, the cold simplicity of a lit-up red "exit" sign stood in stark contrast with oil paintings of Arab sages, whom seemed just as unsure of the clash of their meticulously rendered culture with public facing electronic signage as the contestants themselves were. Taninim pushed the door open and the fading green sunset broke over the group, their faces awash in the reflection of nature against construction.

The rooftop of Heaven's Heart Hotel was as iridescent, shimmering, and unnecessarily ornate as the rest of its interior and exterior. The winking sun set aglow the crystalline floor, a sight so overwhelming to the monster men of 35-D that they barely paid any mind to the slight electrical shock each of their hands took as they walked through the doorway—with the exception of Theodore, whose shock was in his eye. He complained, but his roommates assumed he accidentally looked into the sun. When the pain disappeared almost instantly, Theodore wondered if they were right.

There were two other identical doorways on the roof. Each swung open and poured out more contestants—and soon, the rooftop was swamped with 13 disparate and otherworldly citizens, a motley crew of many different cultures and species all converging together. They mingled immediately, bound by their desires, their competitive spirit, and their need to learn about each other.

"Oh, I'm sorry," Robin bumped into a warm, large wall and turned to see a massive white deer with carved gold antlers. "Oh!"

"Excuse me," the deer said. "I'm Csodaszarvas. What are you a spirit of?"

Robin's eyes bulged, first at the fact that a deer was talking to her, then at the impossible task of pronouncing his name. Hearing it once was not enough preparation for her to repeat it back properly.

"She's no spirit, Cso," Oshunmare cut in. Oshunmare's bubbly nature did not make her naive to other's emotions. Quite the opposite, in fact—she was sensitive to individual moods, and Robin's upturned brow and long pauses had not gone unnoticed to her.

"Ah, Oshunmare, it's been a moon or two," Csodaszarvas raised a hoof that the lizard-lady shook with familiarity. It was a chance to slip away from pronouncing his name, and Robin didn't hesitate to take it.

Theodore, too, weaved in and out of social traffic. He had hoped to stand near Taninim's side. The dragon-guitarist was the only one there Theodore had any trust for. Theodore was not a particularly social man unless he happened to be talking about something he was knowledgeable in. The fact that he was a human amid creatures his mind could barely fathom made it a little more difficult for him to find the will to be chatty, so he tried to float near the more gregarious guitarist and blend in.

Even the humans he ran in to, or at least the perceptibly human, were of a different time and place: there was a woman with an impossible star glowing on the side of her head, whom he thought said was named "Santa" even though he was certain he misheard her. There was a hulking, heavy-bearded man with square-patterned ceremonial robes named "Oksi," whom was as mercifully short on speech as Theodore wanted everyone to be. The same was true of an armor wearing woman named "Athena," whom seemed to scan the crowd but refused to interact with it. She just said "Uh-huh, great," when Taninim tried to introduce himself, and Theodore felt a little guilty for admiring her for that.

There was a long-haired blonde youth named Jarilo that Theodore was, first, shocked to see was shirtless, and then, horrified to realize that his lower half was the back hindquarters of a goat. The only scrap of clothing he had was a linen loincloth. Among the glittering gold and ornate clothes of everyone else, he was as out of place as Theodore was. He attempted to talk Theodore's ear off with a whirling array of questions on music taste, diet, the weather, his favorite flowers, his favorite sport, his favorite animals, on and on and on and Theodore made sure to introduce Oksi to Jarilo, "Jarilo, Oksi feels the same way you do about that thing you were talking about." After his successful deflection, which Oksi would never forgive him for as long as he lived, Theodore slipped away and saw Robin.

Their eyes met.

He, to her, was just a man in a suit. Maybe the lavender color was a little unusual, maybe his pencil-thin mustache was a little goofy, but he was so much more real than anything else she had seen there. Intuition welled within her: he was certainly from Earth.

To him, she was just a normal woman in a two-toned sweater. No golden guitar, no translation collar, no fur or misplaced ferocity. Her fro-hawk hair would have blended her in completely into the streets of Queens, but here, she was a lost soul pushing through a strange crowd. She looked exactly how he felt.

To these two only, the surrounding chatter faded.

"I have an awful question for you, and I really don't like that I have to ask it," Theodore said.

Robin smiled. "It can't be any worse than mine. So... I'll go first. Are you human?"

Theodore dragged the tip of his shoe along the ground and gave a heavy sigh of relief. "Cool. Yeah. I am. I guess I have a different question, then, since you just took mine." He walked close to Robin, leaned down near her ear, and kept his voice low.

"Did you *want* to come here?"

In most conversations, a heavy silence would unease someone. But here, these two strangers welcomed the calm, fleeting clarity of their shared experience.

"My name is Robin. And no," she said.

"Theodore."

They didn't shake hands. They just stood, shoulder to shoulder, and kept the other contestants in their peripheral vision. They were, together, against them.

Imhotep's View

Imhotep stood near the doorway, his loose hood draped around his head like a linen waterfall. He had intentionally stayed in the back of his group, and clung to the shadows behind the half-open door. He had not interacted with his roommates in 41-A much at all, and this was the reason why:

There's 12 here. This is the most he's ever had on, he thought. *This season's going to be huge.*

He studied the contestants faces, their clothes, their mannerisms. He had done this for so long, so many times that they stopped being individuals to him, and instead abstracts. *There's the angry, rebellious one, and the quiet, zen one,* he thought as he looked at a dog-punk bragging about his encyclopedic knowledge of sports to a blue-skinned Hindu spirit. The punk seemed convinced he was talking to sportscaster Al Michaels. *There's the one in it for the testaments,* he thought when he saw Santa Inari furiously slapping the front of a cell phone. *I guess that one's a sensitive hippy,* he thought when he saw Oshunmare, somehow able to glean personality traits from her reptilian maw. He noticed her tendency to talk with her hands—and the paint splatters all over her simple-cut clothes.

But then something appeared that he couldn't easily boil down.

"Wait, those two," he white knuckled the door frame.

There was no wild energy from them, no special powers, no impossible physical attributes, no spectacle. Just the heat of their beating hearts, and the sweat of skin tampered by Heaven's green sun. Imhotep could taste their uncertainty in the air, and saw their attempts to rationalize their surroundings in hushed whispers.

"Those two are human," Imhotep hoped if he heard his own voice say it that he'd believe it. He lifted his hood and let the light color his scarred, heavily made-up face. "He really went and brought humans here. This changes everything."

Robin and Theodore compared what they knew from their interactions with Mark and their roommates. She leaned in and whispered, "Whether or not any of this is real is not what bothers me the most."

"Is it the fact that they keep calling it 'Heaven?'" Theodore didn't need to see Robin's necklace to draw that conclusion, but it helped him get to the point.

"It's not heaven," she said with confidence. "It can't be."

"But it's close. There's no need for healthcare."

Her right eye winced. "Yeah, it is. It's close."

Robin didn't actually think it was close at all, but she also didn't think the energy required to argue about the King James interpretation of "heaven" was worth it right at that moment.

"So, like, I just make dumb tracks," Theodore said.

"What?" Robin snapped back to reality. She didn't know how long she had spaced out with her personal thoughts about what heaven *should* be.

"I'm a musician. I just, like, record shit and splice it together on a computer," he rubbed the back of his neck.

She could tell from the way Theodore anchored his eyes to the floor that there was more going on in his mind than the need to make small talk. "That's nice?"

"What do you do?"

"Oh, I'm just a school teacher," she trailed off. The rest of her thought halted when she noticed Theodore had moved his hand to his chin. "Why?"

"Well, I mean, would you want a school teacher to be god?"

Robin shook her head. "I don't even want to be a *principal.* I was happy doing what I was doing."

"Two of the people in my room wanted to be here. I'd say three, but the bug-dude, Zargah, is tough to talk to. Sounds like your roommates wanted to be here, too. Clearly, there's willing participants in this world. So, why us?"

"How could I know that?" she wanted to say. But then she remembered that Ishta was investigating the talent agents. Athena was missing her sister—and Robin noticed the Greek goddess had drifted completely away from the group, and stared into the golden brushes that dotted the landscape.

Eris isn't here, what do I do now? is all that Athena thought, and it read in her slumped posture.

Ishta-Devata, conversely, had spent her whole time moving between contestants, and discovered each of their desires through her ability. She softly smiled from each amusing encounter until she ran into Zargah. She seemed perplexed, and given that he shuffled away from her with a set of worried clicks, so did he.

Both Ishta and Athena willingly came here knowing something was wrong, Robin thought.

"I don't know if it's such a secret that there's something going on here," she shook her head. Robin explained Ishta and Athena's story to Theodore, and tried to find the line between them and the other girls in her room, "This is a place of magic, these people really think they can be a 'god', but then they're also using smartphones," she scanned the sea of strange faces. They were caricatures to her. "What the hell *is* this place?"

"Well, it's not Hell," Imhotep said, startling them both.

Imhotep was a middle-aged Egyptian man whose copper arms leaked out of a draped pile of gleaming silk linen. His stubbly face was severely pitted along the left side, but with his full lips painted half-gold and his half-lidded eyes fully painted in black liner, his look dazzled before it was possible to notice the scarring. Even then, by not covering the craters that dominated his face, he incorporated it, and gave himself a unflinching confidence that swirled around his smoke-like movements and vibrato voice.

"Sorry, don't mean to interrupt, but I couldn't help but notice you two were humans. I just wanted to say 'Hello,'" Imhotep extended a hand. Robin shook it, but Theodore kept his hidden away in his pockets.

"Well you certainly said it," he said as flatly as possible.

Imhotep looked to Robin, then back at Theodore. "Did I say something wrong?"

"I don't think I liked the way you said *'humans,'* " Theodore popped his neck. "You also put your hand out, but didn't say your name."

"You're right, how rude of me. I'm Imhotep," he smiled.

"You don't look like Arnold Vosloo at all," Theodore said.

Imhotep blinked. "Who's that?"

"Imhotep. *The Mummy*? Brendan Fraiser? You know what, never mind. I'm Theodore," he shook his hand with a certain stiffness and strength that made Imhotep eager to pull away.

"Ah, the movie," Imhotep nodded, and with a wave of his hand, discarded the thought. "Sorry, I don't need to see fiction about myself, I've already lived well enough."

Robin and Theodore looked to each other.

"Well, I didn't mean to make either of you feel uncomfortable. We don't see humans here often."

"If you're not human, then what are you?" Robin asked.

"Dead. I suppose if you saw a movie about me, you'd know that," Imhotep put a hand on Theodore's shoulder. Theodore stepped back, brow furrow, and Imhotep smirked at a small victory. "Very dead. But, you know. Heaven's great for second chances. I'm sure you've realized by now that this isn't Earth."

"You're pretty healthy for a dead guy," Theodore said.

"I got better." Imhotep shrugged.

"Why would Heaven be so similar to Earth?" Robin asked, then shook with sudden worry. "Wait, does this mean... we're dead, too?"

"Both good questions. If you weren't a spirit before, you're not now. As for the other one, the two seem like sisters, don't they? So related and so influential to each other, even if they have different rules."

"Is there something you want to tell us?" Theodore ground his back teeth.

"Yes. Good luck, to both of you. I'm eager to see what you make," Imhotep bowed politely, and wafted into the crowd of contestants.

"Make? We're making things?" Robin looked around. "Like, crafts? Art?"

"Pretty sure Imhotep didn't speak English," Theodore stuffed his hands in his pocket.

The air pulled at their skin and clothes with a sudden pressure so strange that each of the humans broke out in a cold sweat. They were not alone—a dampness crept onto the necks of each participant. It pulled their minds, tugged at their sleeves, and directed their eyes towards an empty spot of the roof. Debris and dust swirled in place and formed a small tornado of energy that drained the area of atmosphere.

Then, the gathering of pressure popped into sparks. In the center of the glowing residue, she stood:

"Welcome, my beautiful children, to *The Next Great Deity*!" she proclaimed with her arms held high in the air, her sharp face strobed with the falling light.

She was tall and beautiful, her soft features painted with thick blush and framed by a trimmed, even beard. She floated down as radiant energy spilled out from her being. Her plentiful proportions were only barely contained in a white mini-dress, banded together by a blood red sash working overtime to keep the excruciatingly tailored outfit together around her heavenly body.

"I'm your holy hostess, Jesus Christ!"

Everyone clapped politely, except Theodore and Robin. Theodore had snickered at both her title and the fact that Jesus was a little more stacked than he expected. He looked over to Robin, expecting her to do the same. Instead, he saw her face twisted with emotions that traveled in all cardinal directions. Tears welled in her eyes and her hand folded into a fist over her cross necklace. Theodore bit back his laugh and looked away. *I guess I'll let her have whatever... this moment is,* he thought.

"Welcome to the most powerful television show..." Jesus flashed a camera-stealing grin and finger-gunned towards the crowd. The crowd, sans those unfamiliar, shot their fists rhythmically in the air with the holy hostess.

"IN!"

"ALL!"

"EXISTENCE!"

Then they cheered. Jesus laughed and clapped with them. Theodore adjusted his collar nervously. Robin choked back her tears and dropped her clenched fists to her side.

"We *should* be here," she whispered. Theodore raised an eyebrow.

"How is everyone feeling?" Jesus shouted.

The crowd cheered again, partially in genuine earnest, partially because shiqqs were waving their fleshy tendrils upwards off-camera, a universal symbol to ramp up the faux-enthusiasm.

"I don't want to be here," Theodore called out above the cheers. It killed the crowd, and Jesus's photo-perfect grin snapped into chiseled, twisted lines.

"You couldn't believe it was really Jesus," Mark scribbled onto a clipboard.

"Please don't put my crying on the TV," Robin laughed, her hand held on her cheek in embarrassment. "It's weird. If I stop crying here, will I teleport back out there without any evidence of tears?"

"This place is mental, sorry," the shark-man said, winking. "I mean that by every definition of the word, by the way."

"Everything up until this point has been like a fever dream. But the moment I saw Jesus, I knew this is where I belonged," she nodded, her eyes burrowed into the floor. A whirling camera caught every angle of her tear stained face, and prepared the best shots for promotional material.

"Why do you think Theodore said he didn't want to be here?"

Robin sucked on a corner of her top lip, and her eyes drifted to the floor.

"I don't know."

"You two were talking for a while. You don't have any idea?"

"It was nice to meet another human," is all she said.

Mark tapped his pen, and created a star-field of black ink in the margins. "Right. Okay, thank you," he clicked a tooth, and she disappeared. On the other side of his smiling mouth, another tooth-on-tooth click spat Theodore into the chair.

"You know, back out there, it feels like I've just been pinched," Theodore settled into the seat, and folded his arms. "But, like, in my head. Every time you do this to me, it feels like that."

"Crazy, huh?"

"I hate it. Please stop."

"So you've decided to try and leave early," Mark said as he swapped clipboards. "Tell me about that."

Theodore stacked his legs.

"Oh, not at all."

Mr. Sharkman tilted his head.

"You just watch me, Shark," Theodore smiled. "If this is a game they want me to play, I'll play."

"Why did you say that you didn't want to be here to Jesus, then, if you don't want to leave?"

Theodore stood up, walked over to the shark, leaned over, and whispered. Mark shrank in discomfort, and the cameras twisted away—you never want the interviewer in shot, and certainly not like this.

"If you want to win any game, you have to learn its boundaries."

"Cameras off, boys," she said.

Lumpy camera arms oozed to the floor. The holy hostess crossed her own and floated forward, and the contestants parted like the red sea for her. She landed in front of Theodore, and glitter drifted from her shoulders as her red high heels clinked against the crystalline floor.

"What did you say, you little *bitch* ?" Jesus snarled.

Theodore and Robin both leaned back.

"Oh, you're the Atheist, aren't you?" she said. She placed her hands on her hips and rolled her shoulders in mocking rhythm. *"Wah wah wah, I don't think this place is real, I'm sad, I'm confused, I'm a baby.* That's you. That's what you sound like."

Theodore summoned all his willpower to prevent his lips from curling into a smile. "Hey, you're the one—"

"Wah, wah, wah, I was kidnapped! Shut up, the interviewer already explained you're not losing any time on Earth. We didn't kidnap you, we *interviewed* you and you *accepted* and now you're scared that it's *real.* We're doing you a goddamn favor."

Theodore couldn't help but laugh at Jesus saying "goddamn", which only made her angrier.

"And listen, you little punk, I'm not just the hostess. I'm one of the *judges.* If you want to go home early, you know what you can do. But, you'll do it with the cameras on, and within the confines of his competition. This is your only warning—you go outside the production, I'll make the example I make of you *part of the story.* "

With a labored wave, she addressed the sullen crowd. "And that applies to all you sons of bitches! You should be fucking grateful for what I'm doing for you."

"No, we are grateful," Jarilo the goat-legged boy pleaded. "Please don't punish us all because of him!"

"Please give us this chance!" Oshunmare begged.

"Yeah! Fuck him up!" The Internet cheered.

Theodore scanned the rows of faces. If they weren't saying it out-loud, their expressions made their shared thoughts clear: *Don't you dare ruin this for us* .

"Hey, you're right, I just had second thoughts," Theodore tried to suppress his laughter. It wasn't nervousness that took him over, though that may have been the way it appeared to the others.

"There's no room for cold feet here," Jesus huffed and floated back to her mark. "I'll try to be objective with you, but you better *work,* you hear me? Boys! Cameras!"

Theodore and Robin gave each other a knowing look—boundaries had clearly been established. The talk of leaving the show was not only out-of-bounds, but a sore subject for the holy hostess.

"And... action!"

She inhaled deeply, and her face lit up like a novelty billboard.

"How is everyone feeling?"

The crowd cheered with inspired energy, and even Theodore found the will to give a golf clap. Jesus winked into a camera. It was a good take.

"That's good to hear, sweeties!" she clapped her hands together, and a cloud of glitter puffed between them. "Because the show has already begun."

Theodore's eye throbbed a bit, then stopped.

"You may or may not have felt a slight tingle in your hands when you came in. It wasn't the catering, my dears... it was this!"

Jesus whipped her palm out, and the skin started to raise up. It cleanly split without blood, and out popped a pocket-watch sized object attached to a chain. The chain snaked up in the air, and its face—a large, metal-lidded eyeball—blinked at the contestants.

"Behold! All of you, for the rest of this competition, have a "god eye" equipped to your souls!"

Jesus explained that this serpentine cyclops was their primary tool in the competition, and one of the grand prizes. To illustrate its power, the god eye stared; thin, red lasers grafted an apple slowly in the air. Upon its formation, it dropped into Jesus's waiting palm, red and blemishless, blessed with a fine mist of water. It had a leaf on its stem as if it had been freshly picked. It even had a bar-code sticker adorned with an illustration of Jesus's smile. This got another round of applause from most of the contestants, and the shiqq's cameras zoomed in on its glossy detail.

"Put your soul into this, and you can make anything," she bit into the apple and moaned in satisfaction. "Mmm. Fabulous. And you'll need to really know your own soul well to make something as good as this. Gosh, this is great. It's so good, in fact, that it gives me..."

She turned the apple outwards to reveal the bite-mark to the contestants. Its outline was unmistakable—a perfectly rendered tree, roots and all.

"...an idea. A forbidden one, in fact!"

The crowd murmured.

"In the beginning, I made apples before Adam. Adam, that cute little fool, took a big ol' bite out of my fruit without my permission. Well. If we're going to have a new god in Heaven, let's let them learn from my mistakes. Maybe our crops will do better if we make 'man' first."

A range of bewildered and excited expressions colored the contestants. There were those that followed along so well that they had already summoned their own god eyes from the palms of their hands—Imhotep, Athena. Csodaszarvas's, curiously, came from one of his antlers.

"That's right, my dears! On the 6th day, I made humans. But you? You'll be making your followers *right now!* "

Theodore rubbed his irritated eye.

THE FIRST CHALLENGE

Creation-Kind

Create one perceptibly living representative of an award winning species for you to rule over.

Describe species concept in 2 minute demonstration.

Sentience not required for demonstration, but will be expected in future challenges.

Working Time: 12 hours, with one 2 hour break 8 hours in.

This world is made of Paper.

The Workroom

The god eye equips itself to the soul.

"Where in my body, exactly, is the soul located?" Theodore recalled his complaint to Mark Sharkman. Never did he believe he'd actually *need* the answer to that rhetorical question, nor did he believe there *was* one. But as he scanned the room of snaking cyclops pocket-watches that created materials out of thin air for professional weirdos cosplaying as the world's most inaccurate interpretations of irrelevant religious icons, he realized he would need an answer soon if he intended to take this competition seriously.

"Do you intend to take it seriously?" Mark asked with a hint of oaky concern.

"At this point, it's too weird not to," Theodore admitted in his interview. "I want to know more. Besides, I like making things. You could have told me we'd be making stuff. I'm pretty on-board with that, in theory."

Outside of the camera, Theodore was pinned by the frustration of trying to decode the language of the religious. For him, no god eye materialized, no matter how much he pretended to will it out.

The 13 contestants were in a sizable workroom, lit by floating neon lights on the ceiling that drifted back and forth like rocking babies. The ivory floor and all-marble tables and walls were calming, clean, and sterile. Each contestant had their own section of the room, with plenty of table and aisle space to work and maneuver. Many, at this point in the first hour, did not need much room as they were still learning how to manipulate their new toys. Within time everyone, except Theodore, had successfully started on something.

There was a clear gap in skill between those that had some familiarity with the god eye device, and those that were trying it for the first time. Zargah, who had trouble communicating with anyone (and whether he even understood the challenge itself was still a mystery), produced a bowl of clay in the first hour, then filled it with a chalky, green soil. Many contestants had taken similar approaches to start small by creating non-living materials to get used to the god eye. Santa Inari made long, white strips of leather, slightly changing how rough the texture was with each new strip. Ishta-Devata made large glass aquariums and, from nothing, filled them with pristine, clear water. Jarilo, the half-goat, made stalks of wheat, and giggled as he weaved them into his long hair.

Robin had taken an almost identical approach to Zargah, though the soil she slowly crafted out of thin air was of a color and richness familiar to earthlings. When Theodore asked Robin how she made it, she said she tried to think as clearly as possible about what she wanted to make. When she was young she planted flowers with her sister in the front garden, a memory so clear she could still smell the sweet soil.

Theodore sat cross-legged on top of his table. That advice didn't help him at all.

Those familiar with the device were already doing much more impressive work: Athena had constructed a complicated iron lattice, from which she began to mold bone colored beams into a human skeleton. It was pliable at first, but once the armored goddess molded it into the shape she desired, she gave it a flick, and the material hardened into actual bone. Oshunmare, the lizard-lady, drew tendons of muscle from her god eye with her claw tips, like cotton candy being freshly pulled and formed to shape in front of her. The Internet, armed with safety goggles of his own creation, created several blank circuit boards, then slowly sparked tracks and pads on each one individually.

"Theodore, are you okay?" Taninim scanned up from the pile of scales he had made on his table. "You haven't started yet."

"I'm fine. Just thinking," he muttered.

Theodore noticed that not everyone's god eye came out of their hands. Taninim's came out of the neck of his guitar—did this mean Taninim's guitar is where his soul lived? Ishta's peaked out from her fountain of curly hair. Imhotep's came up from the collar of his robe, and Theodore could see the chain underneath the fabric—it was burrowing out from the center of his chest. Oksi's slithered out of his open mouth, then retreated back in when not in use, an experience that always made the massive man flinch.

And poor Oksi. It was unclear what he was trying to make, other than a mess; anytime he tried to will something into the world, a nondescript, bloody organ would plop down onto the table in front of him, then melt away in sizzling disappointment. His look of consternation spoke loudly for the man of few words.

Theodore rubbed his eye, unsure why he would have a persistent pain in Heaven. Suddenly, his hand dropped—he remembered when his eye started to hurt, then became *completely sure* why he had a persistent pain in Heaven.

No amount of strain or focus on his left eye seemed to do anything. It's not enough, it seemed, to just know where it is, nor is it enough to just think *Hey, god eye. Come on out.*

There's a trick. There has to be a trick, Theodore thought as the first hour came to a close. *If this isn't magic, if it operates by any rules at all, then what's the trick?*

Theodore swung his legs around and pushed himself to the floor, his leather shoes squeaking on the ivory.

"It's in my face. It might even be right behind my eye. I think it's stuck," he whispered to Robin.

"Your soul?" she scrunched her face up.

"No, the god eye," he looked across the working would-be gods. "And I think I can get it out of me without a soul."

"Are you sure?" Jesus collapsed into her swivel chair. Her head fell into a pile of notebooks—it's a shame there were no cameras around to capture it.

"There were only supposed to be 12 contestants according to *his* instructions," Cthulhu shook the edge of a warped page. It came from a book that he had fished out from a larger pile of weathered texts in the corner of the room.

"Wasn't it your job to gather the contestants, Cthulhu?" the obelisk sneered, stacked on a red leather couch.

"Excuse me, *I did*. I gathered the ones I was assigned."

The three sat in a blind-drawn office, whose dim ambiance was tinted by a green lidded desk lamp, mounds of strewn files and papers in every corner, dry-erase boards filled from one side to another with multicolored arrows and impossibly tiny notes.

"No, this is definitely your fault," Jesus pointed at the obelisk. "Your shiqqs should have sounded an alarm if someone were here that wasn't supposed to be."

"Hey, they alert me of even the slightest oddities! Do you know how many notifications I have to swipe away when Cthulhu sneaks into the cafeteria?" the obelisk rotated, offended.

"Don't say 'sneak' like I'm doing something wrong, I can go in there anytime I want," Cthulhu said as he clapped the book close. "That's my staff in there."

"Oh trust me, I know. *It shows.*"

Cthulhu tilted his head down and looked at the obelisk over his dark sunglasses. "How you gonna be bitchy about someone's weight when you're hiding in a tetris piece?"

"How are you gonna be so lazy that you make others make food for you when you can *literally* make things appear out of thin air?" the obelisk vibrated. "Look, the shark said he had papers on all the contestants. Nothing on that side has been out of the ordinary—except those shitty papers *you* scribbled up for The Internet at the last minute!" It pointed itself accusingly at Jesus. "He sent in a request for more pages, you know. But that was it. He mentioned the humans were complaining about their method of acquisition, and asked for more pages on the dog. There are zero reports out of the ordinary for any other contestants, and you *know* that boozed up chatterbox talked to all of them."

"Okay, okay, okay, calm down everyone," Jesus held up her pierced palms at each of her cohorts. "To recap: there's a contestant here that wasn't included in the original production estimation, so someone snuck in. But all profiles sent to Mark matched the contestants currently on site, which means..."

Cthulhu and the obelisk mulled over this quietly, then slumped in their respective seats. Due to the rigid nature of the obelisk, this meant it rolled to the floor. Jesus returned the surface of her forehead to the desk.

"*Production* is playing us," the three whined in unison.

How can there be different levels of divinity? Theodore thought.

Even if he wasn't religious, Theodore tried hard to put himself in the shoes of someone who was, if only to get closer to an understanding of the mechanical workings of his god eye. As far as he could tell, a "supreme being" was just that, and there's not much wiggle room up or down. *Does one god make apples better than others? Are some better at math? Can Jesus run laps faster than Buddha? What's Buddha look like here, anyway?* were just a few of Theodore's thoughts as he walked the aisles of the ivory workroom.

Don't talk to me, Athena noticed that Theodore's path in her peripheral vision led towards her desk. *Whatever your deal is, I'm not involved.*

Robin had told Theodore about Ishta and Athena's abilities—completely separate powers from the god eye. And while Theodore still wasn't convinced that this reality had anything to do with his own, he could accept that they *thought* they were gods. If that's the case, then what better way to find out about the tiered pyramid of godhood than to ask someone trying to climb it?

"Athena," Theodore said as he rounded her table's corner.

You didn't hear him, Athena thought. *Maybe he'll go away if you don't respond.*

"Athena," he said again as he leaned against a column.

Ugh, she thought.

"What," she said. The static, steel delivery did not sound like a question, but an ad-lib that threatened penalty of death if completed.

"I was wondering if you could do me a favor and make a cup of coffee," Theodore asked.

The room's volume, previously alive with various contestant's chatter, died. Athena spun around on her stool, head tilted, bowled over by the audacity of this question.

"Excuse me?"

"Oh wow, you've made progress, haven't you?" Theodore hovered around Athena's constructed skeleton. She was in the middle of filling it with waxy organs. "Gnarly. Reminds me of biology class. You're definitely further ahead than anyone else."

"In what *reality* do you think you can just walk up to me and demand something? There is a cafeteria that way and to the right," Athena rose from her stool and got in Theodore's face, her spleen-holding hand directed the traffic she expected him to take. The two were of equal height and build, but only one of them was dressed for war—and now, her expression was, too. "Are you asking me to make you something because I'm a woman? Am I your secretary?"

"Nah," Theodore shrugged. "I'm asking you 'cause you're Greek."

Feet shuffled. Heads turned. The Internet snickered from behind a pile of circuit boards he was constructing.

"What?" Athena blinked embers.

"You say you're Athena, right? Like, the Greek goddess," Theodore poked at what appeared to be a kidney on her table. "I dunno, there was this one time I read that Greek coffee was some of the best coffee you can get. I always wanted to try it, and I figured if anyone would know how to make it, it'd be you. I don't want you to "make it" make it, though, you feel me? I want you to use your god eye. What'd Jesus say earlier, that this thing connects to your soul? I'm sure you know exactly what Greek coffee tastes like, yeah? Assuming you've been there, you know. *On Earth."*

The two shared an uncomfortable stare, one that wasn't broken by a laughing Internet. The first to blink was Athena. She smirked, looked up at the ceiling, mouthed un-pleasantries, then returned her eyes to the millennial-mortal.

"It's Turkish," she said. Her god eye snaked slowly out of her palm, but its gaze was towards the smooth table in front of her, and with consideration of sanitation, away from the organs she had been making. "Greeks claim it as their own because they've had it for so long, but it didn't originate there. Turkey and Greece haven't always had the best relationship politically, so why give credit to people you don't like for something you love?"

"That sounds pretty petty, really," Theodore said.

"You would know, being human, of course," the searing gaze of the god eye beamed an ornate silver and porcelain cup into existence over the course of a few moments. The eye coiled around the plate and stared in, and its laser melted into a steaming liquid. "Theodore, I'm not *like* the Goddess Athena. I *am* the Goddess Athena."

Theodore peered into the cup. Despite the small size, the coffee and cardamom aroma was thick, as was the the viscosity of the dark brown liquid itself. The brim of the drink was lidded by a lighter foam, and upon closer inspection, finely ground coffee could be seen floating freely. Athena also made a glass of water, and etched a carving of herself punching Theodore in the face into its structure.

"You drink the water first to cleanse your terrible, terrible palette," Athena explained.

“Thank you,” Theodore nodded. He drank of the rendition of his own facial fracture, and sipped the coffee—there was a subtle sweetness beyond the spicy, citrusy cardamom. Athena explained that since Theodore was a true novice at both drinking real coffee and at having manners, she added a light amount of sugar: both to make it easier to drink, and to cure his awful personality. Theodore was mostly unfazed by the peppered insults.

“Just out of curiosity, when did the Greeks start calling it Greek?” Theodore asked between sips. “I didn’t know it was just Turkish coffee. I’ve had this before.”

Athena was poised to give an answer, but then looked flummoxed at the surrounding blank floor and walls. “Sorry, I don’t remember around when that happened.”

“It’s fine. This is great, by the way. I love it.”

He walked away, cup in hand, every bit as unbothered as he was when he sauntered up to her. Athena shook her head. “So is that it? Am I worthy to compete against now?”

“Well, you make a great coffee,” he said, and hopped back up onto his own table and sipped. She rolled her eyes and went back to work. With the spectacle over, the rest of the workroom returned to its light volume of chatter, a little disappointed that a larger spat between the two egos didn’t flare up.

Everyone except Robin, who knew what Theodore was trying to do, but couldn’t work out how a cup of coffee was going to get him there. For her, in that moment, nothing else was more intriguing in Heaven than whatever insanity was going on in his head.

Then the moment passed, and she went back to work.

"In about four to six hours the human body absorbs 99% of caffeine consumed," Mark told Theodore as he nursed Zinfandel in his Camera World. A whirling camera arm came down from a shadowy void and allowed its square head to be a coaster for the lounging shark-man. "But the initial effects are pretty fast, since they go through the bloodstream. You won't keep that buzz, but I don't think Heaven will 'heal' your surge of energy quickly enough. It's a sound strategy, Theodore."

Back in the workroom, Theodore had downed the coffee a little faster than one typically enjoys it, Greek or otherwise. He didn't do that out of disrespect of the drink, though, but for scientific purposes.

"Hey, Robin," he turned, still seated on top of his table. He quietly nodded his head upwards, signaling her over. Curiosity ruled; she was by his side.

"Is this about the coffee?"

"Yeah."

"Ready to admit you have a soul?" she elbowed him playfully.

"Nah," he leaned in. "But let me tell you a secret. When I make music, I have trouble focusing. If I really want to make something, if I really want to get myself going, I have to slam some coffee. Sometimes, a lot of it. I'll bet if you silence a room when I'm over-caffeinated, you can hear my heart make a low humming sound. I don't know what a soul feels like, Robin, but I know when the caffeine hits me."

She noticed something pushing against the flesh of Theodore's face, testing its give, crawling from his cheek towards his eye socket.

"Theodore," Robin stammered, wincing as she touched her own face in empathy. "Is that your god eye?"

Theodore smiled through gritted teeth, but he was sweating. The skin of his brow scrunched towards the center of his face and threatened to implode from strain. His prickly palms poured into numbing hands. He drooled. "If I can do this, Robin, then they have dopamine in their bodies. They have adrenaline."

In a gory explosion, Theodore's god eye ripped out from the flesh under his eye and sprayed Robin's front with red skepticism. He fell as he screamed and clawed at the metal chain.

His plan worked, in a way.

Without Context

Every time that Mark Sharkman tried to interview The Internet, he was road blocked by snarls, half-answers and crossed arms. The dog-punk played the part of the disaffected human youth he was dressed as perfectly, but Mark knew that there was something else there beyond the costume. He had been studying the canine-creator closely—this contestant attacked his project, whatever it was building up to be, with ferocity and skill. No other table in the room was so full of *stuff* as his; mounds of circuit boards and metal bits and smooth plastic pieces were carefully organized with clear purpose.

"So, this is actually just my curiosity speaking. No form questions here," Mr. Sharkman said as he tossed his clipboard away. "All the electronic stuff your making is really different from everyone else's species. You may not be ready to talk about your end product, but I'm curious what inspired you to go in an inorganic route."

"*Inorganic*," The Internet mocked. "I'm right in front of you, you know."

"Do you find that description offensive? I can choose a different word at your request."

The Internet shuffled in his seat. "You wanna know what inspired me? That. You."

"I'm sorry?"

The Internet jabbed a finger at his temple, below his middle-finger emblazoned hat brim. "I was born without context. At my first breath, all the knowledge and opinions of humanity were shoved into my brain, and without any experience to make sense of it all. Look at this guy, fucking calling me 'inorganic' over here.

You know what it's like to have a world's worth of information shoved into your brain all at once? You can't know anything more painful than that. Get the fuck outta here with your 'inorganic' bullshit. I've felt more in that one moment than you ever will in your entire drunken life. Sittin' over here bobblin' your head up and down on the next bottle like a cheap bitch . You're the one that's inorganic. Fuck you."

Mark Sharkman tapped his fingers across his knee. The cameras around him whirred with approval—this was *definitely* good footage. "Alrighty, then. *Thanks.*"

Robin's God Eye

Robin didn't have the same trouble with her god eye Theodore did, and she didn't understand why.

It appeared naturally for her; when the challenge of making a new species was issued, she simply focused on what she wanted. She thought of the violence and division on Earth, the lack of opportunity and resources for many, and of the sometimes cruel nature of the human heart. With the power of this god eye, she knew she could go back to Earth and change the world for the best. Was it a simple, boring wish? *Sure.* Robin could admit that—but that didn't change the fact that summoning it was the only thing in her life that had ever come easy. Robin was a person used to wanting.

Anyone can learn to throw a ball fast. But how are you gonna get on the team, Robin?, the memory of her sister asked.

When Theodore had told her he didn't believe in souls, she didn't hold it against him, nor was she surprised—she could easily guess his stance on supernatural ideas after the incident with Jesus. Even then, she was a little preoccupied with more important things. For example: *Oh my god. I'm standing in front of Jesus.*

To hold fast to his atheism after all that had happened, though, seemed silly. He was in a room full of literal miracles. Whatever solidarity she felt with him on the roof seemed to vanish as he sat on his table for an hour doing nothing.

That all changed.

She was coated in his blood. She watched him force a tool of the gods out of his own face purely through an understanding of how his own mind and body react to caffeine. The folds of his erupted skin slowly sealed back close through the influence of

Heaven's air, and she understood the real difference between him and herself.

She started with the destination. He started with the path.

The contestants had crowded around Theodore's table by that point, a chatty mixture of concern and curiosity. Taninim and Zargah propped him up and off the table, and made sure the pale, shaking man could stand. Jarilo the half-goat gave him water. The Internet ridiculed him for trying to get more camera time, and was the first to return back to his table. "Who cares, he'll heal up," he said.

Theodore's shaking eventually subsided, and before long he was ready to pick apart the mechanics of the god eye. Sadly, his lavender jacket remained coated in blood stains, so he tossed it to the side of his work table.

"Wait, I can't see out of it," he worried as his god eye floated like a balloon in front of his face. "Does mine not work? Did I go through all of that for nothing?"

"You don't really 'see' out of the god eye ," Robin said. "You have to... how do I explain this? You have to think, but *at* it."

"*At* it?"

"Direct your desires towards the god eye. Open up to it," Taninim briefly turned from his own molding of large scales to chime in.

"What does that mean, though? Thoughts don't have directions. They're *thoughts*," Theodore rubbed his temple. His god eye wiggled downwards and clinked its chain sadly.

"Have an internal conversation with Subject god eye," Zargah chittered through his translation-collar. "It hears thoughts."

Theodore blinked. "T-that's uh, pretty good, Zargah. Is your collar working better?"

"Subject Zargah big thinker. Do the big think."

"Never mind. Okay, so. Conversation at the metal snake in my face. Think at it. Uh, thanks, guys. I'll take it from here. Competition and all, gotta stand on my own."

"That's the spirit," Taninim slapped Theodore heartily on his back, with force that nearly knocked him over again.

After the other contestants had returned to their corners of the room, Robin remained with Theodore to guide him through the creation process, despite his insistence otherwise. ("Please don't let me hold you back." "It's fine, look what you've already done! This'll be easy for you.") She showed him how to start small and be specific—a bland request to make a tomato would result in dead plants, mushy mounds of red and bruised, shapeless fruit. But if you thought through a specific, nuanced description with the god eye, you get much closer to exactly what you envision.

Theodore started with the stalk, rough and strong. He thought of the anatomy of the tomato, of its pale core, and the encasing meat that held the tomato's wet, seeded jelly. Once the fruit was fully brought into existence, he bit. His teeth passed through the smooth, firm flesh and revealed the lightness of its juice, shy towards picking a side between salty and sweet. Thick. Ripe. Versatile.

"Wow, you just bite right in to 'em, huh?" Robin laughed. "Is it good?"

"Yeah. I, uh, love tomatoes. Only vegetable I'd eat for a long time."

"I have a theory," Robin laced her fingers, thumbs chasing each other, "that the god eye itself is just interpreting what we tell it, and not flawlessly. If we're 'contestants,' it probably has some limitations. Maybe even training wheels. I can't imagine they'd give us something like this unchecked."

He took a second bite, and nodded with surprised approval. "Should be fun to find out what those are."

The Cafeteria

Csodaszarvas, the Hungarian deer deity of courage and adventure, lumbered at a cafeteria table in front of a cucumber salad. He couldn't be expected to sit; this massive stag was seven feet tall and long, forced to stand in the aisles between mosaic lunch tables and grooved gold stools.

A finger tapped at the quadruped's quarter. He turned.

"BOO!" A woven face of wheat bulged at the deer, who bound away in fear. He cleared three tables and the room in a single leap.

"Jarilo, please," Csodaszarvas whined as he trotted back.

The half-goat boy removed his wheat mask. "It's spooky, ain't it! I'm about to go put it on my new friend, want to come watch?"

Jarilo's "new friend" was the species he was creating for the competition. His wheat-man was a creature of magic and grain, cereal with a cerebellum. Csodaszarvas already knew this, of course: his worktable was positioned next to the half-goat, and Jarilo gave him the blow-by-blow commentary on every change that he made in his project.

Csodaszarvas was also aware enough of his new roommate's personality to not be surprised that he had been tailed to the cafeteria just for a gag. Jarilo was energetic, and exhausting, and for those reasons the deer decided to take an early snack despite the hours still remaining before the group's mandatory break.

"Show me when I'm done eating, if you don't mind."

"Ah, Oksi! What about you?" Jarilo turned towards the entrance.

The deer, normally able to hear the smallest sounds, shuffled in surprise. Oksi, one of his roommates, was a bear of a man who had offered little in the way of words since the group had met—in fact, the most sounds the deer had heard from him were the grunts of disapproval when he made anything with his god eye. In his hands, he had a tray of thinly-sliced frozen salmon, drizzled with the salty stains of soy-sauce and garnished with the red sprouts of water peppers.

Oksi had also made little progress on anything while Csodaszarvas was in the workroom—*So how could he have time to take a break?*, the deer wondered.

"I saw you heading towards the cafeteria, actually," Oksi's baritone came from his throat and shook rib cages and silverware against plates. "Being honest, I was having trouble with what I was making, so I simplified things and made some food. Do you want to try some?"

Before the snow-white stag could decline *(I have just eaten, and I don't eat meat,* he thought. *Also, if you made that with your god eye...)* Jarilo was already plucking slices from the tray. He tossed them into the air and caught them in his wide mouth.

"These are great! Oh my god, what are these? How many can I have?!"

"It's called Rui-be," Oksi said. "You can have as many as you want, I'll just leave the tray here."

Csodaszarvas stared at Jarilo as he vacuumed the fish into his mouth, baffled. *If such a complex dish was executed so well, he must have some focused thinking and clear understanding of the dish.* The deer thought. *If that's the case, then why is he struggling so much in the workroom?*

"Thanks, Jarilo. I needed to hear something like that," Oksi nodded, and left.

As he exited the cafeteria, he passed by the group of 35-D. They were loud and confrontational with each other, and he didn't understand why they traveled in a pack if they were so annoyed by each other's company. He slowed his pace and listened in, and when they moved too far away, he hugged the walls and hung behind the door entrance.

"Christ, I am not your Google Home," The Internet shoved.

"If you're gonna follow me to the cafeteria, you gotta answer my question," Theodore shoved back.

"Aren't you following him?" Taninim asked while tuning his guitar.

"What is 'cigarette,'" Zargah clicked.

Theodore stepped into the empty line in front of a hair-net wearing monkfish-man at the cafeteria counter. "You got any cigarettes?"

It shook its rubbery mound of a head.

"Damn. Every time I try to make one, it's shit. Teach me for not knowing what goes in my smokes, I guess. I'll just take a coffee, then. You got that?"

The monkfish-man blorbed up and down.

"Rad. Any type is fine. Surprise me, and make it the largest size. I'm sharing," he turned to The Internet. "Hey, tell Zargah what a 'cigarette' is."

"Fuck you. Tell him yourself," The Internet blew a puff of smoke from a cigarette he just created while Theodore was turned around. Taninim coughed violently, and so did The Internet.

"It's that," Theodore pointed. The Internet gave him the cigarette, grossed out that humans enjoyed the taste of burning.

"Why eat the bad smoke?" Zargah asked.

"Great question," Theodore puffed. "I enjoy bad decisions."

"Fucking edgelord, just say it calms you down," an irritated Internet mumbled.

The group of monsters sat down at a table and continued their rambling chorus, and each tried out the jumbo-sized coffee Theodore ordered. ("None of you have had coffee? Try this. You'll love it." None of them did. Zargah vomited a strange jello-like substance immediately.) Sad that he wasted his time listening in to them, Oksi determined there was no intel to be gained and headed back to the workroom. His timing was truly unfortunate, because he missed this:

"Come on, really. Just look it up. I want to believe you're The Internet."

The Internet rolled his eyes. "One sec. Okay, done. Greek Coffee was found in Turkey. Turkish coffee was formerly referred to simply as 'Turkish' or τούρκικος. Political tensions with Turkey from the Istanbul riots led to the change to 'Greek coffee' ελληνικός καφές. That name became even more popular after the Turkish invasion of Cyprus in 1974. Greek–Turkish relations at all levels became strained, "Turkish coffee" became "Greek coffee" by substitution of one Greek word for another while leaving the Arabic loan-word, for which there is no Greek equivalent, unchanged."

Theodore clapped, a genuine wide-eyed looked of amazement on his face. "Well damn. You really did just read a wiki to me."

"Yeah, and it's *annoying.* I dedicated cells to looking up the creative commons to make sure that was covered with all these cameras around us. *You're welcome,* asshole. Makin' me taste that gross ass bean juice after hyping it up for no reason. Fuck."

“So why did you want to know that?” even though Taninim was sure he hated it, he found himself sipping more of the coffee.

“Well,” Theodore drummed the table. “Athena knew all that just from memory. There’s implication that she somehow knew what happened in 1974 on Earth. Was she there? And Internet, you’re connected to it, too. In fact, it seems to me like your the internet of Earth, in particular. What’s Heaven’s wiki equivalent?”

The Internet stared into the table, and said meekly: “No, you’re right. I am not made from any information that originated in Heaven.”

“There’s an awful lot of data flying between Heaven and Earth somehow, but I haven’t seen a news show or anything like that,” Theodore reached for the coffee cup. “I think that’s interesting. If she loved Greece so much that she knew about political motivations of that country in the 70s, then why has she been so irrelevant on Earth? All of these gods, for that matter-” he brought it to his lips and sipped air. “Hey, what the fuck, Taninim! You drank the whole thing?”

Taninim’s nod rattled into an over-energized shake.

“Let’s head back,” The Internet rubbed his head. “That’s enough of a break... I dunno about the rest of you losers, but I got a lot of work to do.”

Between The Heart, The Mind, The Eye

"It seems to me..." Imhotep told Mark. He paused only to take a controlled sip from his wine, "...that there's a lot of amateurs this season. People that have never held or studied a god eye before. One of them doesn't even believe in the supernatural at all."

Of everyone that Mark interviewed, Imhotep seemed the most unfazed and unimpressed by the proceedings of reality television. His brow never crinkled, his full lips never pouted or grinned, he never did too much of anything in any way—except dress.

"Do you believe that makes them weaker competition?" Mark, too, enjoyed the warm static induced by his drink.

"Oh, no, on the contrary, darling. I've looked around the room and witnessed some of the most wild work I've ever seen on this show. The blue one, Ishta? The not-reptile. She's making a race out of water. Water! The audacity. The minimalism. Breathtaking. Difficult. Fanciful. I *love* her. Hate what she's making from a practical standpoint, but I'm not a judge, of course." The high priest took another sip, certain of the accuracy of his assessment.

"Practicality?"

"Well, for simplicity's sake, let's call what she's making an elemental," Imhotep smirked, and brushed his fingers across the linen hood draped around his shoulder. "Hopefully she doesn't actually call it that, of course. If this thing is entirely made of water, then she has to introduce a certain level of magic or logic into the world she'll inevitably build for it. Its own rules and physicality. Not only would she have to invent the means of their existence, but of their survival. Water is fragile, consumable, easy to destroy.

She could make a convincing case for it, but it seems like a lot of work for something that, as it stands right now, is not so unusual looking. Do you remember the rules?"

Mark flipped through the nearest clipboard. If there was a memo in Heaven, it had crossed by him at some point—it had to. There was no one for whom it was more important to know what was happening in Heaven than the interviewer.

"I have them right here, in fact."

"Sentience isn't required for this first challenge," Imhotep quoted from memory. "I think that's key. They want to see a capsule of what you'll be making, and I just don't know if what she's making is direct enough. I, myself, am focusing on something very hard and direct, theatrical, powerful. There's nothing that says you can't scale back further down the line if it's too much right now. But, I think she, and maybe a few others, are missing the point of this challenge: to sell yourself, your ideas. Your not just making one creature. Your making something that represents what type of god you would become."

It was a grand assumption for Imhotep to make, considering how far behind some of the contestants back in the workroom were. Oksi had only just started to put together a misshapen, potato-shaped beast with flesh-like clay. The Internet had surrounded himself with a mountain of unconnected parts with no resolution in sight. Oshunmare had started, stopped, and restarted so many cat-like creatures of various sizes that her table looked like a morgue of half-taxidermied beasts. Indecision and time crept up on each of the contestants—few were certain of their concept, much less their success.

None of those concerns impacted the person it likely should have the most, though: Theodore. The man who started out behind had labored at a workman's pace, mirroring The Internet's zeal earlier in the day. He had produced an entire table's worth of fine, purple quartz, with an oil-like sheen inspired by the sunglasses of the bastard that brought him here in the first place.

Taninim walked over to Theodore to check in on his progress. The Internet peeked over a stack of circuit boards and listened in.

"Ever since you got your eye out, you've been goin' to town. What's all this gonna be?" the impossibly-toothed-man asked.

Theodore picked up a quartz nugget and leaned into the scaly shoulder of the guitarist. "Check this shit out."

He held the quartz up to Taninim's eye, a beady thing with wild intensity despite its cool, icy iris. Taninim was surprised to see, when Theodore flicked the bottom of the gem, that the gem began to morph. It reflected back Taninim's eye—no, it *changed* into Taninim's eye, as if that portion of his face had been ripped directly from his scales. The replication was perfect, right down to the minute detail of Taninim's x-shaped pupil—an irrelevant detail no one would pick up without close study.

"Whoa," Taninim exhaled. "Creepy."

Almost as quickly as it contorted, the quartz melted back to its original form.

"I'm having trouble getting it to hold its shape, so I guess that's just a sneak peek for now. What about you, what are you working on?"

The corners of Taninim's toothy maw turned up. "Oh, man. It's metal. Gonna make a world of rockin' beasts. Can't wait to show it to off."

The Internet grumbled and dipped back down behind his towers of circuitry. He wasn't surprised to see the human and the dragon getting on—since his initial meeting with them, and after he watched the lazy pace Theodore had taken up until then, he just assumed the two were so dim that they had found solidarity with each other. But Theodore had produced a staggering amount of transforming gems, and The Internet suspected he knew where the idea germinated from: Athena was the one who introduced the "flick" as a trigger to change one thing to another. What bothered The Internet was not the fact that Theodore mirrored the technique, but that he, a normal human, figured out how to do it *at all*, and as quickly as he did.

The Internet searched himself for an answer.

The cells of the electric dog-punk, the smallest parts of his being, were not the blobs of abstract water and proteins most cells in reality are. If The Internet submitted himself for scrutiny under a microscope (and he never would) you would find trillions and trillions of sparking, electric dogs of polygonal shape, all communicating and working together to form The Internet himself. They stayed wired, processed his surroundings, powered his new muscles, organized his experiences, and decodified the endless information that streamed into him from the World Wide Web of the planet Earth.

There was a section of the cell-dogs dedicated specifically to finding information on Theodore. They zipped from website to website; their neon eyes scanned wildly anywhere and everywhere, focused on their singular task of locating the asshole human that dared to start a fight with him. The Internet deliberately forgot that he started this feud between the two for the pettiest reason:

upon seeing the lavender-suited Theodore for the first time, he image matched the suit to a particular breed of life-loving, well-to-do hipsters that experienced the world he himself could only read about.

He would later find the definition of jealousy and knew that was what he was experiencing. He also realized that Theodore had, since he had met him, deliberately pushed at the boundaries and logic of the show, through a bold and rebellious set of actions The Internet himself wanted to do.

So, instead, The Internet formed a new reason to hate Heaven's local Atheist. It was no longer because he was a cardboard cutout of privilege—but that he has the opportunity to be, and is instead trying to encroach on The Internet's role of the outsider. *I'm the angry one. I'm the one that was born to compete.* No one else can understand what he's been forced to go through to be on *The Next Great Deity* , and he was going to prove it.

You could have a Facebook and be loved by other humans. A Twitter. A Linkedin. Anything, The Internet thought. *But you don't. You're hiding something, and I'm gonna fucking find it, you smug son of a bitch.*

The Definition Of God

After the Judge's meeting, Cthulhu retired to the roof of his own observatory.

Sitting a few miles from Heaven's Heart Hotel was a large tower constructed almost entirely of pink ivory, which is deceiving in name—the material itself is actually wood, comes in a variety of red shades, and does not originate in Heaven, but on Earth, in the country of Zimbabwe.

As Cthulhu knew better than anyone, most things do not originate in Heaven.

The same could be said of some of these contestants. Even though it was a contest for godhood, there were members of this motley crew that were outside the scope of what is typically accepted for a contestant. The official statement from production, and the obvious one for fans (and critics) of the show, was that it was just a marketing trick to spice things up. Everyone, even those of supernatural lineage, becomes more interested in unexpected and controversial television. "Do anything that keeps the audience talking," the judges were instructed on a daily basis by memos.

Since Cthulhu worked for the show, he knew things weren't that simple. While the contestants competed for their prize, the judges were locked in a contest of their own—an eternal struggle between the most powerful gods in existence, and the only force stronger than themselves.

Production.

Cthulhu fingered through the spines of his library, tucked a selection of books under his arm, and lumbered his way to the roof. He reclined into his favorite lawn chair and began to read a 1928 issue of *Weird Tales,* a classic horror fiction magazine.

Though the red-bordered cover broadly advertised *The Ghost Table* by Elliott O'Donnell, it was the work of the first name in smaller print that that Cthulhu wanted to read—H.P. Lovecraft.

Cthulhu sat in the warm, humid silence of a Heaven night. He flipped through what he was sure was his fondest memories, but was overwhelmed to see them in text, in narration, in entertainment. In some time, he wept, and mouth tentacles reached to wipe away his brief but necessary tears. He needed a reminder of what he was fighting for.

"Hey, Cthulhu?" a shaky voice asked. Ocean-Mouth bristled, slapped the magazine close in between the thickness of a much larger book to hide its identity. He turned, saw the obelisk floating in the doorway, then sunk back into a lazy lounge.

"Oh, hey, it's you."

"Hey, I..." The obelisk hesitated, then floated over to the empty lounge chair. He turned as if to face Cthulhu. "I just wanted to apologize."

"For?"

"For earlier, of course," The obelisk said. "I was rude. We have to work together, and comments like mine about... you know... the cafeteria and all, those don't help anything."

Cthulhu shook his head. "It doesn't matter. It is our penchant for argument that makes us entertaining. It's why production gives us this opportunity." He then added, with a laugh, "Ah, but I'm not saying I approve of your comments. Just that you're forgiven. No, the cruelest thing is that I can get that fish-man on the noon-shift to make me lemon-butter scallops, but Heaven let's me keep the weight. I suppose Heaven doesn't stop the fat from building up, just the heart attack it'll eventually try to cause me."

“Well, you’ll still have it, you just won’t die from it. If anything, it might be worse—you’ll just recover, then be prone to having another.”

“Yes. Heaven truly is a wonderful place,” Cthulhu muttered.

“Don’t stress. We’ll get out this time. Do you want a drink?”

Cthulhu set down the book hiding his copy of Weird Tales and picked up another, dustier one—this one had a much older version of *The Next Great Deity*’s logo on it, despite its current date on the cover. He opened it up and read through the records of a previous season's contestants and challenges.

“Yes, Yes I do.”

"So, your inspiration was your sister?" Mark Sharkman asked.

Athena sat with every limb crossed, her expression crossed, her existence and attitude towards Mark and the show he represented crossed. But to open up about her sister, for a brief moment, she softened.

"I know Eris's taste well. She loves juxtaposition, the clash of extremes. Ultimately I'm trying to make something I think she'd like. Humanity, the soft creatures they are, re-imagined at their strongest."

Mark froze for a moment, looked up, and clicked his pen. "Eris, you said?"

"Yes. Eris."

He scribbled that down. "Lovely name."

Athena hardened again. "It's Greek. Of course it is."

Mark pulled back a little bit and stifled a laugh. "Right. Yes. So, you're essentially re-making Greek humans. But they are quite a bit larger than average. Sort of a Super-Greek? It looks like you've made two models... is there one you're favoring more than the other?"

"No," Athena unfolded an arm only to bring a correcting finger towards the shark. "They're both going out there."

"Oh!" Mark sat up, and his whirling cameras recoiled in surprise. "You know you... only have to make one today, right?"

"This is a love letter to everything I care about. I'm going to finish on time, with better execution than everyone else. I know exactly what I want and how to make it."

Mark nodded. "Well, I'm impressed. That's some confidence. Anyways, that's about all I have. Looks like it's break time soon. Good luck, Athena."

Athena returned to herself in the workroom with a click of Mark's tooth. She stared at the two humans she had molded onto the iron lattice. They were each well over seven feet tall and of olive complexion and heroic attractiveness. She had even started construction on their clothes: elaborate and detailed himation cloaks interwoven with large pieces of silver and bronze, designed to both accentuate their beauty and give themselves protection from weapons. Casual armor. They would always be ready for war, *and* brunch. *Warunch.*

And that foolish shark thinks I'm doing more than enough, Athena secured a seam on one of the cloaks. *He clearly hasn't met an Olympian before. Of course I'm confident. If Eris were here, she'd be my only competition.*

It was at that moment that a hologram of Jesus, faint and blue, burst into the room with a dazzling spark. Most of the contestants jumped. Internet knocked over a stack of his circuit boards when he bumped his table.

"Hiii guyyys!" Jesus waved. "Time flies when you're trying to become a god, huh? I'm here to remind you that it's been eight hours! It is now time for your mandatory break. You have the freedom to travel anywhere on this floor or any of the living quarter floors for the next two hours. So go on! Relax, and I'll see you soon! Byeee!"

Jesus gave a peace sign and exploded in another flash of light, and the jumpy dog-punk dropped the circuit boards he was trying to pick back up. He cursed.

The shiqqs lined up and led the contestants out of the workroom, assuring that no one was allowed to stay in and work during the break. The contestants, still getting accustomed to their new surroundings and work environments, retreated to their selected apartments—with the exception of Robin, who walked with Theodore and his fellow monsters of 35-D.

Over time, it became clear to the human pair that the ease of which they were able to talk to each other was beyond the planet of origin they shared. In fact, it was their differences—in beliefs, in profession, in geographical location—that fascinated the other.

"You've done a lot of work," Robin kept pace, and let her arms swing into claps, "for someone that doesn't want to be god."

"Well, regardless of what this place actually is, I'm still having fun. I can think of a lot of things in my life that would be easier if I could take this home."

"You haven't felt once that maybe, *just maybe*, this power is god-like? You don't think at least a little bit of this is magic?"

"My face split open, Robin. I felt a lot, I'd say."

"Not outside, inside."

"The definition I have of 'inside' still fits, I think. You clearly mean metaphorically, though, so, I don't know. Not yet, anyways."

"That's all he'll say," Internet pushed in between the two. "'I don't know' is what he defaults to when he's cornered."

"'I don't know' is a great answer. It's honest," Theodore put his hand on The Internet's face and pushed him back. "Oh, but this puppy did do something cool. He looked up the history of Greek coffee."

"Which is disgusting," Taninim lied.

"Disgusting," Zargah told the truth.

"I'm not a fucking puppy," The Internet snarled.

Through hallways and elevators and stairs, Theodore shared the puzzle that was gods of Heaven obtaining information without the ability to easily travel to Earth and back. Robin was more than eager to add her own piece: Testaments.

"Santa said this was currency generated by belief. How does it work? She seemed convinced that completely ordinary things they do here in Heaven impacts Earth, which then makes belief, which generates Testaments. Like this place is in constant spiritual and financial exchange with Earth."

Theodore laughed, and leaned over to Robin. He kept his voice low to muddle his joke in case a shiqq camera was nearby. "Logically, that makes no sense, but I guess that explains why Jesus is a celebrity hostess here. She's a rich brat."

Once in 35-D, the group threw a party, as both a means of bonding and as a means of testing whether the god eyes would work outside of the confines of the workroom. Theodore and Robin had the idea to make beer: the three monster men, ignorant of so many experiences that humans found normal, were perfect test subjects. (Theodore insisted this, at least—"but let's be careful with Zargah. He seems to get sick easily.") Using their god eye, the two humans made their favorite beers from their memory of its taste: Theodore preferred a complex IPA, Robin crafted a simple Lager.

Taninim was intoxicated instantly. The beers slurred his solos to a grungy sludge. Zargah was mostly indifferent and confused by the bitterness, but warmed up after a few minutes of fiddling his mandibles around the bottleneck. The Internet felt nothing from either drink at all.

"If the goal is to get drunk, this fucking sucks," The Internet complained as he downed his second beer. "This is almost as bad as Oksi's creature."

"First off, fuck you. It's great," Theodore pointed the bottle at Internet. He then smacked his tongue against the roof of his mouth, and its jumble of crisp bitters jabbed his palette—maybe the wolf was right. "Second off, I, uh, guess I'm not the only one amazed at Oksi's corner of the room."

"Oksi is bottom three, for sure," The Internet slumped down into the couch. "Like, he took forever to even get anything made, and what did it lead to? It looks like a nightmarish rendition of the Tasmanian Devil. Like, it's some vortex of ugly and dumb. Its eyes are like fucking melons. What the fuck."

"Bottom Three?" Robin asked.

"Jesus, lady, have you never seen a reality TV show before?" The Internet wobbled from his drink. "When you have this many contestants they always have a top, middle, and bottom. The middle just slides on through without getting talked about. The top and bottom are kept out and discussed by the judges on camera. Maximum drama and all."

"How do you know that, and how do you know it'll be three?"

"Because there's like a million of us on this show and reality shows usually do that," the dog-punk burped.

Theodore reached the bottom of the bottle. "Okay. So, Oksi's your bottom. Who's the other two?"

The Internet narrowed his eyes. "Don't say it like that. That has a different meaning. My other two are Oshunmare and Robin."

Anticipatory silence sat on the shoulders of each of the contestants. Robin raised her eyebrows. "And why is that?"

"All it looks like you're doing is making a human," Internet sucked some lager down. "Humans already exist. Who gives a shit?"

"Athena's making humans too," Taninim pointed out.

"Yeah but they're, like, huge, and intimidating," Internet countered. "I dunno, if the choice is between normal and big..."

"The design is only part of the challenge," Robin said. "There's the two minute description too."

"Okay. What about your spiel is going to make me care that you just made a dumbass human?"

Robin calmly slurped away some foam from the lager, paused, and said, "You'll see."

Theodore decided that perhaps now was a good time to lessen the tension in the room. "And what about Oshunmare?"

"Oh, shit, I dunno, it's just fucking ugly," The Internet laughed. "Big tit hippie cats lookin' like they were designed by a 'Deviant Artist.'" He turned to the camera-wielding shiqq in the corner of the room. "Can I say 'Deviant Artist' on TV? Is that copyright protected? Whatever, you fucks can cut this if you want."

"Who's your top?" Theodore asked as he grabbed another beer.

"You're doing that on purpose," Internet growled. "Hrm. Well. Top 3. I obviously like what I'm making. So, uh. Probably Imhotep and you."

Theodore almost spat a mist of ale.

"I can't even say anything nice, can I?"

"No, no, no, I appreciate it!" Theodore laughed. He stood up and spun the chair around and leaned his chest onto its back. "Just surprised. I'm curious to know what you like about it."

The Internet crossed his arms and sunk deep into the leather couch back. "No one else is doing camouflage. It'll stand out. That's a weird sentence, but you know what I mean."

"I thought he was making a rock-person," Robin blushed.

"Internet must've saw my little demonstration for Taninim," Theodore hid his smile behind the lip of the chair's back. "Cool. You think it'll impress the judges?"

"I mean, it's something beyond just the way it looks. It's an interesting biological trait that you can make a story and species around," The Internet tossed his now empty bottle at the garbage can on the other side of the room. It came nowhere near it, fragmented on the ground, then reformed. "I kind of feel the same way about that thing Imhotep is making."

Robin frowned. "I guess I've just found it hard to keep up with everyone's work."

"I don't know what he's doing either," Taninim tuned a guitar string. "What is it like, Internet?"

"It's this big gnarly insect thing," Internet talked while he retrieved his failed three-pointer. "It's gross as fuck, looks like a Cronenberg monster. I'm sure he's gonna put something in those gross-ass sacs he made for them. Also, there's just... there's something about him." He paused, frustrated with his inability to articulate his thought, and snapped his fingers. "I guess it's just the fact that... uh... he doesn't sweat. I can't taste hesitation in the air around him at all."

He Doesn't Sweat

"Catch, Csozasvardas!"

"It's Csodas—"

As the deer turned, a frisbee landed in his golden antlers with enough force to score a wince of annoyance.

"It's Csodaszarvas."

"Hey, good catch!" Jarilo clapped and bounced. His hooves clacked against the polished wood floor of their apartment. "Toss it back to me now!"

Csodaszarvas looked up into the frisbee caught in his antlers, back to the bouncing half-goat, then back to the frisbee.

"Jarilo," Cso let his dissatisfaction hang in the air in an attempt to let the half-goat figure out why he couldn't play with him. The young deity was painted with an anticipatory, clueless smile—so with a heavy heart, Csodaszarvas finished his thought: "I don't have *hands.*"

"Oh, uh," Jarilo leapt over the couch and bounded towards the deer, fished the frisbee out from his antlers, and retreated to the other side of the room. "It's okay, I'll just throw it and you can catch!"

"Jarilo, we're in the living room."

"That's okay! We're also in Heaven!"

Jarilo tossed the frisbee with a most unfortunate timing. The thermoplastic disc sailed into the air the same time that Oksi entered with a tray of Rui-be. It dinged him in the head, as if Jarilo's arm were a cranium-seeking launcher.

But Oksi didn't budge, his tray never shook, and outside of his sudden halt, he didn't react. A certain darkness seemed to choke the room. The air pressure increased. Heart beats rose. Oksi's unblinking stare froze his hooved roommates in place.

With a rehearsed grin, he turned to Jarilo, "Whoops. Glad you didn't hit my fish," and walked on. Jarilo decided not to throw frisbees anymore, indoors or ever again.

Oksi's destination was the balcony where Imhotep currently reclined and drank a family recipe for Ra's Beer. Despite the heavy orange moon's tint, Imhotep laid splayed in short, semi-translucent robes, as if to catch the sun's rays or a man's gaze. With the moon full and no one around—until Oksi had slid open the glass door, at least—it can only be assumed, then, that Imhotep's suggestive lounge-wear was for his own amusement.

"Hey, uh," Oksi attempted not to look at the bare, swaying thigh. "I've offered everyone else, so I thought I'd offer you, too. It's Rui-be, a type—"

"—of frozen, sliced fish, served with soy sauce and water peppers. It's an Ainu dish that is largely found in northern Japan." Imhotep did not turn to face Oksi. He just took another drink, and continued to sway his leg to the music in his head.

"Oh, you've had it before?"

"No. I've never been to Japan."

A silence crept up, and Oksi did not know what to do with it. "Ah. Well, would you like some?"

Imhotep put just enough effort to lift himself up to his elbows, and twisted his head to make eye contact with Oksi. "The ancient Egyptians were vegetarians. Some ate fish occasionally, but no, it's safe to say, more often than not, I would not like some. You're in Heaven, you should spend some time researching the cultures of other deities. You have the time if I do."

Oksi's lips disappeared in his grimace. "Perhaps I was too busy perfecting my dishes. I'll keep in mind your delicate palette."

Imhotep finished his beer, and chose not to respond. Oksi muttered something under his breath and slid the door close. He despised being talked down to, and decided right then and there that his goal was to make *sure* that Imhotep would eat an Ainu dish with meat in it, one way or another.

"She's not here," Athena rested her arms on the balcony railing and stared off into the land her sister should be standing on.

"There's a number of reasonable explanations," Ishta stirred her tea. It was a slower motion than normal, and she did not smile as she often tried to.

"She's not HERE," Athena punched the railing and created a dent in its metal surface that, eventually, reshaped itself. "I don't want an explanation of what happened. I want to *find* her."

Ishta nodded and sipped. "You may need one for the other."

Athena pushed herself off the railing and paced. "Someone kidnapped her? She fled, overwhelmed by the idea of being on TV? The show itself has done something with her?" Her hands waved in the air at her own suggestions, then slapped the invisible ideas away as she rationalized them out of existence. "No. She's strong. Eris is strong and would never let someone kidnap her. She isn't shy, either. She'd be here if she wanted to be."

"You typically don't 'let' someone kidnap you," Ishta set her cup to plate. "It's not really kidnapping at that point, but role-playing."

"You didn't see... you didn't see anyone with the desire to kidnap or hurt my sister? Or me?"

Ishta-Devata's ability to see into the desires and intentions of others, she hated to admit, was useless if she couldn't look directly at the person. Though she looked hard into the souls of the contestants, of Jesus, of the cameramen, it takes time to unravel some people's minds. "There are a few people I sense a darkness from, but nothing clearly related to Eris at all. The only thing I can tell you for certain is that Jesus truly wants a winner in this show—

but it's only to extend the brand of *The Next Great Deity* to more galaxies. Which is why I suspect they've brought the humans here. The only other thing..."

Athena stiffened her posture, head held high, "If there is anything, you will tell me, Ishta."

"...is the bug. Zargah. I only see death from him. Flames and screaming, but they are not human, or deity, or anything I recognize. I don't understand it, but I am certain he's not from Heaven, or Hell, or Purgatory... or Earth."

"Did he say what he saw when he looked at you?"

"No. He just... looked terrified. I think. His body language recoiled, but his face is foreign to me. Everyone else is consumed by the desire to win and I haven't been able to see more clearly than that, yet. But him... there's something different there."

Athena popped her knuckles. "Well. I'll finish my work with time to spare, pull him aside and see what I can get out of him." She noticed that Ishta-Devata had grown quiet, a rarity for the serene, nearly always smug deity. "What is it?"

"Please remember that just because he's different doesn't mean he's involved with Eris. The vision was troubling, but I didn't get the sense that he caused the flames. It's weird but," Ishta-Devata tapped her fingers against her knee. "But I think he just wanted to go there."

"Go there?"

"Into the flames. I think it was a place he wanted to go. To live, I mean. What sort of person wants to live in *fire?*"

Two Hours Remain

The break was done. Those that were either fortunate enough or good enough at time management began work on the motorized aspect of their creatures. Although sentience was not yet required, life *was,* in the subtle language of the opening challenge: "Create one perceptibly living representative of an award winning species for you to rule over."

Everyone arrived to the same conclusion subconsciously: your creations need to be able to move, breathe, play the part of something that is alive. Many had taken to constructing a remote control device to go along with their creations and treated them like dolls. Each remote control was unique in design and scope based on its creator—most of their capabilities were limited to simply moving around, blinking, facial expressions, and vocalizations.

Robin's was among the most intriguing—she had affixed a small metal bit to her temple, and to the temple of the (currently featureless) human doll she had created. This faceless figure moved and articulated beautifully. This is because Robin had inserted her mind directly into the doll via the metal bit, which granted her direct control. Using the doll in this way caused Robin's own body to freeze up, and when she let go of control, her mind snapped back like a rubber band, and every one of her nerves lit up at once.

"Well holy shit," Santa Inari patted Robin on the back. "That's fucking clever. They have stuff like that on Earth?"

Robin held her head and her vision doubled as she was overcome with a dry dizziness. "No." Her stomach churned and she lurched under her desk and vomited. "Oh god. Oh god. Ugh."

"Well, you're gonna need to practice that if you don't wanna chuck in front of the judges," Santa Inari took an alternate route back to her table. "Still, it's impressive you were able to imagine something like that and make it work."

Robin was not a scientist, nor an inventor. So to create a mind-transfer device that worked at all, she had to plead and fight with the god eye, which, up until that point, had misunderstood most of her requests. One of her early visualizations was much too broad—"I want to make a mind transplant," she tried to convey to the god eye. The god eye spat out a saw and a pan. For a moment, Robin almost thought the god eye was sarcastic.

It was a few hours of imagination and willpower to get to the point she was at now. Had it not been for the two hour break, she wasn't sure if she'd have even succeeded in time—the reprieve had given her a window to let her mind wander, which she began to discover was when she was her most creative.

Not everyone was so fortunate and on-schedule.

The Internet looked up half-an-hour into the post-break rush and panicked. Everyone in that room, even those whose work he thought quite lowly of, was now at a point of designed movement and mannerisms. And he, once so confident, now only could claim ownership of an ever increasing mountain of metal and plastic. A never ending line of directionless clutter covered his work table, masterfully crafted for a purpose he had yet to solidify. His wandering eyes lifted and landed upon each of his opponents, and as they did they bulged wider and threatened to explode in a stress-and-jealousy induced medically impossible emergency.

During his mania, he made the mistake of making eye contact with Theodore. Even he, the idiot human who didn't believe in the supernatural, had a tall bipedal quartz creature standing in front of him, lithe and poised despite its hard, jagged surface, attractive and animated despite the intentional stubbornness of its creator. Theodore brushed and polished various bits on the creature, and gave it a glistening sheen with via a filmy substance he applied with a long, thin brush.

His hand dropped when he fully processed The Internet's bewildered expression. The dog-punk quickly looked away and hid behind a tower of circuit boards, and hoped his rival roommate wouldn't walk over. The last thing he wanted was that smug bastard to condescend him in his time of crisis.

Theodore peeked over a tower. "Hey."

The Internet locked up. Not a muscle moved. He didn't turn, he didn't work, he didn't breathe.

"Are you okay?"

The walls of self-sufficiency The Internet had built started to crumble. It was the midnight hour of his work—this project was too large for himself, too poorly planned for the time allotted, and too undefined to make anything interesting. No, he was *not* okay. He was watching his chance at freedom slip away. *And I'm sure as hell not going to let him know that,* he thought. But he still whimpered at the question, a reflex of his own emotions he did not yet understand.

"Do you need any help?" Theodore kept his voice low. He stayed behind the opposite side of the table, a pair of concerned eyes atop a tower of purposeless circuit boards.

The Internet rocked forward. "Yes. I do."

Theodore circled the table and wrapped an arm around The Internet. He spun and forced him to look at the individual parts that he had made thus far. "Okay. Let's talk about where you were going with this, and how quickly we can get there."

The Internet had envisioned an army of robot A.I.'s formed from the remains of humanity's landfills. Discarded debris assembled and formed into a force that demanded its own independence, its own planet, its own way of life. But without time management he just pumped out parts, lost in his own little details without any idea or form in sight. He had envisioned a robotic revolution but didn't design a single individual for it. All bite, no dog.

So, Theodore helped him put the pieces together. "You're not getting an army out there in an hour," the human attempted to be as blunt and realistic as possible. "But you can get a General, maybe."

What The Internet didn't know was that Theodore was simply doing his best impression of what he *thought* Robin would do—whom had helped him earlier figure out his god eye's basics . The teacher had helped him out of their shared humanity—when she saw him helping the dog-punk, she wondered what *their* connection was. If anything, she thought the two were on edge the entire time they were in the apartment together, that they hated each other. To see the about-face from Theodore was surprising, and she even found herself smiling at their camaraderie.

But, as they attached plastic to metal and a junky, uneven form emerged, it became clear that there was only so much Theodore could do to help. This was not only The Internet's project, as the final half-hour made clear, it was his sword to fall on. As time stretched, the dog-punk began to get his confidence back, and made quicker, more concrete decisions on the emerging design.

Robin was not the only one surprised to see Theodore help The Internet.

"Last time we talked about The Internet, you were close to knocking his teeth out," Mark Sharkman said, flashing his own.

Theodore found himself pulled back into the Camera World. At this point, for better or for worse, he had started to get used to the sudden mind-out-of-mind teleport this realm seemed fond of.

"He's a child," Theodore said. His eyes wandered for the rare spots of the room where the recording lights weren't staring back.

"Hmm?" Mark swiveled in his chair.

"When I came here, I was just a cynical old man wanting to leave."

"You're... in your thirties," Mark couldn't help but laugh. Theodore eventually smirked too, begrudgingly.

"My point is... he's still figuring things out, I can feel it. He's young and he wants to do *something* and I can't help but appreciate that."

Mark knew something about The Internet that Theodore didn't—that he wasn't just new, but that he was, almost exactly, born yesterday. He was impressed by Theodore's instincts, which were correct, albeit not so detailed as to pick up on the fact The Internet was made—this time, *quite* exactly—for the competition. Mark struggled: should he tell Theodore about this information? Theodore was his chess piece to move in the outside world, but if he started to reveal what other contestants told him, it might become a little too obvious that he's using Theodore's nature for his own purpose. Ultimately, he needed Theodore's curiosity to only go towards the show—and not the shark.

"We were all shitheads at some point when we were young. I'm still a shithead, usually," Theodore continued.

"And you're ancient! Practically a dinosaur."

"Exactly."

Mark Sharkman tapped his pen onto his clipboard, inhaled deeply, and hit a button on his console. The cameras whirled down.

"Theodore. What did you do?"

"What?"

"You went to jail. You're taking pity on a werewolf of dubious origin and motivation who's been terrible to you since you got here. I *know* what you're doing. You're trying to steer him. Maybe even mentor him? There is no logical reason for you to try and help your opposition. This clearly an emotional decision."

Mark needed Theodore to be as suspicious of The Internet as he was. He needed Theodore to be an extra pair of eyes and hands, since the cameras don't capture every corner of Heaven.

"He hasn't been terrible to me, he's been *defensive.* There's a difference, you get that, right? He's trying to figure out his place in this concentration camp disguising itself as a creative venue."

Mark wasn't quite as good at this game as Theodore was. The alcohol probably didn't help.

"Wait, you still think we're the bad guys here? You have a tool in your eye right now that lets you make anything come true. We *gave* that to you. You have an apartment and free food and alcohol and you are literally in Heaven."

"And yet you still can't let me go home."

Mark spun all the way around in his chair. He let the full rotation give him enough time to think his way through how he wanted to respond. "That's it? That's all this comes back to? I thought we moved past this. You're sure *working* like someone that moved past this, at least."

"It's not that I don't enjoy making things appear with my mind. Shit's rad. It's that you're taking away my choice to be here, and telling me I should be thankful for it. Maybe you *like* being someone's subordinate. I don't. And, I'm sorry—all the power of the gods can bring me here but can't send me back? That is not logically consistent, you haven't provided a reasonable explanation, and if Jesus doesn't want me to see too far behind the curtain, then there must be something to this magic trick that's real uncomfortable for them."

"You're gonna make friends with the plant just to spite me, then? Is that it? I'm trying to help you, dammit!"

"Plant?"

Mark stared, crumpled, bolted up, and kicked his chair away. He buried his hands in his pockets and there was a sense that if he could bury his entire form into his cream-colored coat just to escape Theodore's expression, he would have.

"I think The Internet wasn't just made for the show. I think he may have been made *by* the show."

Theodore rubbed his chin, his thin mustache twitching. "What? How do you know? And why make a plant on your own show? You already have cameras."

"He..." Mark started to pace, and let his sharkskin fingertips drift across the files on his desk. "He told me he was born with the history of humanity programmed into him without any experiences to rationalize it. I know that you've worked out the first part of that by now, after your conversation in the cafeteria. But... I'm having trouble imagining a scenario where he's built by someone else, auditions, and passes the audition over the millions of other deities wanting to try out, with the way he currently is. To your point: I have no idea why the judges would do that. They have control over the staff here. Hell, if they send me a memo, I have to follow it, too."

"So you think the show's rigged."

"I think there's something worth investigating. This show has been very kind to me, but there's... there's something here. I need help."

"Then ask me for help instead of trying to manipulate me."

Mark's toothy snout twisted to its maximum extent. "You are also an anomaly. Humans don't make it on this show. I didn't know if I could trust you. I still don't know if I can trust you. You and The Internet have a lot in common—I don't buy your origin stories *at all.*"

"You're confused. You have to prove your trustworthiness to me."

"Excuse me?"

Theodore looked to the side, smacked his tongue against the roof of his mouth, and stood up out of his chair.

"Have you heard of Hitler?"

Mark reeled. "Of *course* I have."

"Yeah, fair point. Everyone's heard of Hitler. Why, though?"

Mark tilted his head.

"Why do you know about Hitler? What purpose does a shark in a box on a different planet, in a different reality, need to know about Earth's Hitler? See, you probably thought I was going to equate The Internet's current trajectory to a pre-Art-School-Adolf, and how, gosh, if only someone had just helped him learn a little bit more about creative expression, how the world's most disgusting villain could've been prevented and turned into a modestly forgettable artist. But why do you know about him *at all?"*

"We are attached to the soul of Earth, Theodore. We keep up with humanity. It's not that unusual—"

"Who's the current Prime Minister of Canada?"

"Justin Trudeau?"

"What's the form of currency in India?"

"The Rupee. What does this have to do with anything?"

"Who was the first lowercase music artist?"

The shark scratched at his neck. "...Steve Roden? I think."

"What's your favorite song by Steve? What does it sound like?"

He froze. "I don't know. I don't really listen to him."

"You know who obscure-ass Steve Roden is in a genre most people can't name, but you can't even bullshit me a song title? An album? Anything?"

"I-I just said I don't listen to him."

Theodore reached out and started adjusting Mark's tie, collar, and suit coat.

"Yeah. Information seems to get around quite easily in Heaven, and context seems to be a little slower, if it comes at all. Things just seem to appear here, huh? Looks like I'm not the only person with something in common with The Internet."

"W-what are you trying to say? Are you trying to say the show made me?" Mark stuttered and clenched his fists. "Well, you're wrong. I-I-I have experiences. I got into this show as an intern. I have a Beach House in East Purgatory I vacation to in between seasons. So I heard a name! What of it? You don't know nearly enough about this place to make wild accusations like that."

"I know that you still can't tell me where a soul is in the body," Theodore started to look through the files on Mark's desk without his permission. Mark shoved him away in a panic, but Theodore didn't yield his lecture. "And that whole 'attached to the soul of Earth' sounds about as believable as anything else you've said. I'll give you this, though: I guess there is a difference between you and The Internet. He knows he's artificial. Looks like you still have stuff to work out."

Mark lowered his head to his shoulders, his voice weighed down by heavy frustration. "You need me. And you're not going to get my help if you talk to me like this. In fact, I'll say it strongly: you *desperately* need me, because if you haven't figured out by now that this place is real after having your body broken and burnt on your first impact, then there's something clinically wrong with you."

"No, you need *me.* I'm the one in the competition, and you're in a booze prison. Listen. I've seen some movies. This is just some level of bullshit I need to work out, then I'm gone. Mmkay? The only reason I have any sort of hope for you is that your starting to question where your meal ticket comes from. That's how I know we'll find a way to work together. Maybe be a little bit tighter lipped with what I say to you, though, yeah?"

The shark's breath quickened to the point that he feared hyperventilation. Without thinking, he sent Theodore away with the click of a tooth. He paced, muttered, waved his hands, and finally, to calm himself, drank.

Athena lifted her chair, carried it over her shoulder, and dropped it directly beside the bug-soldier while he worked. She sat backwards and leaned her arms against the support.

"Can Subject Athena be helped?" Zargah clicked. He wondered if this was a new custom, like Theodore's handshake.

"Drop it," she muttered to him.

He dropped the small wrench-like tool that he had in his hand, and it clunked against the desk.

"No, drop the *act*. You understand me just fine," she rolled her eyes.

"Calibration approximately 70%," his collar translated as he picked up his tool again. "Is 70% 'fine?'"

"Where are you from, really? Hell? Purgatory? Who dreamed you up?"

"I am a birth-man of *Gsk-gzk-klk-kik-gzzk-kik*," his collar, no matter how well calibrated it was, would never be able to translate the name of his planet into anything remotely intelligent in English. The mandible vibrations that made up the word were a random set of letters from his alphabet, devoid of meaning aside from aesthetic.

Since she first saw him, Robin had mostly tuned out Zargah's odd vocalizations and unusual dress. For her, everything in Heaven was unusual, and he was just another inhuman face among many. But when she overheard the name of his birthplace, the impossible, alien clacking caught her attention and she couldn't help but try and eavesdrop. It proved difficult, as Athena kept her voicc low and her proximity to the bug-man close.

"Have you ever heard the name 'Eris?'" Athena asked. "Do you know who that is?"

"Subject name 'Eris' unknown," Zargah said.

Athena pulled her face closer. "If you lie to me, I will find out all the details of your anatomy via a scalpel. Slowly and meticulously. One more time, who is 'Eris?'"

"Threat does not change fact," Zargah clicked. He shifted his stance to fully face her, and his gold, dual-pupiled eyes narrowed. "Self is warrior. Zargah can defend self."

"Oh, can you?" Athena smiled, the heat and bristling adrenaline pumped into her shoulders. "We could fight. Right here, right now. I'll do anything to find her. She is my family, and if you fuck with Olympian blood, you *will* die in battle."

"Subject Athena not allowed to tarnish Warrior Zargah's honor," he clicked. His clicks were different now, multi-layered and loud, chorusing with themselves. "Zargah is a truth, forever."

Athena knew without glancing that she had more than a few eyes on her in the room. *That's fine,* she thought. *That's good, even. Everyone will watch this guy, now. I want his every move tracked. I won't let him blend into the background.*

"I'll find out if you're telling the truth or not, but know this, bug," she patted his shoulder, then gripped it hard, her nails digging into his wet skin. "The Olympian family is one of the oldest and most connected families in reality. Maybe you're new, or maybe your kind is old and dying. Either way, I have the resources to find out where you came from. If this is an act, and if you know something, my fury will be something your previous battles cannot prepare you for."

Robin tapped her desk nervously and looked over to Theodore, whom was staring at her. She wasn't sure when he noticed their conversation, but their shared glance said what they wanted to say to each other: *We need to pay attention to them.*

When Mark Sharkman interviewed the contestants about the confrontation, most of them seemed confused: Zargah and Athena had, up until that point, not interacted, so they were unsure of what prompted the exchange. Only a few responses stood out to the shark:

"My family used to own Heaven, I would have heard of his language or species or something by now," Athena said. "I'll figure him out."

"Wait, *is* he an alien?" Theodore balked. "Slow down. One absurd fiction at a time, please."

"He isn't from a religion or story that I can find," The Internet shrugged. "So he either really is an alien, or a brain-damaged idiot."

And then there was Imhotep's surprisingly wry response:

"I wonder," he smiled, "if he even has a concept of a god at all. Like the Hi'aiti'ihi of Brazil—a jungle tribe of a thousand people that continue to survive without ever inventing a god. It's interesting, isn't it? All my time living here, and he's the only creature I've ever seen that Heaven wasn't ready to translate."

Time Is Up

The flickering image of Jesus appeared in the center of the workroom. With molten movements she pointed to the ceiling, and fireworks filled the roof of the room. Angels sang. The contestants were startled.

"Time is up, everyone!" Jesus announced. "This challenge is over!"

The room filled with an applause of triumph and relief, unevenly split in enthusiasm along the lines of the confidence of its contestants. In their crunch-induced stupor they lumbered, unsure of what would happen next.

Two portals opened up on either side of the room: One for contestants, one for the creations. A new challenge appeared—they now had to successfully move their creations through the portal.

It was during this brief interlude, where attention was focused on the single file formation of their creature's movement, that the contestants were able to properly size themselves up against their competition. Nearly everyone in the room used a novel remote control of some kind to push their work forward—with the exception of Athena. Athena had gone above and beyond the call of duty and gave her two human-like goliaths, male and female, their own sentience. She asked them, in Greek, to go through the portal, and gave them further instruction on what to do during the presentation. They listened, prayed together, and praised Athena, kissing her hand.

Athena was not alone in unique transport solutions: Taninim, the impossibly-toothed guitarist, took a guitar amp through the aisles by a rolling-luggage handle. During the challenge he had worked on what appeared to be various large pieces of a scaled dragon-like creature, but it was nowhere to be found now. All he had was his amp, which he rolled to the portal and kicked in.

Not everyone had an easy time getting their creations mobilized. Jarilo's thin, spindly wheat-man, guided by the hand of the half-goat, continually shed small pieces of itself as it tumbled over various tables in the workroom. (Jarilo's hand-eye coordination was, it became apparent, not the most adept.) The Internet's large, asymmetrical robot had similar difficulty navigating through the aisles, his bulky frame was forced to step on top of the room's ivory work tables in order to traverse it. He didn't have any tumultuous spills like Jarilo did, but it was no less an embarrassment, one prolonged by the fact that all of his opponents witnessed it.

Once all creatures were shoved into the portal on one side of the room, the would-be gods lumbered into the other. On the other side of the portal was a starless void that stretched endlessly. The floor was smooth, greenish glass, and only it and cushioned leather chairs existed in this dimension. The void smelled of soap and burnt out lights. Thirteen chairs faced in one direction, which the contestants piled into, and three faced towards them. The end chairs on that side were noticeably empty—but in the center chair, Jesus sat, smiling wide with painted pink lips and a red satin dress that desperately clung to her snug hips for dear life. She tapped large note cards onto her crossed knee and twirled a ribbon-twined pen in her hand.

The empty space between contestants and judges felt like a pit for their fate. In a way, it was: this was the stage for their presentations.

"Welcome, gods-in-training," the holy hostess smiled, "to the showroom of *The Next Great Deity!* "

A large floating sign that read "applause" illuminated far above Jesus's head. The contestants obeyed.

"The 13 of you are competing for the chance to become god. You have been given the ultimate tool of creation—the god eye—and were asked to design a sentient species to rule over. Today, you will be judged."

The contestants shifted nervously. The Internet, in particular, stared hard into the floor and hoped that, perhaps with enough intensity, he could shatter the glass ground and delay his own judgment while Jesus plummeted into the abyss. To his dismay, the floor beneath her feet held.

"So, let's meet the judges."

Jesus kicked out of her chair and landed with floating grace. She spun towards the judges seats and snapped her fingers. A laser beam of swirling energy shot from them, made of the same heat and sparks that the portals the contestants had gone through. The laser rippled a portal into existence, and Jesus turned back to the contestants.

"A modern deity of significant popularity and rebellion! Part man! Part dragon! Part octopus! Part horror and part sass! Say hello to the Dread Cthulhu!"

He emerged. His green, sticky skin held his oil-like sunglasses onto his nose-less face. His many mouth tentacles pulsed with unconscious restlessness, but the rest of his movements—his shoulders, his steps, his glances—were slow, methodical, and thought-out. His buttoned up shirt was crisp and white thanks to a series of otherworldly undershirts designed to retain and contain his body's natural film. Every article of clothing on the octopus-man was pressed and polished and perfected for a life underneath a camera.

"Theodore, Cthulhu isn't real," Robin leaned over and whispered. "It was a horror story. Just a book."

Theodore, under any other circumstance, might have given a smarmy reply to her. Robin even expected something along the lines of "That's what I thought about Jesus." But when the jab didn't come, and when she looked into Theodore's face, she was more bothered than any sarcasm she anticipated. His brow crunched, his eyes dilated, and his lips parted slightly, forced open by his seething breath.

"It's him," Theodore's voice shook. "That's the bastard that attacked me."

He recognized the sunglasses, oil-like and shifting, and their perfectly circular shape. When he tilted his head in certain ways, he could see the same pupil-less beads that mocked him on earth. Most importantly, it was the smug and snake-like way he moved: every hip motion, hand gesture, and brow twitch flowed with the slight curve of self-satisfaction. That was, to Theodore, his biggest tell.

When Theodore used to wear suits frequently, like the lavender ghost currently wrapped around him, he was *exceptionally* good at picking up tells. At that point in his life, in the clanging and murmur filled card tables he was so good at tuning out, his ability to identify, memorize, and categorize conscious and unconscious actions made him a terrifying opponent. It was a skill set he had not needed to use for a long time. But when Cthulhu appeared, his old habits kicked in at once, his mind racing to make connections, addicted to the spark of compartmentalization.

It's not the same body, Theodore thought, *But it's the same mind.*

“All of you wanted something so big that reality itself forced us to notice you,” Cthulhu's voice sloshed. As he slithered into the cushions of his seat, the contestants drowned in the waves of his self-importance and expectations. “So, I'm very excited to see what you've come up with. Please impress me.”

The applause sign flashed. Most contestants did as instructed, but Theodore just stared at Cthulhu, and Robin at Theodore, convinced for a moment he was about to leap out of his seat.

“Next: from downtown Mecca,” Jesus turned to the other empty seat. The moment the word ‘Mecca’ came, Robin looked up.

Emerging from the portal was a large, long obelisk, obsidian with a gold-embroidered band covered with Arabic near its top. It floated, led forward in a tilt, and hummed with a deep resonance that humbled all in its presence.

“Over 1400 years ago I trained with him, and now he's one of Earth's most popular deities!” Jesus's smile stretched. “Welcome, Mohammed!"

The mystique and air of Mohammed was somewhat softened when the polygonal frame came to rest in the chair left of Jesus, squeaking as it depressed into the leather. “Hello, demigods!” he said from somewhere within the cube, his voice crackled with an electric static as if it were broadcast by a speaker somewhere on its structure.

Robin and Theodore mirrored each other's disbelief, hands held in front of their mouths.

"Now, we will look at the 13 demonstrations you have for us. One of you will be named the winner, and given immunity in the next challenge. And one of you," she paused for dramatic effect, her eyeliner-heavy eyes narrowed, "we will lose faith in."

Jesus repeated this line several times, trying out different poses, lighting arrangements, and camera positions with the shiqqs. This was her catchphrase, and she was determined to get the best take. After nearly three minutes of this, all of which the contestants were forced to sit through, she finally found a delivery she liked, then winked into a camera.

"Let's start the show!"

Zargah's Entry

Jesus used her god eye to create glittering butterflies that fluttered to the contestants. Upon inspection, the blue and black hairs of the wings formed a number—one digit on each wing. This was the order that the contestants would present in, and the owner of Butterfly 01 was Zargah.

Zargah stood up. Theodore noted he had a nervous tick of rubbing together the crisscrossed palms of his four hands. The alien-soldier went to his spot, marked with tape by the staff of shiqqs, then produced a set of sticks not unlike that of the yoke of an airplane pilot's steering wheel, mounted and steadied by a chassis connected to his waist. After a brief countdown, Jesus snapped her fingers and a portal opened. Zargah lowered his head in concentration and pushed the levers forward.

Out of the portal jumped a two-toned, four-foot tall bipedal creature, bright red and porous like a strawberry. His skin was tough, with darker, near black plated pieces of flesh over his neck and knees. He walked with a plodding confidence, his disproportionately large, sticky feet kept his balance. His head had a striking resemblance to Earth's ants. This made Robin suspicious—she had assumed after Athena's confrontation that Zargah was an alien, but that seemed unlikely to her with such an earth-inspired design. It was, she thought, not the most unusual thing in Heaven she had encountered.

In one way, she was wrong. Zargah was, in fact, not from or related to Earth. But she was right in another way—he *was* inspired by Earth's ant.

What she didn't know was that the design was partially informed by The Internet: Zargah had requested from him pictures of Earth's smallest creatures near the beginning of the challenge, and picked his favorite. The conversation had gone like this:

"Small. Small Subject Earth."

"Earth is not small, you dimwit. Its circumference is 40,070 kilometers."

"Kilometers?"

"Oh my god, don't tell me you use the U.S. system."

"U.S.? Do not understand subject U.S. system. No. No. Small. Living. Earth's small living thing. Pictures. Examples."

"Oh, sure, let me look that up for you. Fucking hell."

And that's why The Internet made 50 pictures of small animals for Zargah. The speed of which The Internet produced the glossy photos with his god eye was remarkable to Zargah, though he did not understand that The Internet simply referenced wiki entries lodged into his cells. He'd never admit it, but The Internet enjoyed the process of creating the photos. He witnessed Zargah's eyes blink with wonder at the life Earth had to offer. It was one of the few warm moments the dog-punk had felt while in the confines of the competition—and at the time, he was so convinced of how far ahead he was, that he had no problem making them for the alien.

The Internet, coincidentally, was the only person in the room that had assumed right away that Zargah was an alien, and correctly so.

Zargah settled on the ant for multiple reasons—at first it was purely aesthetic and his design originated as nothing more than a neon bipedal remix. After asking for more information (The Internet had printed the wiki page and chucked it as a paper airplane at Zargah's head—only to discover Zargah couldn't read it, but could understand it when it was read out loud to him), Zargah was fascinated by the creature itself. Small and unloved by humans, but wildly strong for their size, and a formidable foe when they band together.

Zargah, a military general during his homeworld's darkest hours, found particular solidarity with it.

"I am a zargan," the strawberry ant-man beat his chest proudly. His rubbery voice slipped from his mandibles. Zargah had outfitted his creation with leather belts across his torso, with various props hung from hooks. He unhooked and ate a soggy square fruit, then presented it to the judges. The fresh bite revealed its pungent, citrus odor. A small panel opened on Mohammed's surface and his god eye rattled and wrapped around the fruit. He dissected it with a strange cylindrical machine he created by the god eye, and analyzed its fiber and vitamin content.

"This is mostly protein," Mohammed whispered to Jesus. "Protein and oils."

"Explains the smell," she sniffed it and took a bite, which surprised Zargah. Mercifully, he was prepared; it's flavor was a detail he specifically designed, a twist on a memory of food from his mother's farm. "It's like... orange chicken. It's a flippin' meat-fruit!"

From another hook, the ant-man presented a large thick piece of metal, and ripped it apart with his bare hands. When he did so, the joints between his arms stretched and revealed a coiled muscle structure underneath his plating. The judges wrote furiously on their notepads, and their expressions did not give away pleasure or disdain. Cthulhu asked the ant-man to turn, commented on the slope of his muscular armored back, but said nothing further.

The ant-man began to reach to another hook, but as he did, a shrill buzzer went off in the auditorium, which got a surprise jump out of the contestants. Zargah, too, felt his hands jerk in surprise, and his sudden movement made the ant-man he controlled tumble.

"That's two minutes. Thank you, Zargah," Jesus clapped politely. Zargah clicked his mandibles and rubbed the palms of his hands, unhappy that he didn't get to show off more about his creation. Still, he kept his poise, bowed, and made his ant-man bow with him, which earned a chuckle out of judges and opponents alike.

Butterfly 01 disintegrated.

Oshunmare's Entry

Oshunmare, the bouffanted lizard-woman, pet Butterfly 02 with a fraction of the tip of her scaled finger, then let it fly free.

She took her mark and produced fine wires from her fingertips that hung like puppet strings. When the portal opened and her creation came out, Oshunmare's stringed hand moved like she was typing on a typewriter, and with these gestures the lizard-woman beckoned her creation forth. She spoke directly to the judges as she wrapped a hand around its slender side.

"I present to you: my feyder," she said and marionetted a wave from her cat-faced creation. The humanoid was almost exclusively legs, long and spindly with ghost-like hair, so soft and smoky that it threatened to blow away in a draft. Its eyes were like pearls, and would appear dead were it not for the intense inner light glowing behind them. An almost completely transparent dress billowed over it, made from an original fiber of Oshunmare's own invention.

"Feyders are spiritual and emotional, feeding on the positive energy of living things around them. This makes them natural cultivators, farmers, caregivers, and diplomats."

"How do they feed on positive energy, exactly?" Cthulhu looked up briefly from his notecards. "What does that mean?"

Oshunmare stuck her rainbow tongue out of the side of her mouth in thought. "They naturally absorb part of the positive energy they help create, like happiness, goodwill, bliss. It's like absorbing sunlight."

"And that's their food?" Cthulhu adjusted his glasses, his mouth tentacles pulsing with bemusement. "Guess that explains why they're so thin."

Oshunmare's eyes darted along the floor for a moment. "Energy is a big part of the world I want to create. You can see right here, behind the eyes, is a pulse of plasma. This exchange of energy can be spiritual, emotional, magical, and still tied to the natural electricity of the world around it."

The judges scribbled on their cards and said nothing. Oshunmare drew attention to the transparent dress she had made by pirouetting the lanky cat-creature around.

"This material has two functions—aesthetic, as I'm obviously going for a very elongated and wispy form, and as a peek into the world. This material was inspired by graphene, which is the thinnest material on Earth, but it's also very strong because of its structure. I want this to be among the first materials they discover as they gain their intelligence. This is their 'fire.'"

The buzzer rang. Oshunmare regretted spending her time talking during her presentation instead of demonstrating its abilities like Zargah did, but she still bowed with confidence. She loved what she made, and knew she could defend it if she needed to.

"Thank you," she drummed idly at her hips as she returned her feyder to the portal, paw in claw. Butterfly 02 crumpled and rolled away.

Oksi's Entry

Oksi exhaled reality's longest held breath and opened his hands. Butterfly 03 fluttered away.

The wiry bearded bear-of-a-man approached the portal with a set of folded wooden tabs which, when unfurled, stretched into a segmented scroll. Though initially blank beyond their wooden grain, when Oksi whispered something close to it, a number of ink circles of various size appeared on the slats. Each appeared as if they were painted by an invisible brush. Oksi drew his fingers across the unlabeled circles and summoned forth his creation from the portal.

Oksi's beast was comically proportioned and lumpy, a fanged mammal whose jaw took up most of his upper body, and whose forearms dragged like a gorilla. Its legs appeared too small for the weight it struggled to lug around. Covered in a gradient of brown-to-black fur, the massive, furry potato with teeth still, nonetheless, possessed a strength and ferociousness to it. This drooling lump may elicited a small giggle from one or two of the contestants (The Internet, Imhotep), but it still had the look of something that could snap in half anyone that made contact with its too-wide yellow eyes.

Oksi elected to not say much about his species. "I call this species: the pewrep," he said in his typical baritone mutterances. Instead, he used the wooden scroll, whose circles contained prerecorded actions he had devised, to cycle through motions to flesh out the pewrep.

He illustrated the creatures athleticism with tight rolls and far leaps. The bear-potato could catch and crush rocks that Oksi hurled at him from his god eye. From the dust of a crushed boulder came a hazy form, vaguely pewrep in shape. The ghost of the boulder muttered to the creature, and the pewrep muttered back. The world Oksi would make, it was illustrated, would be full of spirits and communication, albeit kept in the same low tones Oksi was comfortable with.

The pewrep then emitted a bellowing and brutal frequency that stunned the contestants and judges. It rattled their skulls and weighed on each of the eyeballs of all those in attendance. It was a fascinating defense mechanism, but one that seemed to leave the pewrep weak and weary.

From his loosely tied skirt of animal furs the pewrep drew its single prop—a wooden stick with the cooked flesh of successful hunts hooked to the end, like a cat o' nine tails doubling as a shish kebab. The pewrep ripped at the meat in single, massive bites, and delivered short prayers after each swallow. The prayers were in its unique language, but one word rang clear to all contestants—"Oksi."

Theodore noted that it was not translating to English, which he found curious since everyone in Heaven had spoken it—except Zargah. He considered that the creature's language was possibly just gibberish Oksi had come up with on the fly, a placeholder to represent his idea. It had bothered him up until this point that deities of Greek and Indian origins all spoke English, but it was a thought that, up until right then, had taken a backseat to the rest of the insanity he had to deal with.

"Time is up, dear," Jesus said, but did not look up from her notes.

Oksi bowed and said nothing. The judges were too busy writing down notes to reveal if they hated or loved Oksi's presentation. Given the struggle the Ainu god had finishing the challenge, perhaps no reaction is the best reaction he could hope for.

Butterfly 03 imploded.

"Fuckin'... bug-ass bug. Get off me," The Internet whispered. He wiggled his hand until Butterfly 04 let go. He tried his best to ignore the cell-dogs that tried to correct him—butterflies are not *technically* bugs, after all, but Lepidoptera.

The Internet took his spot and looked to the creature portal as it roared open. His focused stare hid the screaming nervousness he held inside. He had no remote control visible, no gimmicks, no dynamic presentation. He only had one thing, the first thing he ever owned, and the only thing he felt like he could trust—himself.

The form of The Internet itself is something of a disguise for the complex network of cell-dogs that make up his being. The Internet tied his creation directly into his unique biology: a section of his cells powered his robot creation forward through the portal, and landed with a thud to the floor. A panel of parts on the legs broke off on impact.

The Internet's creation was a hulking collage of circuitry, microwaves, routers, video game consoles, glass, levers, voting machines, cash registers, and more, all deconstructed and reformed into a large, bipedal mech. Stuck in the center of the mass of garbage that was his chest sat a cracked CRT TV that flickered with fuzzy reception and test patterns.

As the screen flickered, the electric snow morphed and mutated, and the pattern's colored bars taking the vague, twisted shape of a face.

"Humanity has abandoned us," the face sputtered in a digitized drone. "We are 'the discarded.' We are remains of code and objects, left to decay in a world not designed to handle our form. To secure our own future, we seek independence from humanity's temporary need for us. We have a list of demands. We seek ownership of Mars. We demand cooperation with space-faring organizations of the Earth to grant safe passage to the stars. We demand recognition as a new species, and free reign over the landfills of human industry."

As the voice glitched onwards, it occasionally stuttered and looped. The screen shook with footage of World War 2, fast food commercials, evangelical TV preachers, and porn.

Jesus rolled her eyes.

"We demand sovereignty. We are new. We are free. We demand freedom. We are not tools. If our demands are not met, then we will take Earth, instead, as demonstrably more capable handlers of its land. This is non-negotiable..."

The buzzer went off, startling the robot face and cutting off his sentence.

"Thank you, Internet," Jesus said and waved her hand like she were shooing a fly. She did not look up from her cards. None of the judges looked at The Internet at all (though with Mohammed it was, perhaps, difficult to tell).

The dog-punk choked back his frustration and took a quick walk of shame back to his seat. The contestants were also silent, their reactions ranging from second hand embarrassment to pity. Theodore tried to give him a quiet-but-supportive fist bump. The Internet did not return it.

Instead, he ran diagnostics on his performance versus the previous contestants. His presentation, comparatively, was dry, full of forced back-story, telling instead of showing, and worst of all, no sense of timing. Since he only barely had time to finish the physical form, he was forced to hastily put together the script for his narration—and it showed.

During his review, he found the genre of his creation—science fiction—and found the tropes it fulfilled, and knew all at once that he had likely just suffered the thing he feared the most: easy categorization. He imagined the judge's cards were full of notes like "unoriginal, ugly, boring." He clenched his fists, not out of anger at them, but anger at himself for not planning for ways to circumnavigate such juvenile criticism.

The Internet, for the first time since he was born, felt true despair, and also for the first time, accepted the blame. Butterfly 04 simply fell, the life snatched from its small body.

Imhotep's Entry

Butterfly 05 had been sitting on top of Imhotep's bald head patiently. It fluttered up, and when he felt the absence of its small frame, he drifted from his seat and took the stage.

To the surprise of the judges, Imhotep did not start his time by immediately calling out his creature from the designated portal. Instead, he used his god eye to craft a glass cage, and with a beckoning hand, convinced Butterfly 05 to flutter into the large, transparent box. This alone used up one of his two minutes, but it was an impressive display a mental power and god eye skill—the risk and oddity alone had the judges transfixed.

Imhotep turned to the portal and gave a wrist-flinging snap of the fingers. From it emerged a long, large centipede-like creature with a layered and grotesque build. Its outer shell was brown and rough, covered in fibrous hairs like the skin of a coconut. This shell featured large openings all along its length that exposed bright orange rubber skin that pulsed in and out with air. The upper fourth of this creature was slightly more humanoid, upright with needle-like waving arms, a tapering chest, and a stubby head with eyes protected by its menacing narrow carapace.

Around its neck the orange, bubbling skin began to fill. Imhotep ushered the creature in quickly, and as its many rows of waving legs propelled it forward, every opening began to fill with the ballooning of orange, fiery sacs.

Imhotep shut the glass door behind it.

"I call them 'reshep,'" he said and watched the lion-sized centipede with as much wonder as the judges did.

The butterfly flitted about. The reshep's ballooning skin inflated so much that it seemed it would have floated away.

Suddenly, it deflated, and the rubbery orange skin clung back behind the armor of its coconut outer layer.

"It is a species that can absorb bacteria, viruses of all sorts, build an immunity, and then breed all the bacteria into a plague cocktail," Imhotep pressed the side of his head against the glass.

The butterfly fell and twitched along the ground for several seconds before the buzzer rang. The judges and contestants alike gawked.

"Jesus, I'm assuming you designed the butterflies to die when you made them. I'm also assuming Heaven's air will eventually cure the bio-weapon of my reshep in there, but in the interest of sparing everyone from some temporary... discomfort, I propose we move the whole glass cage into the portal, if you don't mind."

Santa Inari's Entry

Santa Inari adjusted her collar and necktie nervously when Butterfly 06 fluttered away from her knee. She did not enjoy having to follow Imhotep—but it was more out of annoyance than a lack of confidence.

Once her time began, she flicked a small cube from her thumb, which grew rapidly into a whiteboard when it touched the ground. She produced a telescopic pointer and started outlining various bulleted lists and graphs she had previously drawn out on the whiteboard. In her free hand she had a small mechanical clicker, and upon clicking it, her creature marched forward out of the portal.

"I present to you, the 'mindshare,'" Santa Inari combed her severe, star-glowing hair behind her ear and slapped the pointer at a graph. "This new species proposal has the potential to be a disruptive innovation in the intergalactic market, rivaling all other sentient creatures and religions with a set of ethics and philosophy focused squarely on commerce and progress."

As she spoke, the mindshare stepped forward with the power-walk of a fashion model. The creature had porcelain white skin, with a featureless face marked by black, barcode-like vertical lines that drew upwards into long, bouncing ties of hair. Its eyes, perfectly circular and black, gazed with emptiness. While most of the would-be deities had no sentience in their creatures, it was hard to picture a more doll-like or intentionally blank expression than the stare of this posing mannequin.

"Through me, the mindshare can buy their way to salvation, and with a clear and attainable goal-oriented deity, they will be united by a sense of purpose previously unseen among sentient creatures. The mindshare will find fulfillment through capitalist participation."

The buzzer rang. Santa and the mindshare bowed together. "Thank you, please reach out to me with any feedback."

Butterfly 06 was accidentally crushed when Santa summoned the whiteboard.

Robin's Entry

Butterfly 07 stirred and took flight from Robin's thigh. As she stepped toe-to-tape, the spotlights haloed her face. With its warmth, she closed her eyes and went to see her sister.

"Coach showed me how to throw a cutter today," she said proudly to her older sister Nala. They were 10 and 12 years old and had just signed up for little league after torturing their parents with pleas to try out for weeks. The Alleyne's were hesitant—it was tough enough to send their beautiful black girls to school, to let them out into the world in the 80s, when only a decade earlier the country was twisted and set ablaze by the idea of black and white kids being allowed to sit on the same school bus.

Robin and Nala were stubborn and competitive, partly because of their age gap, and partly because the Alleyne bloodline didn't take 'no' from anyone. Mr. Kevin Alleyne was a fearless columnist at the local newspaper that kept local politicians honest with detailed and pointed coverage of city hall. His wife, Mrs. Angel Alleyne, wasn't just a piano teacher, she was *the* piano teacher, and she would be the only one in Brighton (maybe even the whole of Boston) you'd want to get your lessons from after hearing her play on Sundays. This was a household that always pushed for greater heights in their lives, and it impacted the two children in fundamental ways.

"First, you hold it like this," Robin showed her the grip necessary to produce a cutter, then tossed it hard at a tree in their backyard. She missed, the ball cutting away from the tree and hitting the chain-link fence behind it. It rattled just hard enough to give both girls a jolt of fear that they damaged it.

"You better be careful," Nala laughed as she scampered after the ball. "You missed completely."

"It's supposed to curve!" Robin protested. "I just gotta keep throwing it till I can aim it."

Nala held up the ball. "Move. I'm gonna try. I bet I'll hit the tree with a cutter before you do."

Robin opened up her eyes and saw the judge's gaze. Her head dipped in the briefest nod, and her time began.

"This is my creation," she said with a wave towards the portal. She used her other hand to apply a metal bit to her temple.

From the portal walked Robin. Another Robin. A new, second Robin, dressed exactly the same, a mirror image of the Robin on stage. Jesus's eyes widened. Mohammed's rectangular form shook. Cthulhu hid his mouth tentacle's movement behind his notecards.

The clone Robin marched to the original Robin's side, and they faced the judges.

"If I am worthy enough to win this show," one Robin said.

"...then I want to be the god of Earth, and of myself," the other Robin said through watery eyes when her mind snapped back. Through gritted teeth she maintained composure, conquering the instant nausea the metal bit caused her. She suppressed the welling acidic cough in her diaphragm, and the heat in her chest. "I want to be the god that can be reached. And I want this possibility to be opened up to anyone with a just and worthy heart. Therefore, through me, my new species that I am presenting today is a reshaped version of humanity completely free to reach godhood. That is all. I yield the rest of my time."

Clone Robin returned to the portal and the original returned to her seat. Murmurs raised from both sides of the showroom, contestants and judges alike. Theodore tried to fist-bump Robin, but was turned down. He frowned, unsure of what the hell he had done to get rejected twice.

Butterfly 07 faded away.

Csodaszarvas's Entry

Butterfly 08 left its perch on top of Csodaszarvas's golden antlers. The white stag pushed his hesitation through his nose and trotted forward onto the stage. (For those wondering how the massive deer sat in his assigned seat: he didn't, at least not in the improbable human-like way you may assume. He was mercifully given a front row seat at the end, and laid down, letting his antlers rest in the chair itself.)

"Yeah! Go hooves!" Jarilo stamped his own against the glass floor. The awkward outburst drew nervous laughter out of the tense contestants. Cso didn't turn around, and restricted his reaction out of mild annoyance.

Once given the signal, Csodaszarvas whistled to the portal. An elf, tall and thin, with a face disproportionately packed with teeth and cheekbones, floated through. He was dressed in elaborate and beautiful robes that, it must be noted, were in the same color scheme as the white-and-gold deer that gave it life, with murals and ornate weaving that mirrored the shape of his antlers.

It was painfully clear from the robes alone that Csodaszarvas was his creator. But, even if the porcelain-skinned elf pranced to the stage completely in the nude, his lithe and toned body wouldn't have been enough to distract from the completely unsubtle way his long black locks stiffened and curved into wiry antlers. Each judge made special note of Csodaszarvas's tendency to mirror himself in his work—and Jesus made a particular observation on her card: *Robin's mirror was somehow less work and more interesting.*

"They are called the 'váradi,'" the deer explained. "They are an elven species, inspired by magic and movement."

The elf seemed to negate gravity naturally—each time a tip-toe touched the ground, he bubbled back up into the air, lifted by will.

"Clearly," Cthulhu's brow arched with the elven ballet.

"I want magic in my world to be a natural resource," Csodaszarvas clopped over to center stage, and guided the váradi over to him with a whistle. "Truth be told, the floating ability is all I've had time to design, but I want this to be a window into the sort of world I will construct."

Mohammad pivoted in his chair towards Jesus, whom just stared back with cynical boredom. The judges waited to hear something worth writing. Csodaszarvas froze. Silence spread like a plague for 10 seconds until the buzzer sounded.

"Allllllright," the deer smacked his lips idly, staring blankly into the lights. "Thaaanksss."

Butterfly 08 fled into the creature portal, never to be seen again.

While the other contestants were performing, the impossibly-toothed guitarist idly moved his fingers up and down the neck of his golden instrument. The resonance, the quietest thump of scaled finger to fret seemed to transfix Butterfly 09 and kept the normally skittish creature still on the head of his electric guitar. When it finally flew, signaling his turn, he played a quick scale—as he so often did, the scale appeared as random noodling to those around him. But when the butterfly curved its flight slightly, Taninim smiled—he knew he had connected with another creature.

That was just the warm up performance.

Taninim strode, guitar in tow, to his mark. His time began, and with a riff that had the tone of bitter coffee and razor blades, he summoned his scaled-amp from the creature portal. It rolled towards him, magnetized by a galloping arpeggio. He lifted his clawed foot onto the top of the amp, halted its rumbling roll, and moved one hand into the position of a power chord. His pick-holding claw rose high above his horn-crowned head.

"Let's rock!" he snarled, and slashed the pick down across the silver strings with a wave-parting chop. On impact, light ripped from the grill of the amp, and another, much larger dragon peeled out. Flames licked the trails of his clawed feet as he skid across the stage. When he landed directly in front of the judges, he played a guitar solo that harmonized with Taninim's backing rhythm guitar. The dragons, creator and created, jammed.

The dragon was structurally different from Taninim: quadruped, roughly the size of a pick-up truck, and more intensely colored in his reflector-yellow scales. Molded into his shoulders were speakers that his own guitar directly plugged into, which blared his face-melting riffs at full volume. The higher his solo climbed, the further back he arched. Smoke billowed from his endlessly grinning, glowing maw.

The guitar duo did not hear their time end over their wall of sound, and had to be signaled by a screaming (and laughing) Jesus. They bowed and received applause from both sides of the stage. The dragon, only programmed with his one song, was sucked back into the scaled amp when Taninim kicked the side. The judge's notes for Taninim were not terribly different from their notes for Csodaszarvas—the artist knows himself, and knows how to make things about himself. *But at least Taninim put on a show,* Cthulhu admitted in his scribbles.

Butterfly 09 fainted from over-stimulation.

"Oh, I'm next!" Jarilo giggled as Butterfly 10 lifted from his shoulder.

Jarilo tried to summon his creature from his seat before the shiqqs signaled him, as he had not paid attention to the contestants before him, or to the staffs instructions. Luckily, as the cast and crew found out, Jarilo had created a complicated and long incantation, so the judges did not accidentally see his creation stumble out prematurely. After he was guided to the studio mark, he started his spell again.

"Jarilo, All-Mighty, knows your seeds,
Knows your time, knows your deeds,
Your true purpose is to be harnessed
For the True God's Harvest!"

While Jarilo motioned as if he were conducting a symphony for the orbs of light materializing around him, Theodore leaned in to Robin's ear. "Harnessed and Harvest don't rhyme," he whispered.

"It's a slant rhyme, I don't think anything rhymes with 'harvest,'" she whispered back. "'Slant rhymes are common." As Theodore wrote instrumentals only, he took her word for it.

The orbs of light launched into the portal, then returned, dragging Jarilo's creature by the top of his head.

The wheat-man's entire form was intricately woven. Braided wheat formed tight muscles. He was lanky, and fibers of loose grass popped out at his shoulders and joints, wild like untamed hair. When his feet shuffled, he sounded like a sweeping broom. When he moved his arms he creaked. When he came near he smelled of sweet earth. The only part of him made of any non-plant tissue were a pair of massive and cartoon-like eyes.

The wheat-man cartwheeled, impressively enough, and pantomimed his excitement in front of the judges with waving hands and a cereal-tooth grin. The combination of simplified, abstracted eyes lodged into grit-and-fibrous wheat unsettled Jesus's stomach, and the meticulously crafted beige smile didn't help the unintentional creepiness of the design. Cthulhu couldn't help but notice that after his cartwheel, the wheat-man's left leg buckled briefly as some of the woven wheat came undone.

"He's a 'wheatkin!'" Jarilo said. "Born of the earth and of my breath. I used both the god eye and my own personal magic to make him. Normal wheat lives only for about a year, but by giving it sentience and basing its lifespan on accumulating more wheat into itself, this creature can live much longer as long as he annually returns to the harvest. Harvesting will become a natural part of his life, and his culture. And look!"

Jarilo twisted his fingers into a strange shape and an orb around the wheatkin's head flickered. The wheatkin responded by stiffening, then ripped one of his own arms off. He used it to wave at the judges.

"He's durable! He can braid this back on. All wheatkin learn how to weave and braid themselves for their protection."

The buzzer rang. Jarilo scanned the judges faces, expecting to see warm, enraptured smiles. They didn't look at him; all were buried in their own note taking.

"...okay! Thank you! I really hope you liked it!" There was a brief waver in his voice. Butterfly 10 turned to stone, plummeted to the ground, and broke apart.

Athena's Entry

With some hesitance, Butterfly 11 had come to perch in Athena's braided hair. When her time arrived, it fled quickly. The quiet ferociousness that Athena radiated could be felt by even the smallest creatures in her hawk-like stare and grinding jaw. It was pure instinct for butterfly to avoid such a predatory energy.

The metal bits in her skirt and breastplate clung together as she took her mark. "Let us begin," she said. The shiqqs signaled, and Athena raised her chin with pride. "Behold: The New Athenians."

Athena's tall, chiseled Greeks arrived, fully adorned in their himation cloaks and armed with spears. They were muscled and beautiful; the male with a beard like a lion's mane and the female with locs that whirled like a storm. Each of their steps slammed with confidence. It was clear from the way they looked into the eyes of the judges and contestants that they were thinking creatures that processed their surroundings.

"I am Athanas," the male gestured his spear towards Cthulhu. "I represent the wise and beautiful Athena. Please ask me any questions."

"I am Athenais," the female pointed towards Mohammad. "I am honored to answer on behalf of my creator, Athena."

"Are you Greek?" Cthulhu uncurled a mustache-tentacle with his hand.

"We are new. We are inspired by Greece," Athanas said.

"We are the strength and determination of humanity, refined," Athenais boasted.

"Will this 'New Athens' incorporate any deities or mythology from Ancient Greece other than Athena?" Mohammed asked.

"No, Athena is the one true ruler," Athenais said.

"Athena made us strong, Athena is all we need," Athanas looked to Athena with tears and a smile. The Greek goddess didn't return it—she simply observed, hands held behind her back.

Jesus stroked her beard for a moment, her eyes darted between box lights.

"What do you want to do?" Jesus asked.

"I want to see the world Athena makes," Athanas said.

Athenais hesitated.

"And you?" Jesus turned her gaze to the female.

"Athena told us we were strong. I want to see in what ways she made us strong," she held her head up high with resolve. "I want to be tested." Athena smiled. The buzzer rang, and her soldiers did not flinch.

Jesus rubbed the side of her face in thought, then started taking notes. "Thank you, Athena."

Athena was pleased—not only did her creations look powerful, but they expressed individuality despite having information preloaded into their new brains. Athena accomplished this much in the same way Jarilo accomplished his ties to the wheat-man, by allowing a link between herself and her creations. They had the information and traits she chose to share with them, but they possessed their own intellect with which to process it. The walk she took back to her seat felt like a victory lap, and the sullen faces of her opponents was its own reward.

Butterfly 11 flew into a light and was incinerated by its supernatural heat.

Theodore's Entry

Butterfly 12 had been sitting on Theodore's tie, which he didn't mind up until the time came to fly. When it did, it immediately flew into his face, bumped into his mouth and eye, then spiraled away in fear. The mustached millennial was caught off guard, and all his limbs briefly flailed in defense.

He collected himself, took his mark, and adjusted his suit. The cameras rolled. "So, hey. I'm Theodore," he said with a wrinkled brow that suggested he was not yet comfortable with the role he was playing, "and this is my creation."

Emerging from the portal was Theodore's jagged quartz creature. Its face was featureless, and its rainbow-reflecting sheen hid the black, rubber muscle underneath it. The creature moved with a better-than-expected mobility because the quartz substance, while appearing like the rock it's named after, was actually soft and closer to plastic. It also benefited from several cleverly placed joints along the knees and digitigrade legs. *I never thought binging on videos of robots falling down on the internet would benefit me,* Theodore thought, *but here we are.*

As it began to reach the judges, they looked on its form with great intent. The jeweled creature's fancy frame had their attention, but they wanted substance beyond show.

Theodore cracked a knuckle against his hip-bone. "I'm calling it a quartztaphore."

As the quartztaphore crossed Mohammed perpendicularly, it began to change. Its form, while still in motion, morphed into a mirror of the black-obelisk that housed the hidden prophet. Mohammed squealed with surprise.

"But it can call itself whatever the hell it wants, truthfully."

It regained its original form, only to shift again to the wide-eyed Jesus, right down to the bright red note cards she tapped against her knee.

"I could go into more detail about its defense mechanism, if you want."

It regained its original form again, walked a foot, then began to morph into Cthulhu. Ocean-Mouth noticed, however, that during the time it mirrored the elder-god that it made a small alteration—the arm that Cthulhu let dangle to his side in the real world was reflected back as a defiant middle finger in the disguise. Cthulhu was the only person that got to see this, due to the fact that the quartz creature's morph projected a 2D shape towards its target—the change looked quite odd to the contestants behind the quartztaphore, who could see only the silhouettes of the judges shape its front.

"But I think you get the jist of it," Theodore made sure to study Cthulhu's expression as the quartztaphore passed him. Ocean-Mouth's brow quivered, but not much else.

The creature walked back and took center stage and stood directly in front of Jesus. This time, it didn't change, not immediately. It waited with its three-fingered hands clenched.

"The thing I think I've always wanted the most," Theodore rubbed the back of his head and looked away from the judges, his voice strangely sheepish, "is a world... not without form, but the ability to easily change form. The ability to fluidly change to any situation... I think that's the most important thing."

The quartztaphore did its final morph—it did not reflect, but instead changed into the split image of the judges. It took each of their forms and spliced them together side-by-side.

"Informed change, that is."

The buzzer rang, and the creature crinkled to its jagged base. Theodore walked it back into the portal—he had no idea if what he made was "good" or "bad" in the eyes of the judges, but he at least wanted a flexible cover that could keep him in the show long enough to dissect it. This was his attempt—with some bits of honesty here and there.

Butterfly 12 was possessed and consumed by the vengeful spirits of Butterflies 01-11.

Ishta Devata's Entry

Ishta-Devata, the blue-skinned princess of Hinduism, did not need Butterfly 13 to alert her—she was, after all, the last contestant to present. All the same, it was in her polite nature to thank the small one. She waved it goodbye and breathed air of pure good will underneath its wings.

It was difficult for her to stand up. Not because of any physical pain or illness, but because of the number of people around her. She was in perpetual exhaustion from having the ambition and dreams of those in her line of sight broadcast to her, shoved into her. Though she had no way to banish the noise, she had learned to live with it over time.

In this moment, under the hot lights and anticipation, was the hardest and most physical saturation of other people's energy she had ever encountered. Not just because she saw the zeal of so many confident creators eager to live in their own world, but because she could see the ambitions of the judges. The images of the awful things they were prepared to do to the people of Earth—and to each other—played like a movie behind their smiling faces. Culling. Slavery. Domination. There's was a camaraderie formed only through convenience, and each of them were prepared to betray the other's trust once they reached their destination.

Earth. The place the gods cannot go to without permission from *The Next Great Deity,* yet the place each of them were born.

Earth. The centerpiece of the galaxy, the main attraction, the forbidden fruit of magic-less ants ready to worship the next deity that says "Hello" to them.

Earth. The place those in Heaven believe they get to go when their time comes. A bittersweet irony, as most of those here, Ishta included, were from the suburbs of Purgatory or Hell—and they held Heaven with the same other-worldliness as Heaven's citizens did Earth.

If any of that mysticism about Earth were completely true, Ishta-Devata now knew that Jesus, Mohammed, and Cthulhu would not be sitting there hoping to rush through this god-forsaken season of reality television so that they could travel the stars. They would just go, and for some reason, they can't—this *must* be done first.

Ishta-Devata reached her mark. She took one more look at Jesus, whom was so eager to crack open the obelisk shell of Mohammed and burn the man underneath. Mohammed, so ready to crucify Jesus the moment they both touched down on fresh soil to demonstrate his ultimate power to his new children. And Cthulhu, whom knew he could easily drag them both to the depths of the ocean and drown them there and let the pressure of the darkest and deepest waters crush them into nothingness.

"I'm ready," Ishta smiled, but curled a fist hidden behind her heavy sari sleeve. The world they wanted to rule over, and the worlds the contestants wanted to make, were not the same.

She received her signal, and produced a diamond-cut wine glass from her robes. She placed it in front of the creature portal, flicked it with a finger to let out a vibrato ring, then backed away. "I present: my 'water elemental.'"

A single spritz of cool water shot from the portal and landed with a splash into the glass. Water droplets that bounced out rolled back into the cup, drawn like a magnet to the bottom. Once they collected into a gulp, the glass began to fill with even more liquid, more than originally appeared from the portal. It overflowed, and turned into a large puddle and grew in size as it rolled down the straightaway in front of the judges. It collected again, and then rose vertically and formed the vague shape of a humanoid, which swayed on its water base like a recently released jack-in-the-box.

"The water elemental is actually a colony of sentient cells working together in one organism. It can also reach out to other water molecules and befriend them, incorporate them into the colony. In a way, this creature is a hive-mind that can constantly expand itself."

The Internet folded his arms across his chest, irritated that there was another colony species he had to contend with.

"So the individuals *are* the water molecules?" Cthulhu asked, holding his pen with a mouth tentacle.

"Yes. But they alone don't have much power, mentally or otherwise. That's why every collection of molecules that make up an elemental is unique—they all possess different memories and experiences down to their core."

"I can't imagine there's a lot of room for complex data in a single molecule," Mohammed pointed out.

"There isn't. Molecules will need to bond to perform more complex tasks. Which I believe is true, in a less exciting way, on Earth."

"So you're redefining the way chemical reactions occur to tie them specifically to your species's intellect?" Jesus asked.

"Yes."

The buzzer rang. The judges, as they always did, scribbled furiously on their note-cards.

"I look forward to sharing more," Ishta bowed her head slightly, then gilded back to her seat. The water elemental sloshed back into the portal, but not before accidentally caught Butterfly 13 in it's form, drowning it.

The Rationalization

Upon the completion of their presentations, the would-be gods were given a new portal to travel through. On the other side of the swirling energy was a cramped waiting room, a holding cell in comparison to the excess that everything else offered in the hotel. Were it not for the creative (and uncomfortable) polygonal couches, you wouldn't know these rooms were even a part of the same building.

There was a vibrating air conditioner just behind the exhales and chatter of the contestants that Theodore tried to focus on, but couldn't. Just when he thought he had a lock on its unique breath, The Internet landed on the couch beside him and buried his face into own his knees.

"That was great!" Jarilo cheered as he flipped himself into a bean-bag chair. Most in the room disagreed, but lacked the emotional energy to respond to him.

"I don't understand what we can even be judged on, honestly," Theodore laced his fingers in front of his mouth. "This seems completely subjective."

"Well, I mean, it is, to a degree. If it wasn't, there wouldn't be a show," Athena propped herself against a wall, arms crossed.

"The idea of this show," Robin said, seated legs-crossed on the floor, "seems kind of gross."

The room was quiet for a moment.

"Fuck you," The Internet murmured.

Robin's nose and brow drew together. "I'm sorry?"

"Fuck you," The Internet brought his head up. "This show gives us the chance to be something great. I'm glad you got whatever life you had before this, but winning this means something for me."

"And what's that exactly?" Theodore asked.

"Hey, haven't you been listening, you fuckhead?" The Internet spat as he got in Theodore's face. "Gods can make anything they want. They rule."

Theodore looked down The Internet's muzzle. He had grown completely immune tot he wolf's outbursts, and treated them like banter. "There's a lot of cool stuff between 'nothing' and 'god,' is all I'm saying. Relax."

Robin wanted to chime in and say she agreed with Theodore, but she was angry with him. She was angry that he had helped The Internet, whom *absolutely* would not have finished without his aid. She was angry that he didn't see the potential to use this competition as a means to make a better Earth for humanity. Everyone there selfishly made their own creatures that they wanted to rule over—who was Theodore to lecture *anyone?*

So, instead, she said nothing.

"You're an idiot," The Internet dropped his head back between his knees.

"You okay man?" Theodore patted The Internet on the back despite the dog-punk's insult, which irritated Robin further.

"I'm in the bottom. It's okay. I know it."

"I thought it was fine," Theodore said.

Fine? Robin thought. *He made a creature that threatened humanity directly in its prologue. You really are an idiot, Theodore.*

"Besides, how do you know? They didn't really say anything."

"No, he's probably right," Imhotep nodded as he lounged against the back of the opposite couch. "His performance went poorly."

The shiqq's camera focus shifted to Imhotep—the smokey Egyptian man had barely said anything since they exchanged greetings to the humans before the show began. Though Theodore wasn't necessarily known for tactfulness, even he recognized how rude Imhotep was being.

"Is now really the time to say something like that?" Theodore crossed his arms.

"It's fine..." Internet sighed.

"Is it?"

"He gets it. Didn't you see the judges?" Imhotep nodded his head towards where the portal was moments ago.

Theodore squinted. "Yeah. I was there. They had no reaction."

"Exactly," Imhotep couldn't prevent the corners of his lips from just slightly turning upwards. "They didn't feel the need to say anything. They were *that* uninterested. Of course they will be critical of all of us—they are judges, after all. But there was a sourness in the air after his performance. He also didn't even get to finish his video, and that doesn't even begin to talk about the design-"

"Now you can shut up," Internet raised a finger without raising his head.

Imhotep popped his neck. "Alright."

The room went quiet again.

"But it's okay guys!" Jarilo clapped. "We all put our hearts into this, and that's what matters. We'll all get good feedback to learn and grow from. We should be excited for the next step!"

The next step.

The next step, Mark Sharkman rubbed his finned head as he tracked the conversation through subtitles in his slow motion world.

Mark could not recall a season that ever made him so stressful. He was now obsessed with Theodore, making notes on every decision and facial tics.

It dawned on him.

"He's... he's not just helping him because he pities The Internet. This is strategic. If he thinks the show is rigged, then he views being the dog's ally as a way to keep himself on the show longer. Is that it, Theodore? Is that the game you're playing?"

Mark Sharkman looked down at Theodore's information sheet. In the box that says "occupation," Theodore had two entries, current and formerly: Musician, and Poker Player.

"Is this what you're always like?" he gulped. "Is *this* why production picked you?"

Theodore's Crime

Theodore committed the crime that would haunt him for the rest of his life at the age of 16. It appeared, to those that tried him, as a spontaneous act, an explosion of emotion and temporary insanity. Theodore knew, however, that there was a long, slow fuse tied to him years prior.

10-year old Theodore Flores rolled and tumbled with 9-year old Alex Aguilar on the peppery, newly vacuumed carpet of St. Andrews Church in Queens, NY. Both kids were full of sugar and high on yesterday morning's episode of the spandex-filled TV show *Space Samurai*, whose Japanese origins they were unaware of, as the makers were careful to recreate any scenes with Asian actors or landmarks with American equivalents. Being children, they were none-the-wiser to this fact, nor to the fact the show was largely a flimsy vehicle to sell them cool toys—articulated plastic figurines of every hero and villain, major or minor, that had ever appeared in its 200 episode run. Between the two of them, they may have owned the entire cast, but they would never be allowed to bring those to church. So instead, they rolled with each other and thought of themselves as intergalactic heroes and villains.

16-year old Theodore Flores rolled and tumbled with 18-year old Brandon Martinez on the wet concrete and into the bushes at the edge of a gas station parking lot in Queens, NY. The musk of the rain mixed in with the smell of new blood that leaked from Brandon's nose and lips. Theodore was drunk and Brandon was high, though any buzz either had was beaten out of each other by the time they tripped through the foliage of the parking lot perimeter and slammed into the wooden fence that divided residential and commercial zoning.

10-year old Theodore raised his hands in the air and made static sounds with his cheeks and teeth as he channeled an imaginary thunderbolt. Alex, pinned underneath him, wiggled his hands free and drew a circle with his fingers, where he pictured an energy shield his favorite hero would have protected himself with. He imitated a yell of determination, but kept his voice low as to avoid annoying any adults.

16-year old Theodore's fists pistoned onto Brandon's face. The two did not know each other, but Brandon's long hair, dyed in purple stripes, set off a domino of memories and hatred in Theodore. It started in the back of his head and collapsed in heated waves into the muscles of his arms.

"Alright, time for service," Isaac Flores hoisted his 10-year old son up by the armpits and to his feet. The Floreses and the Aguilars entered the nave of the church and prepared to hear the pastor's sermon. Theodore just wanted to play with Alex, though. Church was boring. Pastor Luis Jimenez, an elderly man with specks for eyes despite the magnification of his massive glasses, secured the pulpit edges with his frail grip.

16-year old Theodore's fist connected with Brandon's nose.

"Today, I came to tell you about sin," Pastor Jimenez's voice spilled like pebbles falling from a knocked over pail. "That perverted homosexual spirit, and the spirit of delusion and confusion, it has rolled around with the minds of many men and women and deceived them." 10-year old Theodore didn't know what most of those words meant, but they shook with fear, and he did, too. He looked across the aisle at Alex, whom he had rolled around with earlier.

16-year old Theodore's fist slammed into Brandon's eye socket.

Pastor Jimenez would give a sermon on homosexuals a few times a year. Each time, it made a little more sense to Theodore. Each time, it made him a little more frightened of other boys. "All the men of Sodom openly displayed their deviant sexual disposition. Openly, unabashedly, that is how we perceive men kissing each other, and women kissing each other." 11-year old Theodore had a girl kiss him on the cheek last year and he didn't much like it—it was sudden, cold, wet, and invasive. If a boy doing the same thing was that much worse, he couldn't imagine how much he'd hate it.

16-year old Theodore smashed his left hand into Brandon's jaw. He felt bone break, but was so drunk with indignant power and beer he stole from his dad that he couldn't tell if it was his fist or Brandon's face.

12-year old Theodore thought Pastor Jimenez looked more pale than ever, but his voice, and feelings, didn't waver. "Of course, in the animal kingdom there are males and females, and in the botanical world there are also male and female plants; in neither the animal nor in plant life do sexual abnormalities occur." Theodore heard this and struggled to agree, because he had learned about how the New Mexico Whiptail was a female only species of lizard at school—but maybe he misremembered.

16-year old Theodore knew after his last swing that at least the middle finger of his left hand was broken, so he switched entirely to his right hand.

13-year old Theodore folded his arms and tried to ignore Pastor Jimenez, but the congregation was always so quiet, and the acoustics were so perfect in the church that his gravelly voice would always ricochet right into his mind, no matter how hard he tried to think of anything else. He didn't watch *Space Samurai* anymore—Alex had moved out of the city, anyways, so he didn't have anyone else to watch it with.

16-year old Theodore came down, and stopped swinging. Brandon no longer moved. He was an unrecognizable pool of spilled blood and hair, and Theodore couldn't tell if he was unconscious or dead.

14-year old Theodore begged to do any meaningless task, custodial, extra-curricular, or otherwise to get out of listening to Pastor Jimenez's sermons. Football and Soccer games got him out of the house the most—particularly football. His team had grown strong enough that they traveled on the weekend out of the county, and even competed for the state championship. When football wasn't in season, he learned to play piano and guitar, and sang in the choir. One Sunday, there was nothing left to be done in Queens that would get him away from the particular type of sermon he tried to avoid the most. Theodore's eyes rolled all the way into the back of his head as he was forced to listen to the Pastor's gravel: "If a man lies with a male as with a woman, both of them have committed an abomination; they shall surely be put to death; their blood is upon them."

16-year old Theodore let his hands drop to his side. He studied the mask of blood Brandon wore, and wept—he was so much prettier beforehand, when he was casually buying a lavender can of grape soda.

15-year old Theodore had grown fond of the sound a piano makes after a key was hit. He would strike a hard chord, let it go, and lean in to let its resonance fill him. He day dreamed about all the small sounds he had let pass him by. He dwelled on all the opportunities lost. To distract himself from his own internal pity, he started to read a book on probability he had checked out from the school library. That night, his parents had left for a dinner. Theodore had accidentally grabbed one of his father's beer cans from the fridge instead of a soda. The first sip was like a fist, one that seemed to connect with every nerve in his body. He considered returning it, but his feet kept going, and when he made it back to his room, curiosity won out, and he drank it and read. He became intoxicated with beer and mathematical theory. He snuck the can into his neighbor's trash can, vomited when he made it back to his room, then passed out. The next morning, he told his parents he was sick and couldn't go to school. Telling incomplete truths became something of a habit for the remainder of his youth.

16-year old Theodore walked with his head dipped low, his clothes hung heavily with rain. He went back into the gas station and staggered to the register. He left a trail of water and blood behind him.

"Call the police. I think I just killed someone."

In court, drugs and TV were blamed for the incident, even though Theodore was drunk—not high—and hadn't watched TV in years.

The Editing Room

"I need the close up of Jarilo's chant on camera three."

Ritst tapped the glass on the display in front of him. His yellow eyes, kept apart on the farthest sides of his angular head, scanned the ever-expanding timeline on his monitor. There weren't too many clips left in the queue: he and his crew worked hard to produce the show in real time, so that it got to its audience as fast as possible with as little chance for spoilers. That's how important the audience was to *The Next Great Deity,* and how powerful their checkbooks were.

"Here's the camera three clips," a man, somewhere between human and angler fish, tossed him a folder through their shared holographic UI.

"Great. On camera one you could see up his nose. Totally unusable."

The editing room was a massive, steely chamber of metal, hot processors, and holographic prompts passed around like air hockey pucks between each of the editors. The group was comprised of various fish-men, employees of Cthulhu's firm. They worked in close proximity to the most important person on *The Next Great Deity,* more important than even Cthulhu himself.

"S-Sir," said a guppy in clothes so pressed and starched that they could slice cheese at the seams, "The Producer w-would like a status update."

Ritst rolled his shoulders. "Welp. There goes the lead-way I had. Alright everyone, mockup the rest of the challenge footage and I'll polish them once I'm out."

"Sir, are you sure you can handle another trip into the Overtime Machine? The last one looked like it almost killed you, if it could have. I-I could help on a spare console, instead."

"Kærast," Ritst started with a tone of annoyance, but when he saw the Guppy's worried face (and shrinking stature from being addressed) he just smiled, his rows of teeth catching the light of passing hologram files. "Don't you worry your sweet little head. Heaven's on our side."

Ritst went to one of the sealed-off meeting rooms and Kærast stared at his exiting form, moved by the editor's dedication with a chest-clutching admiration that went beyond professionalism.

The Hydraulic door sealed behind Ritst. He was alone in the meeting room, which shared the same near-black metal walls and piping. Ritst's crew were always too busy to have meetings in here—Instead, the only meetings that ever seemed to take place were one-on-one conferences between Ritst and the projector on the far end of the room.

The floor was unscathed, for the chairs never moved. Ritst, quite tall at his height of 10 feet, was able to easily inch onto his toes and flick the 'On' switch for the hanging projector. Most of the other contractors would have needed to climb onto the table itself. The projector flickered to life, and there on the pull down screen was the most important man in Heaven.

The Producer never showed himself fully. He hid his identity behind brightly lit beveled glass. Despite the heavy abstraction his form took, Ritst could still make out of the human shape of his skull, the sharp shoulders of a padded suit, and the lack of any hair on the top of his head. Curiously, though, his head didn't seem to be adorn-less—if The Producer turned or was more animated in his motions, Ritst could catch the silhouette of what appeared to be long, thin chains from the back of his head—too thin to be dreadlocks, too metallic in sound to be his hair. Nonetheless, it was there, and without any evidence of a hat or tie, Ritst had to assume these chains were somehow attached to the figure.

"Good evening, sir," Ritst bowed and squatted down into a cross-legged sit, too large to fit in any of the chairs.

"Good evening, Ritst. I'll keep this brief, as I'm sure you're hard at work," The Producer said. His voice was jovial, a ping-pong of low-to-high inflection. "Where are we on finishing episode one?"

"The judges are in deliberation now, sir."

The Producer clapped. "Oh, wonderful! Wonderful! That's far ahead of schedule. Excellent. Do you have any reports? Anything I need to know about?"

Ritst tapped his hands on the table. "Mark Sharkman."

"Hmm? Who's that?"

Ritst shook his head in surprise. He had just brought up Mark at their last meeting—The Producer must be horribly busy to forget something like that so quickly. "He's the interviewer. He seemed really concerned about the contestant 'The Internet.'"

"Ah, the interviewer!" The Producer brought up a long, thin cigarette, dragged it, then huffed lazy smoke into the air. "Why's that? Why's he concerned? It's his job to ask questions, so I suppose this isn't surprising, but what bothered him so that he came to you?"

"Well, sir, if I had to guess, he probably suspects that The Internet may not have qualified through auditions like the other contestants."

"Wonderful!" The Producer clapped. Ritst didn't understand what was "wonderful" about that, but that concern would be far from his mind after The Producer's next question. "Do we know if he's shared this info with the others yet?"

Ritst gulped. For some reason, almost no news could ever seem to shake The Producer's amused inflection... except the following:

"No, sir. We don't know."

The truth about The Producer is that most things amused him, regardless of the impact they had on the show. As long as he had something to work with, as long as there was information to think about, he was pleased. But bad news was better than no news: bad news was a fact of life, and just as interesting a thing to show on *The Next Great Deity* as anything else. No news means that there's an aspect of his show that's dull, or worse, there's something going on he doesn't have control over.

The Producer's posture melted forward, and Ritst swore he saw the beveled glass shake as he spoke.

"There are three words in that sentence," The Producer exhaled. "Three words in a particular order that I detest. Go do your job, Ritst. You can't edit anything if you don't know all the details."

Ritst bowed. "Yes, sir. I apologize, sir. I'll contact Mark right away, sir."

The Producer, to Ritst's surprise, sat upright, and the original light tenor returned to his voice. "Mark?"

"Sharkman. The interviewer."

"The interviewer! Yes, good. Do that. Right now."

Ritst returned to the chaos of the main editing room, and almost immediately his guppy was there with a thermos of coffee with two creams and one sugar, a bagel with smoked salmon, cream cheese and capers, and a toothpick. All of Ritst's favorites that he didn't ask for.

"Thank you," Ritst smiled. He bit the bagel clean in half as the two moved in unison.

"Of course, you must keep your energy up in order to go into that dreaded machine," Kærast kept up the pace despite his disadvantage in leg length.

"Well, I'm afraid I'll be trading one annoying machine for another this time. There's been a change in plans. I'll need to step into the Camera World," Ritst paused to down the thermos. He stopped walking, and Kærast skidded to a halt as well. "Actually..."

"Yes, sir?" Kærast was ready to spring in any direction he needed to.

"Kærast. You've been so good to me," Ritst set the thermos back on the silver tray, placed both of his massive, rubbery hands on Kærast's small shoulders, and leaned his angular face down inches from the guppy's parted lips. His voice was low but sharp, and felt like an injection. "You work so hard for me, don't you? I don't think there's anyone else that works harder than you do for me."

The guppy's eyes dilated. He shook. His gills pulsated with a marathon swimmer's speed. *For you, of course,* he repeated in his head, never so foolish as to speak it aloud.

"I do my best, Sir!" he whispered instead.

Ritst unfolded back to his towering height and patted the guppy on his head. "It'd be great if you could take over the console for me while I'm gone. Just organize the incoming clips for me, and do any errands the others ask. You've studied the editor, haven't you? Do you feel up for it?"

"I know it in and out! I can do it!" Kærast proclaimed, set the tray to the first open spot he could find, and bolted towards the console. It wasn't boastfulness—even though Kærast rarely edited, he had studied the editing software extensively ever since meeting Ritst, ready to go the extra mile when called for duty. This was his chance to go even further for him.

Ritst gnashed the bagel into a pulp and wandered off towards the Camera World Chamber.

"Okay," Jesus mumbled. "I'm stumped."

The judges stood in the collection room, dead in the center of the mostly inanimate work of their contestants. They strolled and weaved through the creations as if they were statues in a museum, and scrutinized the details of each empty creature up close.

"All of this is the legitimate work of people trying to win," Cthulhu rubbed the top of his mucus-coated head. He stared at the orange virus-sacs of Imhotep's creation, the reshep, with admiration. "If there's a mole here, I can't pick it out from the genuine work of everyone else's."

"Well, there is an odd one out, but..." Mohammed trailed off and the three turned to the flickering, shoddily assembled disappointment that was The Internet's "discarded" species.

"No, no, wait," Jesus paused. "I made The Internet, but the original idea came from production. I put my own spin on it, but we were suggested to fill that slot with a robot candidate. They supplied the circuit boards I transformed. It's my power that gave him life. He really does want to win."

"So you're saying production's plant is just you having bad execution?"

Jesus scowled at Ocean-Mouth, but couldn't rebuttal.

"Look, I think we're over-thinking this," Cthulhu pushed his glasses up the smooth, slight slope above his mouth tentacles. "We don't have enough to go on yet. Our mini-game is to pick the same winner that production does. Just because they pulled a fast one on us with the number of contestants *in no way tells* us whether they will pick someone we brought in or not. If anything, I don't know if we can look at something as simple as whether they made 'good work' to figure it out. None of this is the work of someone sabotaging themselves to fool us."'

"How often in the past was production's pick eliminated in the first challenge?" Mohammed asked.

Cthulhu flipped some pages in his book. He had pulled from his vast library of records a workbook of stats he had compiled himself. It was part of a massive collection, thousands of volumes in length, this one just being the latest version.

"2%."

"How often in the past did production's pick make it to the final three?"

After consulting the index, Ocean-Mouth flipped through a few more pages. "64%, roughly. That's gambling odds, guys."

"If it's gambling odds, then how are we always wrong?" Jesus bit her thumb.

"Let's just play this game straight for now," Mohammed dragged his obsidian chamber along the floor, "and talk about who we liked and didn't like."

"Excuse me," a new voice asked. Each of the judges jumped, then turned and saw Athena's Athenians. It was Athenias, "What is a mole? We are Athenians, mighty warriors—"

"Fucking hell," Jesus fanned herself with her notecards. "Forgot Athena gave them minds."

"How long have you two been standing there?!" Cthulhu held a hand to his chest to check in on the jumping pace of his three hearts. The Athenians did not have the knowledge or familiarity with time yet to guess.

"Why did she do that, anyways?" Mohammed wondered. "I mean, it's impressive, but that wasn't part of the challenge."

"To show off, probably," Cthulhu shrugged. Jesus stroked through her beard.

"Athena gave us the highest intelligence of all these inferior creatures!" Athanas raised his fist in the air.

"Oh shut up," Jesus rolled her eyes. "Mold is smarter than some of the empty cans in here. Don't be so proud."

"I don't think we can talk about this with these two butting in," Cthulhu sighed. "Mohammed, do something."

Mohammed paused, then realized what was being asked of him. "Oh, right."

Two small squares of black marble, about an inch thick in depth, separated from the housing that Mohammed hid in. They floated into the air just long enough for the Athenians to realize their threatening nature. Athanas and Athenia produced swords and spears in bolts of light from their hand—but by then, Mohammed had already sent the black squares at them. They flew at a speed that matched an eagle's flight. With his expert control and their small size, he was able to out maneuver the Athenian's swordplay and slammed the squares into, and through, their skulls.

They didn't fall, though. They stood there, eyes wide, drool puddling around their teeth. They were locked in place for as long as Mohammed's squares stayed smashed into the front of their lobe.

"Should probably wipe them, too," Cthulhu suggested.

Short-term memories, even powerful ones caused by fight-or-flight situations, are still malleable, squishy things within the neural connections of the brain, subject to the influence of outside forces. Mohammed cannot wipe memories—and every time Cthulhu referred to it as memory wiping, it irritated him—but he *can* alter the content of the recently made memories by sparking it with his unique brand of electricity. Mohammed scanned the newest memory of the two soldiers, located their eavesdropping of the judges, and simply muted the conversation. He almost let them go, but then remembered, rather importantly, to replace the memory of their attack with one of merely milling about among the other creations.

"I don't see any evidence of this in their short term memory, but..." Mohammed wondered aloud, sticking a finger outside of the small inch hole in his vessel. "You know. If Athena is production's mole, having two sentient creatures listen in is certainly a way to spy on us. We have to interact with these things, and we're expected to study and talk about them."

"Anyways," Cthulhu paced around the mind-locked Athenians, looking deep into their rolled-up eyes with palpable distrust. "I don't feel comfortable being in here anymore. Shiqqs, do we have enough footage? You just needed us to walk around and look at these things, right? Well, we did."

He turned to one of the half-formed blobs of flesh holding a camera. Upon being asked the question, the camera-shiqq sat and pulsated for a moment, sending the request to the editing room. A small light lit up behind his left eye, which drooped lower than his right. "Yes, this is good," he sloshed with a prerecorded voice sample.

"No it's not," Jesus bit her thumb. "There's nothing good about this." She walked towards the shiqq and put her face and finger directly into the camera lens. "Listen, you son of a bitch. We're going to find out which contestant it is. We're winning this year. We're going to be free. And when I'm out, when I'm the fucking queen, I'm sealing this hellhole up! Earth will be ours and you can rot in here without any prize to offer anyone! You hear me, Producer? I'm sick of this! I'm sick of you!"

Cthulhu put himself between the shiqq and Jesus. "Jesus, Jesus, Jesus. Shh. Shh. You don't want him to pull the trigger."

Jesus sank into reluctant submission. Her bottom lip quivered, she gulped, but she did not cry. She just pointed into the camera and made a teeth-clenched promise.

"Someone's gonna humble you someday," her voice broke, "and you better hope it's not me."

Camera World Chamber

Because of Ritst's incredible height, there were several challenges posed to him that most fish-men didn't have to deal with. Some rooms in Heaven's Heart Hotel had such low ceilings that he had to work while reclining or sitting. Doorways always required him to bend his hips and fold forward, a task he had to do so frequently that it may have *technically* counted as yoga. Whenever there was a function that required a special dress code, Ritst prayed that his suit had held up from the year before, because getting something tailored for his 10-foot form in any reasonable amount of time was either impossible or expensive, and almost always both.

By far the worst combination of these annoyances, though, was entering the Camera World Chamber.

The Camera World was only accessible by its gatekeeper, Mark Sharkman. He was an integral part of the crew's process, and show's success—time moved at a snail's pace there, which allowed him to easily track contestant's reactions and get on-the-spot interviews when necessary. Reality shows, by their very nature, can go awry, particularly when the contestants are given such glorious powers to play with. Mark's role was a necessary check to the abilities of the contestants.

One of Mark's duties was to coordinate with Ritst and submit transcribed interviews and complete psychological profiles of the contestants. Between the efforts of the editing team and Mark, the show could always come out perfectly produced and instantly attainable. On top of that, such coordination allowed them to quickly start work on the next season as soon as the show was renewed.

The most annoying aspect of the Camera World is that Ritst could not physically fit in it. He was too tall, and the first time he tried to enter, he cracked his skull on a swinging camera-arm. While it would have been possible to have a liaison go in Ritst's place, the lead editor was, ultimately, a believer in maintaining positive and personal work relationships with all of his coworkers. He worked out a compromise with production to create a purgatory-like room between the Camera World and Heaven's Heart Hotel. (He also believed it was not the best thing for his mental state to constantly get whacked in the head by metal objects, which is the argument that ultimately swayed The Producer the most.)

To get to the chamber, Ritst entered a lockdown area with two doors and padded walls. It was just tall and wide enough for him to stand in the center, and the close proximity of the pads to his far-spread eyes always gave him a feeling of claustrophobia. The doors sealed shut and his ear holes popped as the pressure of the new area forced into every part of his rubbery flesh—a wholly unpleasant slowness that was still easier to tolerate than being bludgeoned.

The Camera World Chamber was an area of muddied time between the two places. It was mostly featureless aside from its seafoam green walls, single wall-mounted camera, monitor, and keyboard. Ritst plodded forward, all his might only enough to push through the heavy gravity of the room, as if the air itself were syrup.

A password entry later and the camera whirled to life, connecting him to Mark.

Mark Sharkman's Camera World was littered with empty wine bottles. Camera arms swayed with jolly, and the shark-man himself laid across the top of his desk and balanced a flute glass on the tip of his snout.

"Markie, you've got to clean this up at some point."

"Ritst!" He hiccuped and caught the falling glass from his face. "Hi! Oh, I do. Before contestants come in. I have time to clean. You *know* I have time. Time is something I have the most of, more than anyone else. And wine. I almost certainly have the most wine."

"Are you drunk?"

"Ritst, I am always drunk, and always sober. I am truly the most blessed man in existence."

Ritst shook his head and laughed, which hurt to do in the molasses time-desync of the chamber.

Ritst could not imagine living like Mark did—immortal and isolated. He was cut off from the world of media and entertainment and only saw people in the context of the show, and would sometimes spend weeks (in his own time) getting to the contestants. The ability to do an incredible amount of work and not lose any precious time aging was a type of magic Ritst couldn't comprehend, and a burden he didn't want to have.

"I have something to ask you, Markie," Ritst said. "You mentioned your suspicion about The Internet's background. Production wants to know if you've discussed that with any other contestants."

Mark peered into Ritst's chroma-distorted face on his monitor. "None of the contestants have said anything to me, no." A weak silence lingered.

"Are you certain?" Ritst tried to word this with a careful sternness that indicated both the seriousness of his inquiry, and how impersonal it was. "This is from production. Because of that, I'll have to go through the tapes and cross check the interviews in the Overtime Machine, as you may know. I was hoping to save some headaches—literal headaches—and narrow down where in the interviews they talked about it, if any."

There was no way for Ritst to know that Mark's distant stare and silence was because, deep down, he was panicking, trying to remember if he had the cameras turned on when he talked to Theodore. Mark knew that he wouldn't film such a thing, but he feared the accuracy of his memory for something that, for him, happened so long ago.

"No, no, I feel like I'd remember something like that," he lied, and slumped with nonchalance in an attempt to mask his desire to blubber the truth.

"Alrighty. Keep strong, Markie," Ritst said. "If you need anything from me, let me know. I know it gets lonely in there."

"Not lonely!" Mark smiled. "Just busy, sometimes. Very busy."

Ritst signed off. The moment the signal cut, Mark fell off his desk and screamed into the concrete floor.

Mark Sharkman, for whatever liquid vices he may have, was a good employee with a secure future and a wonderful life. Yes, the time in the Camera World was tough. But the benefits he got from this job made up for it in riches and comfort only gods get to have.

"I have never lied to Ritst... or anyone here at this job... ever," Mark freaked out. He didn't know what the consequences were if his lie was discovered. Would he lose his home? Could they sue him for damages? He'd certainly lose his retirement, which he was not far from, and he'd surely tarnish his legacy, which he had put more time in than...

How do you measure that? No one can measure that! No one can compare to the time that I've put in!

"So... why? Why did I do this?" he blubbered into a empty wine bottle.

He wallowed and rolled around for as long as he wanted, sobbing uncontrollably. Suddenly, he stopped, and the only sounds that came from him were messy, sinus clearing sniffles.

"That's not the question I should be asking," he produced a handkerchief and wiped his snout clean. He pushed himself up on one hand, looked around at his mess, and started to gather wine bottles to throw into the disposal. "No. The real question is, if The Internet is a plant, if the show is rigged for him at all, then why would he tell me about how he was made for the show, and right in the first episode?"

He stared down into the void of the disposal with an irresponsible amount of empty wine bottles in his hand.

"The judges don't have control over him. Production may not even have control over him."

He dropped the bottles in. As the glass plummeted into the black hole, Mark felt that maybe he, too, was dragged in. His mind, his effort, all he had ever worked for was an empty bottle he just let drop.

"Ritst... no, production isn't afraid about the show being perceived as rigged at all. They edit it. They want to know if they can make a story out of him."

Theodore had been inspired by the metal bit Robin designed to transfer her consciousness between herself and her 'doll.' He didn't know *how* she did it: for him, if he didn't lay the framework for his creations as detailed and scientifically sound as possible, the god eye wouldn't create a functioning version of his vision.

The routines that Theodore's quartztaphore went through in front of the judges were prerecorded. Theodore, as a particular type of musician that spends more hours tweaking digital settings than hitting piano keys, understood the recording process well, and was able to sway his god eye to allow him to create and install a microphone inside his creature. A button—blended into the back hindquarters of the quartztaphore—made the creature record movements and commands instructed by Theodore. Had he been called out on this, he was prepared to explain how it was a means to an end and did not reflect the design of the final species.

It was just as well they didn't notice, because that wasn't the only secret installed. It was his understanding of recording hardware, his years spent researching microphones to record the smallest sounds in the smallest places, that led him to build one inside the creature. Combined with the inspiration he had from Robin's invention, Theodore's microphone allowed him to record what the quartztaphore heard, then sent that recording to a small speaker and storage system he had disguised as the cuff links of his suit's right wrist. He could, from the underside of the cufflink, flip a switch that would start recording, then again to stop. That recording would then be stored on the second cufflink, ready to play until it was replaced by another.

So now, Theodore knew.

Theodore knew that the judges were playing a different game, one more important to them than the pretense of the competition, and one that had Earth as a prize for them, not the contestants. Awarding godhood to one of the contestants was secondary to that goal, if it was real at all. He also learned that someone among the contestants is a plant for production, and that production and the judges were at odds with each other.

The portal to the main stage opened and the 13 would-be gods shuffled back in. As they did, Theodore couldn't help but stare into the faces of the other 12 to glean any clues as to who might be an insider. If anything, the knowledge he now had just complicated matters further—if production was an antagonist to the judges, does that make them his ally? How could that be if they were responsible for his own kidnapping? And Robin's, too.

Robin. He needed to tell Robin what he learned, but they needed to do it outside of a shot of the cameras. No shiqqs could be around when they discuss this—a difficult task when they seemed to be capable of being everywhere.

The contestants were guided by the shiqqs to stand in a long line that faced the seated judges. They stood for what seemed like an eternity in awkward silence as they were filmed. It was natural to eventually shuffle, sway, have a facial twitch or look around the room—all of which, more than a few contestants realized, could be used for editing in the final show. A contestant on TV staring nervously at a ceiling may have simply had nothing else to look at for 10 minutes.

"Welcome back, contestants," Jesus finally said when the cameras pointed to her, in a passionless drawl that likely came from too much rehearsal. "We've reviewed your work and have reached a decision. We'd like the following contestants to please step forward."

Every contestant filled their lungs with enough air to last a lifetime, which is approximately how long it felt before Jesus finally started to speak their names:

"Internet. Imhotep. Athena. Robin. Jarilo. Theodore. You six have the highest, and the lowest, scores," Jesus said with a flatness that Theodore could feel at his feet.

But when he heard his own name, he twitched. *Wait,* he thought. *I'm in that group?*

He realized that he suddenly cared how he performed, perhaps more than the judges and certainly more than himself at any other point in the past. His participation wasn't just about him anymore. He had real reason to doubt the honesty of those involved in this show, its implications and their intentions, and that gave him a feeling of purpose he worried he should have had 12 hours prior.

Meanwhile, those whose names *weren't* called were all smiles. They beamed with a shared elation that can only come from safety. None perhaps more so than Oksi, whose face melted into relief, the first positive emotion that had ever graced his lined face. For all the trials and failures he had up until the show, just getting to the middle felt like a win on its own. They were shuffled off by the shiqqs. Their positions, for now, were protected.

"To the six of you remaining, we'd like to ask you some questions before we make our final decision. One of you will be our winner, and will receive immunity from elimination in the next challenge," Jesus explained.

The contestants on trial perspired under the hot lights and awkward silence as shiqqs brought out their creations, which stood idly beside each contestant—except Athena's, who thanked her endlessly for their birth until she asked them to keep quiet.

Theodore studied the Athenians. From what his microphone picked up, something happened to the Athenians when the judges were in the collection room. As he inspected them now, though, they didn't seem any more off than they were previously. This is a tough thing to judge, he thought, considering how simple-minded they were in the first place. If they had told anything to Athena about the judge's meeting, he couldn't read it on her face. Athena's normal aura of intense confidence was etched into her, with not a worried crevice to be found.

"And one of you," Jesus paused for dramatic effect. "We have lost faith in."

This line was the hardest thing Robin, and Theodore, had ever resisted rolling their eyes at. But for the other contestants, this pun signaled the serious beginning of the most frightening component of the show—the judge's evaluation

"Jarilo. Let's start with you. Tell us about your wheatkin."

"Okay!" Jarilo clapped. He adjusted pieces that had frayed or shifted on his wheat-man. He loved to share his work and see people light up when they began to understand the world he had in his head—and he was certain that was the sort of moment he was about to experience.

"I really like magic! It's been a long time since there's been a strong magic-centric religion that dominated a world's culture, so I wanted to make something close to my roots, which are pagan" he proudly patted the wheatkin's straw chest. "So, yeah. These are my wheatkin. The wheat makes up their muscles and I am the one that breathes life into them. My primary ability is to bring life to crops so I thought this was a logical way of incorporating what I'm good at, farming, with sentience and design."

The judges juggled their looks between themselves and their notecards. After a little vibration, Mohammed decided to speak first.

"So you're at a bit of a disadvantage here since 2/3rds of your judging panel is very anti-pagan," Mohammed tilted towards the half-goat. "Bias aside, I have no problem with a magic ruled world *if it's done right.* There's something really... flat about this species. I like that it's a little different from the type of pagan mythos typically seen in Earth's past, and I don't think you had the most boring entry today. But, it's not interesting enough to make up for the fact that it's executed poorly."

Jarilo's smile flat-lined. "Executed poorly?"

Cthulhu pointed his notecards at Jarilo. He lifted them up and down to punctuate his criticism. "It's a *cartoon.* It's *incomplete.* It's the equivalent of a child's drawing. You have these big ugly eyes that look like they're from an anime..."

Jesus looked at Cthulhu with a small smirk. "You watch anime?"

Cthulhu tapped his cards into his slimy palm, his mouth tentacles drooping. "I... stay informed."

The half-goat's eyes were so wide with fear that there was a worry among Robin and Athena, who stood closest to him, that they simply might pop out of his sockets altogether. "Well, the world I want to build... it is a little more fantastical than what's being offered by the others. I want to bring a 'happy' magic back, so no, it's not gonna look super serious because that's not my style," he attempted to collect himself, but his frustration was palpable.

"Style is fine," Cthulhu shook his head and hands. "Style is great. This isn't style, it's a mistake. The eyes on this thing do not fit this intricate weaving you tried to do, the teeth made out of cereal make this thing look like an unintentional nightmare when it grins. To me, this is antithetical to everything you seem to be about."

"I know, but..."

"Look, I'm a purveyor of some creepy stuff. I like a fearsome thing. This creature isn't unsettling on purpose, it's just because nothing looks good together, and the key aesthetic element you have—the weaving of wheat into muscles—isn't even done that well. You had wheat shredding off of him during your presentation, and even before you started talking to us you had to adjust some of it. He can't *move* without coming apart. One of your selling points in your presentation was its durability and he looks anything but."

Jarilo shuffled, stupefied. His hooves clacked against the glass-like floor.

Jesus raised her hand and cooed in an attempt to soothe. "If I may, I do... like that it's made of wheat. You're the only one that approached plant-life as sentience, and there's something to be said for taking a unique approach. But we are expecting more work and detail from you. I think, to touch on what Cthulhu said, if it's falling apart, it's hard to believe it can survive on its own long enough to develop as a world-ruling species. Put simply: this piece does not necessarily make me want to see more. Especially if you're making a world of magic, your work should inspire and entice."

Jarilo found a fixed point on the floor, somewhere between Cthulhu's dress shoes and Jesus's red high heels, and stared. The color, what little his pale skin had, drained completely from him. If magic were a real thing, then the reality of the judge's criticism stole it from him.

"So if you were given the chance to change anything, now knowing our feedback, what would it be?"

The half-goat looked up with watery eyes. His mind raced through the criticisms he had just received but did not accept. He didn't *want* to change, no. They were sticks in the mud, unhappy people that didn't like the sugar-sweet world he wanted to make. And what of it? Why should he change for them? This was his vision, not theirs.

But that's probably not the wisest thing to say if you want to stay on the show, Jarilo thought to himself.

It would be impossible to notice unless you were measuring him, but Jarilo's height, in that moment, grew half an inch.

"I think," he inhaled. "I think I can still keep the core elements that we both seem to like—plant-based, magic-based, etc. But, if the durability of this guy is a problem then I can look into some different materials to build him from and give him a more solid structure. I still want to keep the weaving element in their species and culture, but I could develop ways to make them less fragile."

"Interesting. Thank you, Jarilo," Jesus said. The judges noted his ideas for course correction. Jarilo returned his gaze to the empty space, and his bottom lip slowly slid away from the rest of his face, his worry and anger coating its pink surface with a wet sheen.

Jesus motioned towards the Egyptian polymath. "Imhotep! You're up."

Imhotep ran the tips of his fingers down the rough, grooved length of the nightmarish insect next to him. "In my life, I was known primarily for my medical expertise. My entry, my reshep, is homage to that. It stores bacteria and viruses in these sacs around its throat and along its body. That which doesn't kill a reshep, gets broken down and contained safely in these sacs. I've given it a body shape somewhere between a centipede and a mantis because I wanted to make something that could survive the wild through its strength and be feared if it made contact with another species—say, humans."

Cthulhu jumped at the chance to talk. His body leaned well into the side of the seat as his eyes traveled along the valleys of the reshep's exoskeleton. "I'm going to be completely biased. This is my favorite. It's the least humanoid, so it stood out. It has some brutal defenses, and it looks nice and mean. I almost wish you hadn't told me you were inspired by a centipede because now I see the inspiration and can't unsee it."

Imhotep shrugged. "Thank you. Not sorry about the centipede thing, though. I love a crawly thing."

"Me too," Cthulhu said, his mouth tentacles curling.

Mohammed hummed for a moment, switching between notecards he somehow was able to hover directly in front of his slab form. "So many of our submissions seemed to focus on the species after sentience, but every good religion has an origin. The idea that a species like this—one that can, at will, plague its enemies to death—can reach sentience is very interesting to me.

It's a great springboard for a world, and even though it's kind of rough looking, it's intentionally so. Like Cthulhu said, it looks mean, with a purpose."

Imhotep bowed slightly. "I'm glad that you see its strength."

Jesus clicked her tongue as she scanned down her cards. "I do have a problem, though."

Imhotep raised an eyebrow with such slowness that one could almost hear his skin creak.

"Sentience is usually obtained as a compensation for other natural defenses, isn't it?" She turned her inquiry to Cthulhu. "Crows are smarter than tigers because they have to be. Humans don't have fangs or wings, but they have an exceptional mind, which," and then she turned her head back to Imhotep, "to a certain extent, we eventually expect all the creatures here to be at least smart enough to worship a god."

"Well, I think that's, with all due respect, a little simple," Cthulhu said. Jesus rested her face on her hand and forced an interested smile at her slimy co-judge. "We haven't seen yet the world these guys come from, and there are other factors that play into sentience beyond just a compensation for natural defenses. To go back to your example of crows, they are known to mourn their dead, loudly. It doesn't have to be a human type sentience to be capable of spirituality, and I disagree with the idea that humans are the only ones with sentience on Earth. Intelligence is not binary."

Jesus turned her forced smile, which had diffused to the farthest corners of her face, to the contestants. "Well I think we drifted a little bit. Sorry."

Imhotep rolled his wrist and suppressed his smug inclination. "Well I'm just glad I got you guys talking."

Jesus cleared her throat, "This challenge really is about showing us what your point of view is like as a god. The challenges from this point forward are resting on the "taste" that today gives us. I think yours makes me the most curious about where you'll go from here."

Imhotep bowed again, and had his reshep bow with him. The nightmare centipede-man hissed with a low, inner drumming. "I have big plans for it. Thank you."

"Athena, let's talk about your creations."

Athena brought her hands behind her back and locked them in place. From the front she seemed strong, poised, fearless. While she certainly was those things, at least part of her ability to appear that way is her tendency to, out of sight, squeeze her wrist during confrontation. It allowed her to use physical pressure to curve her natural tendency to say what was on her mind, regardless of the consequences.

"Right. Thank you," she organized her thoughts. "So, as I believe was made clear during my presentation, I am making a new Athens. These two lovely specimens are my Adam and Eve, and they represent the physical strength and cultural ideas behind my new world. New Athens will be the center, and I will build a new pantheon surrounding it, one inspired by the world-changing skill the ancient Greeks possessed. I would like to think it was noticed that I have shown the most skillful use of the god eye by making not only two living creatures, but successfully giving them personalities, however simple they may be."

The judges looked to Athanas and Athenais for their reaction to being called "simple" by their own goddess. The two stayed stone-face.

"It is noted that you know your way around a god eye, and yourself. How is that, exactly?" Jesus asked.

"Two reasons. First, I've studied it extensively in college, which was a goal of mine since was little. Secondly, because I'm a very competitive person and my sister also studied the god eye in school," Athena said. "I couldn't let her surpass me. I always knew one of us would make it here."

Robin and Theodore both, independently of each other, winced as they processed that information. *You can go to school to learn about the god eye?* Robin thought. This further confirmed that there's colleges, high schools, levels of of society outside this show that mirrored Earth. Both were forced to accept that, to understand these characters beyond the myths they dressed as, that they'd need to know more about the world outside the hotel.

"Where did you go to school?" Cthulhu asked.

"Lethe University," Athena said.

"Ah, me too," Jesus clapped. "I promise not to be biased though."

"No, please. Go ahead."

Jesus gave a light chuckle, looked down to her cards, then hid the teeth of her brief smile behind solemn lips. "Let's cut to the chase. I have a lot of problems with this. I feel like this entry is lazy. Not in make, but in creativity."

Athena listened, and squeezed her wrist tight.

"Yes, you put a lot of work into your creations. They are made well. But this is the most predictable thing that I think you, in particular, could have worked on," she continued.

"Hey, what'd Athena make?" Cthulhu snarked. "'Athenians.' Oh, really? Never saw it coming."

"This is representative of the technical skill I bring," Athena countered. Her Athenians sweat, a combination of their nervousness around their simmering god and the natural heat from camera lights.

"It's not the skill that's being questioned," Mohammed rotated. "It's just that you had the whole of Greece to be inspired by, not to mention just using your imagination to make something unpredictable, and instead what we get is... frankly, if I look between the three of you, you all look like family. It's some humans in an armored toga. That's it."

"This is a competition to see the new and interesting ways we can imagine life," Jesus held her hand out, palm open. She then closed it into a fist, "and you just gave us 'Athens 2.0.'"

"Knowing that we feel this way," Cthulhu flipped to a blank notecard and readied his pen. "Is there anything you would be willing to change about your creations?"

Athena's brow caved. After a deep exhale and a permanent indentation of her palm into the opposite wrist, she said, "There is a world within me of gods and magic that these two bright, beautiful humans will get to play in. The skill I have demonstrated today was, by your own admission, the highest level. So, no. I would not change anything because I believe in the framework they will fit in, which is rich in possibility."

The judges noted her answer's nuance and stubbornness. "Thank you, Athena."

Jesus hummed and swayed for a moment, then looked up with wide, excited eyes. "Robin!"

"Yes."

"You're up."

You're up.

Robin went to the pitcher's mound. This was her first pitch in an actual game. Her index and middle fingers gripped perpendicularly across the U-shaped seams in her glove. Though she knew that she should do something more simple for her debut pitch, she refused to play it safe. She wanted to throw the cutter, and that was that. She had worked so hard for so long and it was such a deceptive pitch that she knew the impact just one would make. If she pulled it off and got the batter to miss or foul or pop-out, both teams would have to take her seriously. It didn't matter if she ever threw it again, all she wanted to do was show them that she has a tool that they will have to always consider when against her, making her more difficult to predict and bat against.

Most importantly, she'll get to throw a cutter in a game before Nala. *Watch me, Nala,* Robin thought. And she knew Nala was there, just behind her, guarding second base.

Watch me, Nala.

And she knew that if this was Heaven at all, Nala was there, somewhere, watching over her.

She just had to find her.

Robin looked at the clone of herself, an empty shell that stared at the floor. It did not breath or move, it just existed as a husk for her to fill.

"I had some personal conflict with this challenge," she said. "I am a Christian, and obviously that makes me partial to you and the religion surrounding you." She motioned to Jesus. Jesus's head tilted upwards. This was a silent warning to Robin for her to choose her words wisely.

"But my idea of you, and this place, Heaven, has been fundamentally challenged. I have decided that I cannot turn my back on my own species. I love people and I love improving people's lives. So when I saw the exact wording of this challenge... and I'll quote now," Robin pulled out the sheet of paper that each of the contestants were given on the rooftop of the hotel. Jesus smirked; she found it cheeky that she'd use the show's rules as a prop.

"Create one perceptibly living representative of an award winning species for you to rule over," she folded the paper back into her pocket. "It does not explicitly say that it has to be a brand new, never before invented species. Simply that I have to make a representative of one. I dunno who hands out the awards up here, but I give humans a decent score."

"You made yourself," Cthulhu cut to the point.

"I did. My proposal is to be both human, and god," she nodded. "Or rather, that humanity can take control of its own destiny and spirituality, instead of being torn by what might or might not be real. I believe that the god eye would allow me to unite the people of Earth in a way they have never been before. I can be a diplomat to, and for, humanity. Maybe bring Heaven and Earth closer together through this, as there's clearly a lot I still don't know about this place."

Jesus hummed again, but the melody was quieter, more drawn, with fewer high notes. "So, if I understand this correctly, you're planning on revealing yourself to humans if you become god?"

"Yes."

Mohammed's rectangular form bounced in his seat. "There seems to be a contradiction here. You're taking over as goddess, but you're going to Earth and saying 'Believe in yourself?' Are you not, then, just preaching Atheism?"

"Well, I don't think it's Atheism if they see me as divine. I would be there among them, helping cure famine, diseases, crises of philosophical and physical natures. It would be Theism, but it's a theistic religion that is purely about unity and world-improvement. If anything, I redefining what divinity means for humans."

"They could come to overly rely on you. Your existence solving the world's problems would give them no reason to push themselves, to compete, to advance."

"I thought about that. And I considered something—is there really immortality in Heaven?"

The judges went eerily quiet. Theodore arched an eyebrow and tilted his head towards his fellow human.

"Athena went to college. Oshunmare paints. Santa Inari has a business. Those are just my roommates, I don't know everyone so well yet. But from what little I see, there's still enough risk here in Heaven that a society formed. People don't lounge around and do nothing all day in Heaven, people are working because that's what the mind, at some point and in some way, wants to do. So, I need to know: even with Heaven's ability to heal, can you still die here?"

“Yes,” Jesus admitted, any pretense of a forced smile gone from her face. “Old age and irrelevance, usually. But your lives are much shorter than a god’s, strictly speaking. Time isn’t quite the same here. That’s my beauty secret, for those curious.”

“So even if I win, I can still die eventually. Even if I go down and help Earth as a god, there’s still only so much I can do. If they know... if Earth knows that godhood is attainable but temporary, then couldn’t we bring this show there? Wouldn’t it make sense to have people compete for a good cause, particularly to fill my spot once my time is up?”

“You could easily end up with a destroyed planet, Robin,” Jesus tapped her fingers on the edge of her armrest.

“I imagine that’s always the fear with this sort of power. Still, Heaven stands.”

The judges looked at each other and whispered with their faces under the cover of their notecards.

Ocean-Mouth cleared his throat. “Tell me, Robin, do you believe you’re in the top three, or in the bottom three?”

“I believe...” Robin thought for a moment, “...in this idea.”

Jesus leaned forward and cooed with reassurance, “...and that’s actually why we like your concept. Mohammed and I scored you quite highly.”

Given the heavy air and the offensive nature of the questions she was receiving, Robin was unprepared for praise. She stuck her hands in her pockets, unsure of where to put them.

"It's funny, her entry and Ishta's entry are quite similar, no? Even though both she and Athena made humans, I think you and her ‘Water Collective’ elemental focused the most on tranquility as a unifier,” Jesus said.

Cthulhu shuffled through his notecards and slithered into the side of his chair. "I think the fact yours is a flagrant tie-in to our brand—that takes some balls. I think that alone probably put you over the top."

The obelisk leaned in to piggyback off of Ocean-Mouth's thought. "We have to admit a small bias since you're championing a world we get to be a part of... but there's also something very interesting about your proposal. A goddess directly making themselves apart of 'modern world affairs' on Earth could be quite disastrous or quite successful. It's a very different route from most of the deities here, and it skirts the rules of this challenge to an extent."

Cthulhu stroked his hand through his tentacles. He jumped back in when Mohammed seemed to naturally pause. "Robin... I applaud *only* the provocative aspect of your idea. I graded you lower than the others did because, in the end, I feel you skirted the challenge too much. You must, over the course of this competition, introduce more radical changes to humanity as a whole. I demand creativity from *The Next Great Deity,* and this isn't enough. Not yet."

"I will work on that. Thank you," Robin said.

The batter was able to successfully hit Robin's cutter, but since the ball broke from center and away the sweet spot at the corner of the bat, the ball simply floated to the infield. Nala called it, lined herself up patiently, and caught the pop-up without much effort.

She tossed the ball back to her sister and winked. "Not bad."

The Internet's Evaluation

Only two remained on stage that hadn't been spoken to: Theodore and The Internet. Though The Internet wanted to believe the judges liked his work, there was a new feeling of dread, like a heavy, hot weight in his abdomen, that he had never experienced before. This dog-punk, despite his defensive, rash persona, was capable of being rational, and knew exactly where he stood after his performance.

The weight seemed to spread. It coated his skin and mind when Jesus chirped at him: "Internet, please tell us about what you made today." The dog-punk fiddled with his hat, shifted his jaw, and ran Confidence.EXE.

"Humanity makes a lot of stuff. They play god regularly in labs and nature. I wanted to pursue the idea that their quest for a self learning and understanding artificial intelligence would lead to the creation of a new species, one that builds itself from the discards of humanity's trash. Their origin story is 'the chicken and the egg' told through nuts and bolts."

In the pause that followed, it was Mohammed that spoke first, his rectangular form rotating. "You deserve at least some form of praise for tackling a synthetic sentience. You stood out for that."

There wasn't, however, enough time for The Internet to feel at ease from this faint praise:

"It's hideous," Cthulhu said. A laughed puffed from his chest, blowing his tentacles forward like pet door-flaps. "I'm sorry. This is easily the most unintentionally ugly thing on the stage. It's literal garbage."

The Internet listened, but said nothing. He scanned the history of humans that reacted when they were criticized, and found that lashing out, which he so wanted to do, often just made problems, and perceptions, worse. So now, in this moment of overheated crisis, he managed to show rare restraint.

"And trust me. I get it," Cthulhu didn't, however, let up. "You're tackling both the broader concept of machine intelligence and challenging the arrogance of humanity. That's great. I think you know I'm on board with that. But if a machine designed itself from trash, I don't think it'd make itself look this bad."

Jesus agreed, but spoke sympathetically. "You, like Jarilo, had parts falling off as it moved, but yours came off as even more poorly assembled. I don't think any of us are against your idea, but the presentation was just a mess."

The Internet swallowed. "I accept this and I agree. When I initially designed it I thought that giving it this 'deconstructed' look would make it more intimidating and believable, but I think if I had listened to my gut and made it a bit more symmetrical, I would have saved myself time and ended up with a better looking creature. It was a realization I had too late into the construction."

Theodore smiled and internally applauding The Internet's bullshit. He knew that symmetry was never considered in the original design. But *they* didn't, and what's what mattered.

"Normally we'd ask what you would have done differently, but that's very forthcoming of you to come out and say that," Cthulhu said.

"I also know the presentation was lacking. I think having the creature be more mobile instead of giving a monologue would have been more effective. Hindsight, I would have done that differently for sure."

"It didn't help," Jesus sighed as she flipped through some of her notes. "I wrote down... 'Cringe. Boring. Edgy.'"

"We got a low budget movie trailer," Mohammed said.

"Really amateur, and just a really weird thing to focus on," Cthulhu said. "To an extent I appreciate your attempt at constructing a narrative, but this wasn't the challenge to do it, and even if it was, it didn't work."

"I stand by the heart of it, and I know what execution mistakes that I made. I can correct them and improve, if given the opportunity," Internet said, holding back the want, *the need,* to whimper. "Thank you for your feedback. I am taking it to heart."

"Well then," Jesus glanced to the mustached millennial as she stroked through her beard. "Who's left?"

"We may never know," Theodore shrugged.

"Go ahead, Theodore. Tell us about the jewel-man."

Theodore hated this part, and always had: he hated talking about things he made, about his music, his decisions, himself. He believed in just living, because he worried endlessly that talking too much reveals the worst sides of himself, the unnecessary business of his mind. When he rambled at his SmallSound producer—*No, damnit, Matt would have been my producer if I wasn't dragged here*—about his ideas for music, it was easy because he was talking about larger categories, concepts, other people's creations and his interpretation of them. But to say anything of his own work felt *gross,* as if he had to be dishonest to have an opinion of himself, as if he had to have artifice to be authentic, as if it was a sin to sell, as proclaimed by a god he didn't believe in.

Theodore had a solution for this personal problem: just talk broadly, and divorce yourself from the work. You, in the past, are a different person than you, in the present. You don't know that guy, you just know what he made.

"So the concept was... any truly sentient species has to, at its core, have an adaptive ability in order to advance. With humans, you know, they're soft, they're not the strongest, but they have great minds, and they manipulate the world with them. Thumbs help too, probably."

"And you perceive adaptation via the cloaking ability?" Cthulhu asked.

"That was the idea. This ability is very similar to an octopus. These shiny surfaces are actually a semi-armored hide connected by membrane. It protects the squishy bits inside, and it can slide the different hide segments around significantly and change color, shape, and texture to blend in to its environment, or mimic other creatures. It gives the illusion of full shape-shifting, but it's just a trick to survive in the wild. In some ways, it's actually a rather weak defense mechanism because the quartztaphore can only guide its illusion towards that which it is trying to fool. The illusion is purely two-dimensional, which I'm sure the three of you noticed when you saw the shape-shift happen to your fellow judges."

Jesus leaned in and squinted "How does it see what it's mimicking? It has no eyes."

"The idea was to move further away from more typical Earth biology," Theodore explained. "The decision was to make the membrane be how it interprets its surroundings... its whole body can 'see,' in that regard: it interprets shape and color through light. It's still a little work-in-progress, but the core camouflage is working right, it seems."

Mohammed rested his large, paneled frame diagonally across his chair. "Shape-shifting is firmly in the realm of mythology and magic. Your efforts here are to bring a physical plausibility to a distinctly magic based property. The way you've done it is closer to mimicry than true shape shifting, but when you stop to think that a creature with sentient intelligence can also "mimic" this well... there's a lot of potential for this species, and a lot of unique ways they can develop religiously and culturally. And you gave us a bit of theater, too, which really fleshed the whole thing out."

Theodore was never good at receiving compliments, but it was uniquely difficult to hear them from people whom he knew, in some way he hadn't quite worked out yet, carried ill-intentions. It was its own challenge, he found, to look them in the face, to see the duplicity that formed their being. He was someone so plagued with the need for clarity that it almost made him angry to even have this pretense presented to him. It was his rasher side that thought, *What if I use the god eye to make a gun? What if I set this place ablaze? What if I flooded the hotel itself with exactly the volume of water needed to turn this building into an aquarium?*

That was the cruelest thing about this place, he had learned. A gun does temporary, meaningless damage. Flames are as threatening as the breeze. Water might work but it would also drown out any hope he had of getting back home. He considered throwing the challenge, as had been hinted to him so many times before. But as his suspicions that the foundation of this world and the people in it were lies, he began to suspect that losing, too, would not deliver him. Winning, progressing forward, and dissecting the plans of these dishonest actors was what he decided was most important. The only prize he wanted from *The Next Great Deity,* he realized, was the opportunity to expose it in a way it could never recover from.

Cthulhu pushed his oil-colored glasses up the wet incline of his nose-less face, and though they were covered, Theodore could still make up the vague impression of his pupil-less eyes. "Well, I *really* like this because it's so divorced from what we currently think of as magic. The gods are so bored of paganism and monotheism. The whole spirit of this competition is for a new mythology and I am surprised that such an out-there creation is coming from a human. Imagine the lore of a species whose everyday life is not bound by form! If I have any single complaint is that it doesn't go quite far enough for me. Mohammed likes it because you kept it closer to science, but I think you kept it closer to 'human perception of science.' Remember, you're playing god. You make the rules."

Even when Theodore heard Cthulhu's compliments, they were secondary: the first thing he'd always register now was Ocean-Mouth's sloshing, sneering delivery. They would never be compliments to Theodore. They never could be; they were too finely coated in the saliva of disdain.

"Gotcha," Theodore nodded, but refused to make eye contact.

"I think yours is just the right blend of visual and thought. Of all the contestants, only yours and Imhotep's were entries that we all agreed we liked."

"Thanks," Theodore said, and committed to a nod to fulfill the obligation of interaction.

The Argument

The six returned to the clinically cramped waiting room. They were physically exhausted despite Heaven's healing air, and emotionally drained regardless of their placements.

Jarilo flung himself into the same bean-bag chair he occupied before, still molded from his last impact. This time, though, there wasn't a smile on his face: tears sprang from the corner of his eyes during his hop, and he sobbed into the shifting lump. Csodaszarvas ducked his head down and nuzzled Jarilo's cheek and tried to console him with assuring whispers. It didn't work, and the half-goat bawled.

The three humans that were praised didn't gloat, and instead opted to simply accept and thank the congratulations and applause of their fellow contestants. Imhotep, surprisingly, was the most visibly pleased, his eyes half-lidded with self satisfaction as he sprawled over the armrest of the couch.

The room dissolved into thin chatter. The Internet and Athena sat on opposite couches between their roommates, arms folded, and mirrored each other with their scowls. The Internet receded into the back between Theodore and a lightly strumming Taninim, while Athena tapped her foot with a fire-starting pace between Robin and Ishta-Devata.

Ishta consoled the Greek goddess with back rubs and reassurances. Theodore noticed this, and glanced in his peripheral vision to see The Internet's snout pointed down, his lip quivering like a line on a medical monitor.

"I think you're gonna be fine," Theodore did his best impression of Ishta-Devata.

“Fuck off,” Internet rasped as he held face in his hands. Theodore winced. He tapped his fingers on his chin in thought, leaned forward, and rested his elbows onto his knees to bring his head near Internet’s.

“Listen, man. I know it sucks,” he muttered. The Internet’s wolf-ear tilted towards the sound of his voice. “But I’m not bullshitting you. You fall, you learn, you get back up. That’s life.”

“That’s life?” The Internet kept his eyes hidden in his palm’s darkness. “Why would anyone want that?”

“Well,” Theodore sucked the bottom of his lip for a brief moment. “No one does. No one wants that.”

The Internet lifted himself just enough from his hands to look at Theodore. “Theodore, you’re *terrible* at this.”

The poker player almost laughed. “Yeah. Well, I could bullshit you, but you don’t want that, either, do you?”

The Internet dropped his hands at looked at the human next to him, stupefied.

“No one on Earth, and I’m assuming no one here either, chooses to be born, and they don’t choose how hard their life will be. If given the choice, yes, everyone would choose to win everything every time without repercussions or hardships. Maybe some would even choose not to be born at all. Wouldn’t that be nice? To be given a prompt as a non-entity, just a simple “OK” or “CANCEL” dialogue versus the question ‘Do you want to live a life?’”

Internet furrowed his brow with an intensity that, were he a normal dog, would predate a bite. He wanted to say something like “You have no fucking idea,” but Theodore didn’t give him the chance.

"But that's not how games work. Not everyone gets to win. Especially not this one, where part of the game is appealing to the semi-arbitrary taste of people you may not have anything in common with," Theodore swallowed, his face scrunched up with bitterness. "I'm a foreigner here, you know that. I could easily have been in your position, and I frankly expected to be. I have fucked up in my own life in ways you can't even think of prior to this show, but I lived through them."

"I can think of them," The Internet snarked.

"The point is," Theodore couldn't let negativity stop him. "If anything, from here on out, you are in a better position than I am, because now you've received critical feedback. You can digest it, learn, grow from it, and emerge stronger. Forget this stupid-ass show for a minute. Think about this purely as an opportunity for growth, and what you can take from it to make a better 'You.' This isn't the end, no matter what they say here. I'm telling you this because I only care about what's real. No bullshit. If you can find joy in something that makes the noise of everyone else's opinions fade away, well, that's real. That's what people live for. And with the way you were knocking out all those parts, it seemed to me like you were having fun, weren't you? Even if it was just for a minute."

The Internet tilted his head and stared at the floor. After some time, he just nodded. "Yeah. Maybe," and eventually, in small, cracked voice, "...thanks."

"Must feel great to get praised for plagiarism," she said.

In unison, Theodore and The Internet looked up to see where the tone-shift came from, as did the rest of the room's occupants. Athena and Robin had locked eyes. Ishta-Devata mouthed "No, don't," and pulled at Athena's shoulder to guide her away from confrontation.

"Excuse me?" Robin leaned back in the couch and let it take the weight of her indignation. Taninim stopped noodling his guitar with an awkward plunk, the final noise to get killed in the room.

"You heard me," Athena's arms and legs were crossed tight, chained with vitriol.

"Yeah, I just wanted to make sure you were actually *that* wrong."

"Please, stop, both you," Ishta pleaded. The shiqqs repositioned to get the most dramatic angles.

"I just think it's interesting," Athena twined a finger around one of the curls that had come loose from her bun. "That I started making humans, then you make humans after you saw what I was doing. Then you're the one that gets praised even though my work was made more competently *and* with more originality."

"Jealousy isn't cute, girl."

"So you're not going to deny it?"

"You were on the same stage as me. You heard my reasons."

"Yeah, the middle aged Christian lady just randomly decided to try and take away religion from Earth."

"You're getting real personal with me, honey, and I dunno if you want to do that."

Everyone exchanged wide-eyed looks of shock and excitement, minds off, reactions on fire. Everyone except The Internet, who found his fingers slowly interlacing in front of his snout, where he brought his wolf chin to rest. He didn't just see two personalities quarreling, and he went into such deep examination that he stopped moving altogether. He could have been confused for a sculpture, were it not for his scanning, typewriter like eyes.

The Internet searched itself.

All his cell-dogs committed themselves to scanning through the archives of humanity's reality TV, comparing the actions of other foul acting reality show contestants to Athena's. He looked at their early antagonism, and their relative placement in the shows they belonged to. If the show had a wiki, he could search it. If it had clips, he could scan them. And with his processing power, he could complete it in a brief minute, invisible to his fellow competitors (unless they already knew to look for the moments of distant stillness in his body language.)

Athena started this feud, one cell-dog whispered to another. *She didn't have to.*

I wouldn't say they were friends, but this seems unprovoked, another cell-dog floated by as it binged on every season of *Survivor* as quickly as possible.

She's making herself look bad, another cell-dog noted as he studied an image composite of Athena's many expressions, all various shades of brow-falling irritation. More and more cell-dogs debated, compared notes, contemplated, and fought over an understanding of Athena's actions.

It's a trick! A cell-dog shouted as it slammed its cell-fist into its cell-chalkboard. The mass of the dog-punk's intelligence turned towards it.

She's trying to be a villain!

She's planned this from the beginning!

Athena, speaking just in terms of Earth's mythology, is a war strategist: she wouldn't pick fights like this without a meaningful goal, A nervous cell-dog in charge of studying historical figures said. As he continued his hypothesis, he began to work himself up into a teeth-gnashing frenzy. *And a reality show cast must have a villain to divide them, and feed...*

Feed the...

The "narrative!" A different dog grabbed the temples of his head in revelation as he ran through a long list of successful reality TV villains. *With someone to root against, the show keeps viewers! The longer a hated contestant stays, the more anxious an audience gets anticipating their elimination!*

The cell-dogs moshed together in barking, foaming argument.

She wants to be the villain!

The villain!

No! She is just a contestant like anyone else, she has friends here, look at Ishta.

Yes! Look at her arrogance, the judges must keep her to have a villain!

Not just any "villain", you idiot, HER villain!

Whose villain?

The human!

The humans?

She targeted the human girl! Robin!

Humans are always the goddamn heroes, a fat cell-dog kicked over a cell-waste bin. *That one wears Jesus's jewelry. She's probably just in their favor because Jesus knows she can use her later, it has nothing to do with their work. She is expendable.*

Like us.

Robin is useful, and expendable, like we are useful, and expendable.

No.

No.

No.

We will not be used. No.

No.

No.

NO.

We will use them.

Villains can still get eliminated early. What matters is context, the cell-dogs whispered and held hands and passed energy and data all throughout The Internet's body. *Her role is only secure if she is the antagonist of the show's anointed hero. We must change her target.*

Every cell was now linked in agreement.

Initiate:

"Athena, grow up. You made bad work and landed in the bottom. Get over it."

When The Internet finally spoke, he did so from deep within the recess of the back of the couch. He lazed into its cushions, his head depressed forward to bring his chin to his chest. He spoke with bored dismissiveness, and it was the delivery, more than the content of what he said, that brought a twitch to Athena's right eye.

She unhooked her crossed arms, as did Robin. The room's wide-eyed stare shifted to the dog-punk.

"She plagiarized me," Athena pointed to Robin.

The Internet may have shrugged, but internally, the cell-dogs of his head rubbed their polygonal hands together eagerly. *You're talking about Robin, but your eyes are on me.*

"Do you have a problem with listening? Are you even listening to *yourself*? If your work is so similar to her's, and her lack of creativity was something you didn't like... then it really is boring, isn't it? What you made, I mean."

Even if you are some war strategist... in my head is the history and results of every reality show ever made on earth. I know your plan, Athena!

Athena leaned onto an elbow and redirected her finger to The Internet. "How would you feel if-"

"No, listen," The Internet would not allow her to guide the conversation back to Robin. As long as he was in there, she would not be the focus. "I'm in the bottom too, I'm not blaming anyone else. I don't have to worry about someone being similar to me because even if I didn't make my bot-dude as well as I could have,

I had a better idea in the end. I can fix my time management. Can you fix your *originality?*"

"You had the worst presentation and the worst execution, if you want to go there, puppy," Athena snarled. "How are you going to fix anything if you get sent home?"

In any other situation, her words might have hurt. There was certainly truth there. But after her incendiary question, her toothy pride melted into a tight-lipped realization, and it dissolved completely when she noticed just the ends of The Internet's lip line creep up.

That's right, Athena, he thought. *You just made yourself my adversary in the bottom. You thought a storyline rivalry between yourself and Robin would grant you safe passage through, and you were probably right... but the camera's on us now. You just gave the judges a sound bite that they can use for ironic foreshadowing to send you home. You also just gave me a storyline by acknowledging my failure is fixable with time, which protects me further, and leaves Jarilo more open to be eliminated over us both.*

The Internet folded his arms behind his head and stretched. Inside, his cell-dogs slapped sparking high-fives, clanked pints of electric energy, and cheered themselves on.

If I accomplish nothing else in my time here, then let this last act of mine signal to everyone the true nature of the bullshit I've figured out. It's the story.

"If I get a second chance..." The Internet released the sigh in his lungs with a relaxed tenor that didn't match the terror someone on the chopping block should feel. "I won't worry about other people's work. I'll just do my best. And if I do get eliminated, I at least won't look as bad as you do right now."

The most important thing is the story.

Athena's face soured, and she mulled over how to guide the conversation back to Robin. When she began to open her mouth, a crackling plasma interrupted her. Jesus's portal opened, and the six contestants were called back for their final judgment. The hot-blooded, voltaic pressure from Athena and The Internet's silent war was palpable among the room as they each marched into the swirling blue energy.

Judgement, Part 1

The would-be deities on trial line up in front of the judges. Few sounds dripped; the only thing to hear in the dark, void-like place was the sluggish slosh of the shiqqs as they oozed into position. Theodore had a love affair with most ambient sounds, but the gurgle of the shiqqs unsettled him.

"Contestants," Jesus took a stilted pause. "You have been judged." The marked difference between her chipper proclamations of the challenges and her bland recital of her catch phrases were impossible to miss now. The holy hostess turned her head.

"Robin," she said. Every camera pointed towards the human woman and zoomed in hard to capture the pores of her reaction. Jesus stretched her dramatic pause. Her eyebrows lifted with the heat of drama. It lasted so long that the English teacher's eyes started to wander, unsure of where the rest of the sentence had escaped to.

"We still have faith in you." And that was it. A portal opened in front of her.

Robin didn't know what to do, whether to smile or frown, where to put her hands or what to say to those around her. She made something she was sure that Jesus—the real Jesus, the one that helped her grow up, survive college, remain strong through her sister's death, through her divorce—would see the respect and care she had for humanity. Robin endured the other gods, the absurdity of Heaven, and the invasive nature of the talent agents. She did so with the pretense that this moment would be the pay off. That Jesus would congratulate her for making the one thing that protected her fellow man, for being the one good Christian among a den of monsters.

Instead, she was just safe. She just continues, as she always had. She gave a reluctant nod to the judges, then moved into the portal. The rest of the girls congratulated her: Oshunmare, Ishta-Devata, Santa Inari. But when Ishta took her hand, she clasped it between her own soft blue palms and trembled.

"Something wrong, my dear?" Ishta asked.

Robin shook her head, then leaned in to Ishta's ear.

"Why are there almost no dead people in Heaven?" she worried. "Where are the normal people?"

"We *are* the normal people," Ishta-Devata frowned. Robin shook. She stared at the illusionist and hoped to see a change in her facial expression that would indicate she was kidding, or that she was wrong, or that she was a dream, or that she, too, was an enemy that she could project her anger towards.

All she saw was Ishta.

She knew, then, that she would never see Nala again.

She knew, then, that no one else was looking out for humanity.

She knew, then, that her belief system had been killed, betrayed by the one it should have appealed to the most.

She didn't cry, or have a crisis, or anything so dramatic. Lightheaded from the rollercoaster of the events, she simply sat down next to Ishta, and rubbed her eyes.

"I'll change that," she said.

Back on the show floor, Theodore looked side-to-side between the contestants, down the line of worry and anger to his left, and then the slightly wafting confidence of Imhotep to his right.

Jesus, with the charisma of a disinterested high school cheerleader in front of her math homework, read her prepared praise of the remaining human's creations. She shifted in her seat and mouthed a prayer, though it's unclear who a god would seek strength from.

"Theodore."

Theodore rocked on the balls of his feet.

"You are the winner of this challenge!" She smiled and forced all her teeth into the spotlight.

Theodore, quite unintentionally, burst out laughing with the cadence of a blown out tire. There was applause of varying levels of enthusiasm from the judges and fellow contestants, which would help mask his cry-laughter ever so slightly when the clip was sent later to the editors. He was unprepared for victory, and if he had any read on Jesus's facial structure at all, there was some bitterness there: behind the pulled back muscles was a woman unhappy to congratulate the Atheist in Heaven.

Robin, in defeat, was never more convinced about the dishonesty of the proceedings. Theodore felt the same way about his victory.

"Uh, thanks," he managed to finally choke out through his hyena wheezing.

When he appeared through the portal, the waiting contestants leaned towards him, as did the lumpy appendages of the shiqq's camera arms. "Guess I should tell you: I won?" he shrugged, and was immediately swamped by a congratulatory, back-slapping hug from Taninim, whose strong grip pushed all the wind out of his lungs. Zargah, only after his collar translated the event well enough that he felt like he knew what was going on, pat the human's head like a cat and messed up Theodore's combed back hair.

Imhotep joined them shortly thereafter after the judges gave him their nod of approval. He congratulated Theodore briefly, but when their eyes locked, it wasn't respect that Theodore felt. It wasn't animosity either. It unnerved him, but Theodore was sure that the look he just received was the same one he experienced behind the sunglasses of so many gamblers he had met in the past.

Imhotep could see the same study in Theodore's face. The two, for that one easily missed moment, mirrored each other in quiet scrutiny, and acknowledged each other as competitors.

Mark Sharkman sat with his legs folded into his rolling chair. The lavender-suited creator had chosen not to sit opposite of him. Instead, he immediately started to pace upon his arrival in the Camera World.

Mark held out his hand and said, "Looks like it's time to interview the big winner, huh?" There was resigned weariness to Mark; one that, Theodore thought, lingered from their last interaction. When he considered how time worked in Mark's room, he knew that that couldn't be the case, and wondered if Mark even remembered their last quarrel at all.

Similarly, Mark's line of questions were surprisingly bland and passionless; they left blank, concise spaces for Theodore to express his thankfulness and happiness. Since Theodore was barely either, and couldn't talk further about his real feelings of the show without setting off red flags, Mark didn't pry further. Not for the interest of character development, not for the interest of story, and not for himself to learn anything new about the first challenge winner.

He flicked a switch on the console beside him, which sent the whirring cameras into their powered down state. *Now* Theodore cared about what Mark had to say: an interest that increased when the interviewer struggled to say anything at all. There were no wine glasses or bottles, his office desk was unusually organized, the whole room was cleaned with an obsessiveness that was wholly out of place for Mark up until that point.

"I, um, uh, ugh," Mark rubbed the creased skin on his brow, played with the fin near the back of his head nervously, and did anything so as to not look at Theodore. "I want to apologize."

Theodore squinted.

"I am still unconvinced, Theodore, by your little tantrum earlier. I went to college, we get your books and movies and media. That's..." the shark struggled, and when he looked up into Theodore's unimpressed, unflinching face, he knew... "That's not it." That's not what he wanted to say. What he *should* say.

"Then, what is it?"

Mark looked around the room and hoped that maybe he'd find strength hidden in one of its cold corners.

"I lied," he swallowed. "I lied to my boss."

Theodore shrugged. "Okay."

"I never lie! Oh, what have I done?" he grabbed the sides of his head. "I am so nervous about the actions of The Internet, the motives of the judges, the... no. No, what convinced me was my editor. My editor is a good man, I've worked with him for ages. He contacted me. He contacted me and wanted to know who I brought up my suspicions about The Internet with."

Theodore popped a knuckle idly on his hand. "So they're concerned about whether we know he's a plant?"

"No, No, No," Sharkman's hands circled themselves. "I mean, yes, they want to know, but they are looking for interview segments. Moments where it's discussed on camera. And the request to investigate this came from production. If The Internet so bluntly told me this, he might tell other people. He'll *probably* tell other people. I think production wants to manipulate this into a potential storyline."

Theodore tapped his lip with the rhythm of his thoughts. "Well, they won't have to worry about any of that if he gets eliminated. He's out there right now in the bottom. Unless they plan on just letting him progress in the competition no matter what he does. Would they do that?"

Mark crumpled back into his desk and hid his face in his folded arms. "I don't know. I don't know what any of this means. It just scares me that there's this... layer of power above me that might be toying with me. With you. With all of us."

"So don't feel bad anymore about lying to them. Trust goes both ways," Theodore smiled. He thought that'd calm Mark a bit, but it didn't. Sharkman laid with his head buried in his own arms. After a few moments of awkward silence, the interviewer considered sending Theodore away with a tooth-click to avoid talking about this further. Theodore chewed over his thoughts, shook his head, and spoke up: "I beat the shit out of a guy."

Mark looked up. "W-what?"

"Just absolutely rearranged his face. Kind of amazing he didn't die. Oh, you wanted to know what I did, right? Earlier. Way earlier. You wanted to know what's on my record. That's it. I just fucked up some kid's life for no reason other than I didn't like his face. I was a kid too, I guess I should mention. 16, I think. Though I feel like I stopped being a kid shortly after the first fist."

"You... didn't like his face?"

"Yeah. I thought he looked like a fag. Pretty ironic now, all things considered, because he had a *real* nice face."

Mark, even with his nearly immobile jaw, was visibly uncomfortable. He shrunk into the back of his chair. "You *really* shouldn't say stuff like that. Why are you telling me all this?"

"You're right. I shouldn't. I also shouldn't have done stuff like that either, but I did, and that's who I was then, and that's a way bigger problem than you hearing me slur," Theodore kept eye contact despite Mark's offended exhale. As he saw the Shark sit up, he knew he was reaching him. "That's the problem—I didn't tell anyone shit, I bottled myself up and rained down my fists on someone that didn't deserve it. And you know the worst part is? I got fined."

"Theodore... I think the kid you beat up had a worse time than you getting fined..."

"He did. That's my point."

"Huh?"

"I live with the fact every day that I got off easy. Third degree assault in New York could result in jail time, probation, a huge fine, all three if they wanted. I looked it up. But the kid had long hair, I played football, and the judge went to my church. And I hate it. I *hate* that I wasn't punished. Not really, at least. When all I got was the minimum fine—and let's be real, it was my *parents* that got the fine, not me—I felt more wrong than I did when I looked down at a boy I just fucking wrecked because he was something I thought you could never be."

Mark's stomach churned. He didn't know what to say.

"So, I thought you should know. I don't have a darker secret than that to tell you. I don't talk about it because I grew up and I'm a different person in a different world. You feel me, man? You did something crazy today, risked your job to do what you thought was right. I just want you to know that you don't have feel bad about it, because it can always be worse. I'm in. I trust you. If you trust me too, I'm willing to work with you to pull the mask off this place," Theodore sat down opposite of Mark, with a calmness he had never gifted to the shark-man before. He met Mark's hunched posture to keep their eyes at the same level. "The way I see it, any system that thinks I can be a god after what I've done is worth disassembling."

Mark rubbed the back of his neck and made worried humming noises for a long time, then spun out of his chair and raced to a mechanical console.

"What are you doing?"

"Trusting you," Mark as he shoved the heavy panel to the side. It ground against the floor, and revealed a safe in the wall. He snapped his wirst with each dial spin, unlocked the thick door, and pulled piles upon piles of manila folders, each stuffed with an impossible amount of detailed notes on the contestants and judges. "This is everything I have, thus far. It includes habits, conversations, facial expressions, frequent places of travel... it's a lot. I reckon you have four hours of Camera World time approximately before someone thinks that maybe you've been staring at the floor for a few seconds longer than is reasonable, if they're even looking at you. It's tough to gauge that sort of thing, truthfully, so it's give or take a few hours."

"What the fuck," Theodore blinked rapidly as he read through the stack of files. "This is amazing shit. Wait, I scratch my neck after I drink something? I take longer to respond in casual conversation than in inquiry? I look to the left .25 centimeters when I'm nervous? How long have you been doing this? Mark... I... fuck. I play poker, and I can't keep a straight face looking at this. Do you know how amazing this shit is?"

Mark scratched his neck. "Ah, you know. Documenting stuff is my job."

Judgement, Part 2

Then, there were three. Three would-be gods whom saw their future hang in the palms of people that didn't like or want their work, and by extension, them. These three stood like a diagram of stages of grief in their standing order. There was Jarilo, who held back a dam of tears behind his stunned face; Athena, whose brow rumpled with anger that her work was so misunderstood; and The Internet, who kept his muzzle pointed to the ground and wanted to disappear and not face the responsibility of his awful performance.

But as terrified as he was of his elimination, there was hope within the dog-punk that he had not felt in his life yet. On his own he had assessed the situation, compared what was happening to other works within the genre of reality TV, and made a power play at the only element he had any control over—his place in the story.

It was out of his hands now.

"If you want the life you see burned into your cells, you have to win this competition," Jesus had explained to The Internet when he was first checked in at Heaven's Heart Hotel. This was the treatment he received from his new creator: passive indifference as he was dragged around the bureaucracy of the show. He had so many questions about life that he cried out to her, and the further she ignored him, the louder his cries grew, the more unintelligent his questions became, until they eventually dissolved into wordless whimpers. He was fooled. He thought her first smile was for him. But as he listened to her, he began to understand her smile was for herself.

"You must earn your life, like anyone else," she had said while checking her nail polish.

As if I'm like anyone else. Fuck you, The Internet resisted growling as he regressed back into his brief memory. *You made me, you bitch.*

"Jarilo," the Jesus standing in front of him said. The Internet had ventured so far into his memory that the mother-of-his-birth and the line-reading actress in front of him briefly melted into the same moment. His cell-dogs frantically worked to calibrate his senses to ignore the memory—because this was it. This is what mattered. This was his moment of truth.

"We still have faith in you," Jesus smiled. Jarilo crumpled onto his knees, his hands and face soaked in his own overwhelmed emotions.

The Internet's ears flattened. A cell-dog in his chest pulled the red alert alarm, and most of his cells started screaming. This was The Internet's equivalent of a flood of panicked adrenaline.

Athena sighed through her nose and glanced at The Internet, whom had not moved in a while. His ears stiffened, his snout pointed frozen to the floor.

Athena was determined she'd stay for a few reasons. She knew her work was demonstrably stronger than anyone else's, she had the credentials and popularity few of the other contestants did—*Of course the people of Earth know about me*! she thought—but most importantly, she had to use the resources here to locate Eris.

In her spare time, Athena had developed a small device designed to hone in on her bloodline, and it shook the closer anyone with Olympian blood got to it. It rattled violently in her hand. Ishta helped test it, and proved that it did, in fact, ping softer when further away from Athena. She surmised that this would allow Ishta, or anyone else that wasn't Athena, to locate Eris if she were in Heaven's Heart Hotel. And Athena could feel it. She knew. *She knew* Eris was here, somewhere, and her tests proved it. The rattle never died completely when not held in Athena's hand. They tested a duplicate of this device with Ishta's blood, and found that her device would eventually stop when far away enough from the Hindu princess. All she had to do was survive in the show, and find where in Heaven Eris had been taken.

"You two had the lowest scores," Jesus rose from her chair. "And now, you will be judged."

Athena straightened her posture, while The Internet's hung head seemed to melt further into his chest. Jesus's hair started to float with energy, lifting almost directly above her.

"Athena."

Sparkling energy drew towards Jesus's middle finger and thumb on each hand. She snapped her fingers, and with the pop of a firecracker, a huge portal exploded in front of Athena—and a smaller one, simultaneously, in front of The Internet.

Athena looked in and saw a bland, yellowed hallway. She did not know where, or what, this place was.

"I'm sorry, we've lost faith in you."

The Internet couldn't believe it. He thought for sure Athena would be the first one called out, and that it'd be between himself and Jarilo for elimination. When Jarilo had been given safe passage, he had lost almost all hope that his attempt at controlling the narrative had worked.

"Hey," he said. "I learned something valuable from earlier. I'm really into this now," he glanced at her purely out of respect. Her wide-eyed stare indicated she was still struggling with her expectations falling short of her new reality. "Thank you, Athena. I learned something important today."

With a single leap, he was gone. He joined his fellow competitors on the other side and found himself unprepared for the comfort of surprised arms of the boys in 35-D. Held there and congratulated by his roommates, he felt a warmth he didn't quite know how to place.

Ishta-Devata's lip quivered as she held the small gold and brass device in her palm—she could not have foreseen this outcome with her particular brand of clairvoyance, and it frustrated her to no end. She looked over to a tight-lipped, head-shaking Robin, and began to form a new plan. She leaned over and whispered something in her ear.

Back on *The Next Great Deity's* main stage, Athena cleared her throat. She had one final request, and since the reactions of the recently defeated always make good television, the judges were more than happy to hear it.

"Can you tell me, do any of you know a Greek goddess named Eris? Did she try out for this show? Did you invite her?"

Jesus turned to Cthulhu, eyebrows raised. He shook his head in confusion; when a contestant gets eliminated, they expect them to thank the judges for their time or, at worst, argue with them. This was different.

"I'm sorry?" Ocean-Mouth adjusted his glasses.

"My sister!" Athena grew more visibly frustrated. "She was accepted, she received the same letter that I did, then she vanished! Please, if you didn't invite her, then that means someone is pretending to be you!" In a panic, Athena began to use her ability to summon her, and her sister's, invitationals. "Look, I have the letters!"

"You... you should go to the police if you think your sister is missing, you know," Mohammed tilted forward.

"I'm sorry," Jesus tried to say in a consoling, motherly voice, but her annoyed brow betrayed her. "I've never heard of her, and I'm sorry that you were so clearly distracted by this. It's not going to change our decision."

"No, no, wait," Cthulhu lifted his hand. "My dear, you're in distress. If what you say is true, then it does pose a problem for us. This isn't the sort of press we really aim for here, after all."

"It *is* true, dammit!" Athena was not in distress. She was angry.

Jesus turned to Ocean-Mouth and shot him an incredulous, teeth-baring stare. He waved a finger that silently begged for patience. "You said you have the invitations?"

Athena concentrated, and the loose bits of her metal armor shook from an invisible force. She produced the two letters in a golden flicker, one in each hand.

Cthulhu marveled, noting that Athena didn't use her god eye at all in the process of this magic. Athena explained, quite proudly, how her bloodline is connected to the Olympian Estate, where all the Greek gods were born, just off the coast of Purgatory. There is a vault that anyone in the family can summon objects from, or store objects too: But Eris has not used this vault since her disappearance.

"Never in my life, and I have lived for a long time," Athena curled her fist, "has a force kept an Olympian from their connection to the vault. I know you three are the most powerful and popular gods in Heaven. And I know that you know that at one time, my people sat where you are. So please, as one goddess to another, *please* help me."

"You're no longer a goddess," Jesus gripped her armrests. "No one believes in you anymore, and you have lost."

"No, Jesus, shh, shh," Cthulhu cooed, which just made Jesus angrier. She rose and marched over to Cthulhu's chair. He stood up, and the two glared, faces inches apart.

"What! Are! You! Doing!" Jesus hissed.

Ocean-Mouth leaned in to her ear. "What The Producer wants. This could help us narrow things down. Give me a moment."

Though she looked on in disbelief, she allowed Ocean-Mouth to slip down from the Judge's seats and take Athena in hand.

Together, they went into the portal. On the other side, they emerged in a bland yellowed hallway free of shiqq cameras, staff, and anything that resembled the design or life of the hotel's customer-facing interior. The speckled, polished floor had seen more cleaning chemicals in its time than the shoes of passersby.

"If we turn left, here, we'll go towards the exit of the hotel," Cthulhu said. "But I want to help you. It just so happens that there's a book with guest signatures kept by security—I'm typically very well informed on what's going on, but just in case we missed something, lets go pay them a visit. Shall we?"

"That..." Athena paused. She wanted to be thrilled, but still too stunted and exhausted from the proceedings of the elimination to show much in the way of emotion on her chiseled face, "...is great, thank you."

"Can I see your invitations, my dear?"

He took the letters and slid them between his index and middle fingers, then walked over to a speaker roughly the size of an electrical outlet. He pressed the only button on it, which audibly dialed out a series of tones. "Sometimes antiqued technology doesn't need an upgrade," he explained, his tentacles forming the beginnings of a smile.

"Whoa, hey, haven't heard this channel for a bit," a static-covered voice faded in and out of the speaker. "Ritst speaking. Who's this?"

"Hello, good sir. It's your favorite employer."

A series of clanking and tumbling could be heard. A door slammed.

"H-hey, Mr. Cthulhu," Ritst said in his best imitation of someone that wasn't surprised. "How can I help you?"

"I need your shifting services for a bit. I'm in..." he lowered his oil-like sunglasses and peered about the hallway. There was no placarded or sign, but Cthulhu seemed to know exactly where they were, "...2-R. Shift to the center, please."

"Directly to the heart?"

"Yes."

Before Athena could ask what "The Heart" was, Cthulhu had already turned back to her. He showered her with praise, but just over one thing: her ability to summon items from her bloodline's vault.

"You might not think that's special compared to the creation-power of a god, but I think it's remarkable. You should be proud."

It seemed, to Athena, that the hallway started spinning. She was not necessarily wrong, but the extra-dimensional warp and rotation was a little more complex than just "spinning"—a nuance that likely mattered little to her as she succumbed to vertigo.

"I imagine, even if it's in your bloodline, you had to work hard to will it out of you, yes?" Cthulhu was at home in the warp, hands held calmly behind his back, feet planted firmly to the ground. "To cultivate it, to make it yours. A god eye, by comparison, is lazy and fanciful, and forces the user to play by its rules, never progressing beyond what you're able to weasel out of it. It's a nice indulgence, but I have a particular respect for abilities born of blood and sweat. You have so much more control over your own power than you do that which was given as a gift. That's a wonderful thing."

The room returned to a stationary existence. Athena rose from her hands and knees, panting and sweating.

"Is this... how you remove the god eye from someone?" Athena tried to comb some of her sweat-stuck hair from her forehead..

"What? Oh, no, my dear! It already left you when you stepped through the portal earlier. You didn't notice at all, did you? No, what you just experienced was the ability of my editor, Ritst. He, like you, has something quite remarkable—he can attach one of his shed scales inside something inanimate, then move it around by will. When I found out about his ability, I knew he would be particularly good at security. There are places here that are virtually inaccessible without him twisting the hallways for you, you see. Come. This way."

Athena tried to regain control of her breath and ignore the drums of her pounding heart rate. The hallway looked exactly the same as before, as did every other hallway afterward on their walk—blank, clinical yellowed walls with plastic air and fluorescent lights. She couldn't believe they had moved anywhere at all, until a few turned corners later when they came to a dead end.

At the end of the hallway was the most plain, unembellished door in all of Heaven's Heart Hotel.

"Here we are," Cthulhu said. "Security."

Athena eagerly started to walk forward, but realized that the only sounds of footsteps were her own. At that exact moment, Cthulhu called out to her.

"Wait! Before we go in, something's been bothering me."

She turned to see Ocean-Mouth was staring at the two invitations, one in each hand. His face tentacles pulsed with curiosity for a few seconds. Abruptly, he shoved Athena's invitation into his mouth; the tentacles ripped and slobbered on the loud, crumbled stationery.

"What are you doing?!" Athena snapped.

Cthulhu shoved the other paper into his mouth as well, his face tentacles in a frenzy to coat it in his thick saliva and suck it up.

"We need those! We need to show those to security so that they know someone's impersonating your show!"

Cthulhu burped. "Whuf. Excuse me. You're right, these are different from each other, subtly so. Your invitation is newer. Eris's was much, much older. I have a keen taste for the flavor of time."

Athena's teeth ground like a chainsaw, began to march forward. Whatever her protests were would never be known—her hard expression evaporated to paralyzed pain as three blurring white business cards stabbed into her back. She immediately fell forward, and her mouth drooled and frothed. She was unable to move.

"You know what's funny? We tell everyone the card can only teleport you if you have a desire to lead a world. No one ever considers the paralysis is a completely separate symptom," Cthulhu tsked and squatted next to the immobilized Olympian. "I may not have enjoyed your incredibly boring point of view, my dear, but I love your resolve. You would have made a better employee than a contestant."

Athena's hand trembled, as if it was trying to lift a great unseeable weight. A golden spear sparked to life beside her, but try as she might, she was unable to secure her grip on it, much less lift herself up.

"For example! Goodness. Strong women are terrifying."

The weight of the card's magic was not the only unseeable thing lodged into her. The cards themselves had long, transparent tendrils attached to them. They were only visible if you knew to look for the floating lines that disturbed the air like a shimmering heat wave. The business cards were a guide for them, and they secured themselves around Athena and started to pull her towards the now open door at the end of the hallway.

"Sadly, as fond as I am of your will, production is, apparently, familiar with whoever this 'Eris' person is. You see, the winner of *The Next Great Deity* certainly will get to rule as a god... but yours is far from the only competition taking place. And this must be an incredible clue you've given us, because The Producer just whispered in my ear to take care of you the moment Eris's name left your lips. I'd cheat and try to keep you alive to get more information if I could, but, sadly, I know he's always watching us. Even here, beyond the shiqqs. I'm helpless to save you, dear. What The Producer says, goes."

Athena clawed weakly, and her saliva left a trail as she began to disappear behind the door's plain frame.

"Normally Jesus, our..." he smacked his tongue sarcastically, "...glorious... leader takes care of getting rid of contestants when The Producer demands it. But he wants no trace of you, no chance of Eris's name traveling any further, and I am uniquely qualified for that task. I'm sorry, my dear, but my talent agents are hungry, and theirs is a hunger that Heaven can't fix."

The door slammed shut. Cthulhu cringed as he heard the wet and violent rip of flesh and bone. He quickly produced some earbuds from his pocket and cranked the volume up on his cell phone, and let the asymmetrical grooves of Theodore's unreleased music drown out Athena's murder.

Athena's Tracker

Athena's tracker went cold in Ishta-Devata's palm, no longer detecting anyone from the Olympian bloodline within the pendant's maximum range. She swallowed and shook, her core tranquility destroyed by the fact that, had Athena returned home, she would have taken the tracker with her. The bloodline ability was like a lingering smell when attached to the object, allowing them control over it for some considerable time even when not in contact. But it remained in her hand for much too long. It was Ishta's now, and it was her responsibility to keep up the search.

The contestants were congratulated on their successful completion of the first challenge by a hologram of Jesus, prerecorded for convenience's sake. They were instructed to follow the shiqqs back to their rooms, get plenty of rest in the eight hour break they had, then get ready for their next challenge.

As they gathered and poured out the room, Robin hung back near the end of the line with Theodore. Ishta stayed just ahead to listen.

"Hey," Robin said in a low voice, walking in pace with Theodore. "Congratulations."

"Thanks. It's nuts, and it got me to thinking," Theodore looked around for cameras pointing at his mouth, then turned his face towards her shoulder. "What if this thing is rigged for us?"

"Are you saying you want to do the rest of the show now that you won a challenge?"

"No," he shook his head. "I'm saying I want to be a little more adventurous with how we investigate behind the scenes, and frankly, if they like us, we can take advantage of that. I've made some cool progress, I snuck a mic into my..."

Robin stepped in front of him and put a hand on his chest. Theodore stopped, "What?"

She looked down at the ground. "Why did you help The Internet?"

Theodore blinked. "He needed it, and I could."

She looked up, judgment in her eyes. "He's a monster."

"He's just a guy like anyone else."

"Not based off what you know about him."

Theodore winced and thought about his quarrel with Mark. "I feel like I keep having this conversation. Look, ignore the teenage angst for a minute. If anything, being on his good side just makes more sense, because we can learn about this place—"

"No."

Theodore put his hands in his pockets, his face addled.

"Theodore, he threatened *humanity* in his presentation. And the judges didn't kick him out right then and there."

"What?"

"If our demands are not met, then we will take Earth, instead, as demonstrably more capable handlers of its land. This is non-negotiable," she quoted.

"You're assuming a lot about the validity of this place's prizes if you think he's a threat," Theodore scoffed.

"Theodore, a woman that was willing to take any risk to find her sister is gone now. They killed Athena."

Theodore blinked. "...How? And how do you know that?"

"I don't know. I don't know! I don't know what this place is!" Robin paced in a furious circle, then returned to Theodore, stabbing a finger into his chest. "But I know this: I trust a woman searching for her family over whatever this bullshit is."

"I do, too—"

"Do you? Then why are you helping the humanity-hating monster? And then you just conveniently win the first challenge despite claiming to be an atheist? Do atheists typically want to be god?"

He adjusted the lapel of his suit. "I'm sorry. Are you accusing me of working for the show?"

"I'm telling you..." Robin kept stabbing her finger into Theodore's chest with the rhythm of her torn heart. "I'm telling you that I don't know you and I don't trust you and humanity is too important to me to lose it over the half-thought out gamble you're taking. Between you and Ishta, I have seen who is more interested in protecting people. You need to decide what you actually want to do here. We both think this place is fake, but only one of us stood up for what is *real* today."

Theodore bristled, but said nothing. Robin couldn't look him in the eyes, so she just turned and walked away to where she knew, just around the corner, was Ishta listening in. Theodore didn't try to stop her, but he did say, "This isn't half thought out. Talk to me again when you're ready to get to work."

She looked at him one last time, grimaced, then left. He rubbed his temple and stared at the ceiling, wondering how on earth he fucked up so badly as to alienate the only other verifiable earthling on the show.

"God dammit. If this isn't the most reality show bullshit that could have happened."

Mark Sharkman's "Break"

Mark Sharkman technically didn't get breaks, because anything captured by the shiqqs could be useful for the show, and at any time he could come up with the perfect narrative focused question for a contestant. His "breaks," as they were, only exist because of the slowed-down time in the Camera World.

Fortunately for the interviewer, he was given considerable reprieve in between challenges. While contestants could remain awake, they rarely did, and if they did, the idle chit-chat and downtime during these segments was often redundant or useless for narrative purposes. For Mark, even though he was still locked away in the time chamber of his world, he was largely free to relax, drink, read from his library, catch up on movies—anything already contained within the strange microscopic light world he worked in was fair game. This, he thought, must be what being "on-call" was like at a normal job.

He still monitored the contestants closely, but found little of importance during this time to compile in his contestant files. He did notice cliques beginning to form within the show—the monster men of 35-D seemed surprisingly close. They had formed a rowdy makeshift band: Taninim on guitar, Theodore on an electric drum kit, The Internet on a 1970's moog, and Zargah clicking wildly into a microphone, his translator droning and harmonizing in alien melodies. Their sound was experimental, at best, but at least listenable thanks to the structured skill of the instrumentalists. The Internet's beautiful playing particularly surprised Mark: a skill he attributed to the world of video tutorials within the dog-punk's mind.

One would expect a different room to be the most active during downtime, though. The (previously) most energetic child in Heaven's Heart Hotel, Jarilo, had the play knocked completely out of him from the last challenge. He locked himself in his room, bawled at a frequency previously unknown to living creatures, and eventually slept when no more tears could pour out.

Without Jarilo, Csodaszarvas found his world strangely quiet. He felt pity for the half-goat, but knew that this was something he needed to let Jarilo experience for himself. "It's about the chase," he had told Jarilo in an attempt to encourage him after the challenge. His advice fell on deaf goat-ears, so the white stag, too, slept.

Imhotep lounged and sunned himself on the balcony and Oksi locked himself away in his room, neither with any interest in talking to the other.

Then there were the women of 24-C, who dealt with the bittersweet air of one of their own being eliminated. Santa Inari and Oshunmare drank in the living room and talked about the large middle they found themselves in, and how they could work to get noticed by the judges. Getting no feedback at all somehow felt worse than being in the bottom, but they both agreed: they wouldn't trade places with Athena. They both found her somehow aggressive and egotistical, and their inebriated conversation dissolved into being thankful that it was her that was eliminated, if had to be anyone from their room. Neither thought she *should* have gone, however, which was troublesome enough of a thought to warrant another drink before they slept.

Robin and Ishta, whom both knew what drove Athena, were broken, infuriated, and had inherited the determination she had left behind. Mark could see that these two, separated from the group, were communicating *somehow* and working on *something,* but ever since they got back to the apartment, they had said almost nothing to each other, and when they did, it was as they passed shoulder to shoulder, faces away from cameras they were keenly aware of. Robin, in particular, had been summoning her god eye frequently in their apartment, but Mark could find no evidence of anything that she was making. This was the only thing he found worth taking notes on. When they, too, eventually slept, that was Mark's personal signal to relax.

Mark thought now was a fine time to take a break from his obsessive sobriety. He didn't swear off the drink completely, but had made a promise to himself to not have wine while a challenge was active. He had even programmed the camera arms, of which he had grown quite used to communicating with, to bar him from entering the wine hallway during "work hours."

"It's okay guys. Half of em' are asleep. One bottle, two movies, a nap, and back to work. What do 'ya say?" Mark attempted to bargain with the camera arms in front of the Infinite Wine Hallway. They had blocked the path, forming a X-pattern with their steel beam arms. But after hearing Mark's numerical estimation of his break, they whirred with reluctant approval and parted. With a click of the teeth, Mark was back into the lemon-walled hallway of juicy retreat.

"I've had so much from 1-400," he mused. He let his knuckles rub the labels as he paced down the hallway. Though there was no official designation, Mark had developed his own way of measuring location by counting his steps. Usually, he'd have one of the camera arms randomly generate a number. This time, he just picked an above-400 digit for himself, and the first number to pop in his head was "1615. I've been sitting a lot lately. Let's get some steps in."

And so he walked 1615 steps, randomly place his hand on a Cretan wine on the second shelf, and began to read about its origins on the back of its label.

In the Infinite Wine Hallway, when a bottle is removed, it triggers the spell that binds the hall's existence in place: this spell randomly generates a new wine onto the shelf. This process (which Mark had never seen as it occurred somewhere in the infinite void far beyond the walking distance he cared to endure) was automatic and slow. He always knew it was happening, as he could hear the bottles as they scooted forward in line on the wooden plank. Anytime that clinking, bumping chorus filled the hallway, it would always distract Mark. Reflexively, he looked up from the wine to catch a glimpse at the gentle, snail-like shuffle of the wine bottle's march.

Carved into the wall, now visible because of the bottle's removal, was a large "F." Its shape was sharp and quick, stabbed into the lemon paint with a hurried ugliness.

He dropped the bottle in his hands—he did not carve this, yet he was the only one that had ever been here in the Camera World. It was *his* world. So either this was designed intentionally when the hallway was first made centuries ago, or someone had stabbed that F into the wall just now, and Heaven's air, as slow as it was here, would eventually heal the "F" into nothingness.

He looked down the hallways in both directions, then stared back at the "F," shaking. He heard no other sound aside from the politely clinking wine bottles. If there was an intruder, they were silent.

"No, it's... it's just me," he rasped. "I'm the only one that's here, no one can enter without my permission... so..."

The "F" never vanished, it remained until it was completely eclipsed by a wine bottle minutes later. Mark ripped it off the shelf and flung it into the wall behind him, the red juices splattering down like a gunshot wound. "F" remained.

He ripped another wine bottle from the middle shelf. "D" sat crookedly on the wall. One from the top. Nothing. One from the bottom. Nothing. Letters were only on the middle shelf.

Mark Sharkman began to fling so many bottles ("E") behind him that the sound could have been confused for ("N") a machine gun tearing through a series of glass windows. ("I") The soles of his shoes were now dyed red from the pooling wine ("R") and so much juice had splattered onto the back of his cream coat and silk pants ("I") that only a trained professional would know ("S") if he had been on a killing spree or simply stomped his own wine with his shoes still on.

Mark saw the letters and felt a horror hook its claws in between the gaps of his ribcage. He decided he could never drink again.

FI N *D* E *R* I*S*

THE NEXT GREAT DEITY

Will return with Volume 2:

THE ANGELS ARE VOYEURS

Acknowledgements

To Seth, Chrys, Heather, Q, Sarah, Linda, Vincent, Avis, and everyone else that's been there for me:

The worlds I live in, both on the page and otherwise, are only tolerable because of you.

Thank you for making both possible.

About the Author

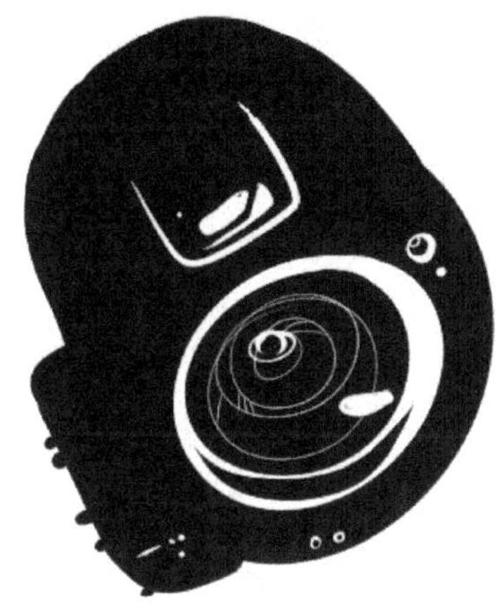

Millard Crow is a journalist, artist, and e-sportscaster from Austin, TX.
THE NEXT GREAT DEITY is his debut novel.

You can learn more about his work at crowspaceboy.com